I Take Thee, a Stranger by Kristy Dykes
Widowed and alone, Corinn McCauley is faced with a desperate decision. Is she willing to marry a stranger in order to survive in a new country? Trevor Parker is a prosperous farmer in Florida, and he and his two daughters need a woman in their life. But Corrin doesn't realize just how acute their needs are until she accepts this stranger's proposal.

Blessed Land by Nancy J. Farrier
Paloma Rivera hates everything American and is determined to convince her sister to move back to Mexico. But first she has to *find* her sister, and no one in the pueblo of Tucson is willing to help her. Can she trust the handsome blacksmith, Antonio Escobar, or is he just toying with her until it is time for her to return home?

Promises Kept by Sally Laity
With the death of her fiancé, all of Kiera MacPherson's hopes for a wonderful life in the New World have vanished. She takes a position as companion to a wealthy matriarch in order to earn her passage back to Ireland. Her leisurely work allows plenty of time for studying an old family Bible, and she asks Devon Hamilton, the master of the mansion, many insightful questions. Will this quest for biblical knowledge upset order in the Hamilton household—and then bless her with everlasting love?

Freedom's Ring by Judith McCoy Miller
Hannah Falcrest missed out on the hope that New World immigrants anticipate. But the sudden death of her abusive husband has granted Hannah the power to map the future for herself and her infant daughter. Now, though, William Winslow seems more than eager to step in and impose his opinions over her plans. Can she trust his friendship? Will her heart ever be free to seek true love?

American
DREAM

Four Historical Love Stories
Celebrating the Faith of American Immigrants

Kristy Dykes
Nancy J. Farrier
Sally Laity
Judith McCoy Miller

BARBOUR
PUBLISHING, INC.
Uhrichsville, Ohio

I Take Thee, a Stranger ©2000 by Kristy Dykes.
Blessed Land ©2000 by Nancy J. Farrier.
Promises Kept ©2000 by Sally Laity.
Freedom's Ring ©2000 by Judith McCoy Miller.

Illustrations by Mari Goering.

ISBN 1-57748-727-3

All Scripture quotations are taken from the King James Version of the Bible.

Published by Barbour Publishing, Inc., P.O. Box 719, Uhrichsville, Ohio 44683 http://www.barbourbooks.com

Member of the
Evangelical Christian
Publishers Association

Printed in the United States of America.

American
DREAM

I Take Thee a Stranger

by Kristy Dykes

Dedication

To my hero husband, Milton,
who is my collaborator in
the deepest sense of the word—
he's believed in me, supported me, and
cheered me on in my quest to be
published in CBA fiction.

Chapter 1

1885—Massachusetts—Large Hill Place

O h, Galen, please don't die," Corinn McCauley said, hovering over the still form of her husband, wiping his brow with a wet cloth. He had lain under their red plaid wedding coverlet for eleven days now, never stirring, her hoping and praying the whole time that he would open his twinkling blue eyes and say, as he'd said many a time, "Corinn, my Scottish lass, all will be well. You'll see. Things will go better for us."

She sat down by the bed and took his limp hand in hers, caressing his wrist, trailing her finger across his palm. "Those calluses, Galen," she choked out, "all for our future. You worked so hard since we came to America. We were going to start a new life. . .a prosperous one."

She had worked, too, toiling from daybreak to dark, taking in washing and ironing and sewing, baking pies and cakes, recaning chair bottoms—anything that would put dollars in the jar at the back of the drawer.

But, between the company boardinghouse and the company mercantile, the level of dollars was always low.

She pleated, then unpleated the edge of the wedding coverlet that lay over her husband, staring at the dingy wall. "Granny Jen, you never dreamed the wedding coverlet you so lovingly made two years ago would one day be a. . .a death blanket."

Tears streamed down her face, but she ignored them and reached, once again, for the damp cloth on her husband's forehead. She dipped it in a basin of water, squeezed it, and lovingly laid the cloth on his fevered brow. If only she could do something more. Anything to help him. But there was nothing she, or anyone, could do.

When the men from the foundry brought her injured husband home to her, announcing that he would be dead within hours, she refused to believe them. Even when one of the soot-blackened men said, "This happened to Albert Rowe and he died before daybreak," Corinn made a quiet resolve that the same plight would *not* befall *her* husband.

She took the hem of her apron and wiped away her blinding tears. Then, with fresh resolve to nurse Galen back to health, she fluffed the small pillows that were wedged on either side of his head. Taking a spoonful of water from the cup on the nightstand, she forced a drop of water between his parched lips.

Dr. Robbins would come soon, as he had each day, to change her husband's bandages and offer his grim prognosis. But, Corinn refused to give in to despair.

Throughout each long, worry-filled day. . .and night, she had stubbornly held onto her optimism. Until now.

"No," she shrieked, slumping to her knees, pounding the hard wooden chair with her fists, not caring if anyone heard through the thin walls. "I won't let you leave me, Galen McCauley. We've loved each other too long. We have plans, remember? We are going to live in a fine home one day, and our sons and daughters are going to be upstanding American citizens. One of our grandsons shall surely be the president of this mighty nation. Oh, Galen, my heart is breaking in two."

She heard him stir and looked over at him, her soul soaring with joy. "Praise be, you've come back to me." Fresh tears—joy tears—sprang to her eyes. She jumped up, smiling, then laughing.

She leaned over him.

And went cold with fear.

It was the death rattle.

❦

At dusk, ten days after her husband's burial, Corinn stood on the doctor's doorstep, wondering why he had summoned her. He already had a housekeeper, the position she was seeking.

After Mrs. Mullins showed her to the parlor and excused herself, Corinn settled in a chair and timidly thrust her feet toward the hearth, enjoying the warmth. Nearly every night, she went to bed with cold feet—a phenomenon that had greatly amused Galen.

Tuck them beneath my legs and get them warm, my Scottish lass, he had whispered as he pulled her close each night.

A sob caught in her chest and a tear threatened to spill over. *Oh, Galen, my bonnie prince. . .*

The door creaked open, and the elderly doctor shuffled toward her. For the first time, she noticed how stiff were his movements, how slow was his gait.

"Good evening, Mrs. McCauley."

"A pleasant evening to you, sir." She made a movement to stand in respect, but he waved her down.

"No need to get up." He shook her hand and sank into the chair opposite hers, pulling an envelope from his coat pocket. "I've an important matter to discuss with you."

He pulled several pages from the envelope and studied them for a moment, then looked up. "I'm concerned about you, Mrs. McCauley. I know what becomes of some women who find themselves in your circumstance. You're an immigrant and a widow. You've no income and no prospects of a job. Soon, you'll be without a roof over your head—"

"How did you know?"

"I made a point of finding out."

She swallowed hard. *Why does this kind man care what happens to me?*

"Women in dire straits sometimes wind up as women of—well, to phrase this as delicately as possible—women of ill repute." He lowered his eyes and stared at the flames. "Or kept women."

Corinn felt her cheeks growing hot as she, too, stared into the fire.

"I don't want you to suffer such a fate." He looked directly into her eyes with fatherly concern. "You are a good woman, one of the kindest and. . .and most industrious I've ever met."

She fidgeted in her chair. She was not accustomed to receiving compliments. Everybody worked hard, didn't they? That was what one was supposed to do.

"I've been impressed with your loyalty to your husband, your diligence. . ."

She fidgeted again.

"Your fortitude, your courage. . ."

She shrugged. "All Scots are brave. It's legendary."

"I've no openings in my household." He hit a sturdy side table with his fist, producing a loud thwacking sound. "If I were a rich man, I'd help you. But, that will never be. I'm tired and old. Soon. . ."

"I'd never ask you for charity." She thrust her shoulders back stiffly. "Even if you were wealthy."

"Yes, I know." His faded gray eyes lit up as he waved the letter he held in his hand, its thin pages rustling. "I have a solution for you—in these pages. The matter is a simple one, really. This letter is from a young man who needs a wife. You are a young woman who needs a husband."

She grasped the arms of the chair, willing herself not to cry out against this travesty, then scolding herself for being outraged. Dr. Robbins was only doing this out of concern.

She stared at the framed landscape above the mantel, not focusing on the details, barely hearing the doctor's words.

He talked on and on, something about how his nephew had gone to Florida, how his mate had recently died from pneumonia, how there were few unattached females in that part of the raw, young state, how he needed a wife. Did his uncle know of a worthy woman who could meet this challenge? In return, he would offer the woman a home—and affection besides. Could the doctor find him such a woman?

"As I said, here is a young man who needs a wife." Dr. Robbins thumped the pages. "And you, my dear, are a young woman who needs a husband. This is the solution to your plight."

"No, Dr. Robbins," she finally said, thoughts of her beloved Galen filling her head and heart.

"Please take time to think about this before you refuse. My nephew is Philadelphia-born and bred and well educated. He's hobnobbed with high society since he was a suckling. Whatever he puts his mind to, he succeeds. Now, it appears he's put his mind to acquiring land in Florida. One day, he'll be an elected official. Mark my words."

She looked down at her worn skirts, at her patched high-top shoes, at her threadbare shawl made of red plaid with a wide band of green. The plaid was her clan's tartan for generations and said by them to be John Knox's tartan—the Great Reformer of Scotland.

What man would want her, especially one with the social standing of which Dr. Robbins spoke? If she looked in a mirror right now, she knew what she would see—not an elegant lady of high society garbed in silks and satins—but a small-statured female with uneven features, thin brown hair, and speckles across her nose.

CORINN, CORINN,
SMALL AND THIN,

SINGS LIKE A ROBIN
BUT LOOKS LIKE A WREN.

The familiar taunt of her schoolmates filled her head, hammering, hammering, hammering. Galen had fallen in love with her when she was a wee sparkly lass, before she had reached womanhood. Even after she had passed the bloom of childhood, Galen had loved her still, despite her plainness.

"Won't you give some serious thought to what I'm offering—what my nephew is offering—Mrs. McCauley? I have no doubt that you could fill the role admirably."

She rubbed her temples in circles, staring at the flames. What had Dr. Robbins called it? A role? Yes, that's what it would be, a role and nothing more, if she were to marry a stranger.

She rose to her feet. "Earlier, I said I could never ask for charity. Something else I could never do is marry a man I don't know, let alone a man I don't love. I may be poor and I may be uncomely, but I still have my wits. Besides, I'm young and strong and. . .and. . .hopeful."

She faced him squarely. "All will be well. As my husband often said, things *will* go better."

❧

Two months after Galen's death, Corinn made her way down a busy street. All *was not* well. Things *had not* gone better. She knew what she must do.

She passed a woman wearing bold face paint, dressed in a gown of flimsy fabric that revealed bare arms and a brazen décolletage. A woman of ill repute.

Corinn felt herself blushing, and she rapidly fanned herself with a handkerchief. What was the other type of woman Dr. Robbins had referred to? *A kept woman?* Last evening, when her laird, no, landlord, they called them here. . .when her landlord had evicted her, he had made her an offer. She fanned more furiously, remembering his abominable words.

Another woman of ill repute passed her on the sidewalk. Yes, she knew what she must do.

Woodenly, she plodded down the street, her empty stomach making a thunderous noise. She trudged up the steep steps and grasped the door knocker on Dr. Robbins's front door.

A strange man in Florida didn't seem nearly as frightening as the prospects here in Massachusetts.

Chapter 2

Florida—The Flowery Land

Corinn sat in the minuscule stateroom, thinking of the last few weeks and the grueling trip to Florida. Days and days on a soot-filled train. More days and days on an ocean-tossed boat.

She withdrew Mr. Parker's letter from the sporran which hung from a belt about her waist. Trembling, she held the page in front of her and read the brief note for, it seemed, the hundredth time.

Dear Mrs. McCauley,

Thank you for agreeing to be my wife. I will do my best by you.

We came to Florida about ten years ago, when land was reasonably priced. I now own 2,000 acres. Much of the land is filled with virgin timber, while other portions have been cultivated and are producing sweet potatoes, my main crop.

I have two daughters, ages seven and four. They are genteel little ladies.

When you arrive, I will meet you. Look for a tall man with two children at his side. My uncle, Dr. Robbins, wrote and described you. We will be married immediately. Then we will travel to Sunny Acres by wagon and arrive before nightfall.

With regard,
Trevor Parker

Corinn shivered as she let the letter drop to her lap. What had she done—committing to marry someone she didn't know?

In an effort to comfort herself, she picked up her lap harp and strummed the strings. Within moments, she was no longer in tight quarters on a sailing vessel somewhere near Florida. . .

She was transported to Scotland, singing and playing a lively folk song over the backdrop of droning bagpipes, members of her clan prancing about her in jigs and reels.

Soon, though, she would be in the midst of strangers in a distant land—far away from Scotland and friends and family. As if in a haze, she looked down at her harp and watched her fingers absently plucking discordant, dirge-like notes.

"No," she said aloud, casting her harp aside. "I mustn't think like that." She looked heavenward. " 'Take no thought for your life, what ye shall eat, or what ye shall drink,' " she quoted as she began packing her belongings into the carpetbag beside her. " 'Nor yet for your body, what ye shall put on. . . . But seek ye first the kingdom of God, and his righteousness; and all these things shall be added unto you.' "

She rose and gathered the remainder of her personal articles. The great boat was about to dock. In Florida.

"I shall seek the Lord with all my heart," she whispered. "And all the things I have need of shall be added unto me."

She stopped at midstride and looked down at her left hand. She touched the spot on her ring finger that, for two years, had been encompassed by a band of gold.

What do I have need of, Lord?
The love of a good man.

❧

The boat behind her, the smells of the harbor around her, the honking and geeking of the birds above her, she paused on the gangplank. As she adjusted the beret atop her head and put her plaid about her shoulders, she was trembling again and couldn't seem to stop.

This is no time to be faint of heart, she lectured herself, her throat suddenly feeling like flax. She had made an agreement—to marry Mr. Parker. She had given her word on the matter, and her word was her bond. Wasn't that what her mother had taught her, had drilled into her?

You made your bed—now lie in it, her mother would say if she were here, meaning, *You made a commitment—now keep it.* No turning back.

Telling herself to be steady, she swallowed hard, then took a tenuous step in Mr. Parker's direction. She easily recognized the tall man with two wee girls on either side.

As she walked toward him, she fiddled with the

fringe on her plaid. In many foreign countries, women commonly married men they didn't know. An arranged marriage, it was called, in which love eventually came to them. And in the Bible, didn't Rebekah agree to marry Isaac, a stranger? And didn't the Scripture say that Isaac loved her at first sight? And that Rebekah comforted Isaac after the death of his mother?

Perhaps things would turn out between her and Mr. Parker that way. Perhaps Mr. Parker would love her at first sight. And, in comforting him after a dear one's death—just as Rebekah had done for Isaac—Corinn would come to love him too.

"Father God, let it be so." She looked up, squared her shoulders, and smiled. She would face this thing with a cheerful countenance and a hopeful outlook.

She was pleased to see Mr. Parker closing the distance that separated them in long, hurried strides, the wee girls running to keep up.

The smaller girl stumbled and Corinn gasped, afraid she would land, face-first, in the mud. But he kept up his pace, seemingly oblivious, and the girl righted herself and ran faster on her chubby little legs.

When he reached Corinn, he stopped abruptly, towering over her.

With your physique, Mr. Parker, you could toss the caber, was her first thought. She visualized him participating in the Highland games where only the strongest, most able-bodied men hurled twenty-foot tree trunks into the air and made them land on opposite ends.

Sometime soon, she would share her first impressions of him, perhaps on the wagon ride home. She smiled at the pleasant thought. His strong-looking stature surely bespoke hard work. . .perseverance. . . indefatibility. Her compliments would please him, she was certain. Surely these fine attributes were the reasons behind his success in this untamed land.

"Welcome to Florida," he said in a deep bass voice, extending his hand for a shake.

With a dip of her chin, she said a quiet, "Thank you," then shook his hand.

"Florida means 'flowery land.' " The older girl's voice was a squeak, her posture mouse-like.

"That must mean flowers bloom everywhere," Corinn said, smiling—though her insides were jiggling like droplets of water on a hot skillet.

"Only where they're planted," Mr. Parker remarked, his features without expression.

After formally introducing his daughters, Edith and Adeline, he collected her bags and helped Corinn and the wee ones into his farm wagon. She sat on the front seat beside him, the children on a built-in bench directly behind.

He picked up the reins. "The parson is expecting us," was all he said. All anybody said.

21

Chapter 3

Sitting in the wagon beside Mr. Parker, Corinn resisted the urge to study him. Proper decorum—well taught by her mother—dictated that she keep her eyes straight ahead. Except for her initial glance and her first impression on the wharf, she had not found an opportune moment to scrutinize his face or even determine his eye color.

From the corner of her eye, she *did* notice that he sported long black sideburns and showed impeccable taste in clothing. From his dark blue broadcloth coat and his gray serge dress pants to his wine-colored satin tie, he appeared finely tailored.

The children, also, modeled the latest fashions. The older girl wore a flouncy yellow silk frock, and the wee one was attired in pink in a similar pattern. Their matching wide-brimmed, ribbon-garnished hats made them look like the genteel little ladies described by Mr. Parker in his letter.

With a sad pang, she looked down at her own clothing, fingering the folds of her travel-stained brown skirt and jacket, lamenting that she didn't have a new gown to be married in. She tucked a strand of hair under her beret. She hadn't even had time to freshen up for her wedding. Before she and Galen married, she had prepared for months, fashioning a wedding gown and making monogrammed linens.

What would marriage be like to this tall man beside her? She moistened her lips and straightened her shoulders, trying to rally her courage.

At the parson's home, Mr. Parker helped her alight. Within a few moments, all four of them were standing inside an octagon-shaped sitting room, the parson reciting marriage vows.

"Please say these words after me," the parson instructed, standing before them with a black book in his hands. He gestured at Corinn. "You first. Say this, 'I, Corinn, take thee, Trevor.' "

"I, Corinn," she said. *Take thee, a stranger...*

"Take thee, Trevor," the parson repeated.

"Take thee, Trevor," she dutifully said.

"To be my lawful wedded husband," he instructed.

"To be my lawful wedded husband." She heard a giggle and looked down to watch the wee girl twist sideways. Then, Mr. Parker snapped his fingers three times. The child grew statue-still.

Corinn repeated the rest of the marriage vows without further prodding from the parson, but her mind was far away.

In Scotland.

At her and Galen's wedding.

Galen, looking lovingly into her eyes.

Family and friends gathered round. Sweet-smelling flowers in her hands. A filmy veil on her head. Music and songs and laughter. . .

"Mrs. Parker?" the parson said.

And then there had been the shivaree after the wedding. . .

"Mrs. Parker, let me be the first person to offer congratulations."

Corinn felt a tugging on her skirts, looked down into bright blue eyes, saw the wee girl pointing at the parson, then glanced up to see the parson holding out his hand.

"Mrs. Parker, congratulations," the parson said.

She offered her hand and squeaked out a timid, "Thank you, sir," enduring his crushing handshake.

"And congratulations to you, Mr. Parker," the parson offered.

Moments later, she walked across the room, the children on her heels. Mr. Parker raced ahead of her and opened the door wide.

As she stepped onto the porch, she adjusted her beret and touched its red pom-pom.

Then, a staggering thought hit her.

This was the first wedding she had ever been to where the groom had not kissed the bride.

❧

The long ride to Sunny Acres started out as a silent one, and Corinn wondered. Even when they stopped and ate the basket supper that Mr. Parker had purchased from the local hotel, somberness hung in the air.

"For the past three years," Mr. Parker said, after swallowing a bite of biscuit and wiping his lips, "a neighbor woman—Mrs. Henderson—has been cooking and cleaning for us, several days a week." He sighed deeply and added, "But, just enough to keep body and soul together. She has her own nine children to attend to. I've been fortunate with clothing, however. A seamstress in town keeps my daughters well clothed."

"But I thought your wife passed away only months ago," Corinn said. *If that was so, why had he hired someone to do housekeeping three years prior?*

He didn't respond, but she noticed his jaw tightening.

She was puzzled. Had she committed a breach of etiquette? If he asked her about Galen, she would freely give him information. She was only trying to learn something about this reticent man. After all, he was her husband now.

Dead silence reigned as they hurriedly finished their supper. On the road again in the gathering twilight, Corinn sat on the wagon seat, bone weary and heart heavy.

The wee girl began bouncing about, chattering to the dolly she held in her arms, as if she couldn't contain herself any longer.

Corinn turned around, suddenly deciding to do what she'd been wanting to since she'd met little Adeline. She didn't care if Mr. Parker subjected her or the girls to another stern stare.

With sheer joy and abandonment, she scooped up the wee girl and plopped her onto her lap, hugging her, then stroking her springy blond curls. "May I hold your dolly, Adeline?"

The girl giggled, her eyes dancing as she handed over the doll.

"What's your wee bairn's name, lassie?"

"Lathee?" Adeline lisped through her snaggle-toothed grin. "Whath a lathee?"

Corinn laughed. "Oh, that. Lassie is a Scottish term for a wee girl."

"You're from Scotland, aren't you?" Edith, the older girl, asked. "Papa said you were."

"That I am." Corinn touched her plaid shawl, the pride of Scotland welling up in her. "So, Adeline, what's your bairn's name?"

Adeline giggled again. "Whath a bairn?"

"A bairn is a wee babe."

"Mama said I was her baby."

"That's enough, Adeline," Mr. Parker said, a dark shadow passing across his face. "Get back to your seat and settle down."

As Adeline clambered over her in unquestioning obedience, Corinn did what Mary, the mother of Jesus, had done at an uncertain time in her life.

She kept all these things and pondered them in her heart.

❧

When they reached Mr. Parker's house, Corinn went inside at his bidding while he saw to the horses.

As she stepped across the threshold, the wee ones dashed past her, apparently to their bedroom. She stood in the parlor for a long moment, hardly able to keep her mouth from dropping open. Everywhere she looked, she saw elegance. A satinwood upright piano. A rose-colored damask settee and matching chair. A massive mahogany dining table and chairs and buffet.

Puffy batiste drapes at the windows. Books galore in glass-fronted cabinets, some with the titles showing, some with the pages facing out.

If clean and organized, the house would have been a showplace. A thick layer of dust covered the piano. Stains spotted the settee. And though the floors appeared to be swept, they begged for a good scrubbing and waxing besides.

Corinn continued in her survey of the room. Apparently the drapes had recently been washed, but their wrinkles cried out for ironing. Ornate gold-framed paintings—landscapes and portraits—hung askew.

She walked over and righted one of the frames. *No picture of the late Mrs. Parker displayed above the mantel? Or on a side table?* Most people who'd lost a mate kept a picture around—at least for a while. She moistened her lips. Perhaps Mr. Parker had put away the late Mrs. Parker's portrait out of respect to her—the new Mrs. Parker.

The kitchen showed the same state of disarray. The cookstove needed scouring. The table needed clearing. The windows needed polishing. The floor needed mopping. Everything screamed out for the touch of a woman. She scanned the room again, resisting the urge to roll up her sleeves and work until everything shone. But she couldn't.

She wasn't the lady of this lair.

Not yet.

"Mrs. Henderson was supposed to come yesterday and tidy things up," Mr. Parker said from behind her as he brought in several boxes from the wagon. "But one

27

of her children fell ill."

Corinn turned and saw that he looked embarrassed. For the first time since she'd met him, she felt kindliness for him welling up inside her.

"I–I apologize," he stammered, still holding one of the boxes as if he didn't realize it was in his arms. "This isn't the way I wanted things to be."

"No need to explain."

"Running the farm," he mumbled. "Seeing to my daughters—" He stopped abruptly and stared through the parted curtains over the window.

"I'll help." Her heart went out to him. "I'm not shy of hard work, Mr. Parker. In my raising, my mother used to say, 'An idle mind is the devil's workshop' and 'The used key is always bright.' By her example, I learned to stay busy always."

"My uncle told me you were of that inclination." Still, he stared out the window. Finally, he turned and faced her. "Welcome to Sunny Acres."

"Why, thank you. Why don't you stow that box in here?" She gestured toward a door behind her. "I assume this is the pantry? That box contains my books. I'll unpack them later." She pulled on the doorknob.

"No." His voice held a loud ring of authority.

"But they'll be out of the way." She jiggled the handle.

In a flash, he set down the box and towered over her, his palm flat on the raised panel of the door, his eyes cold, his mouth drawn into a grim line. "This door always remains locked."

Immediately, she withdrew her hand as if burned by a flame. She could only stare at him. He stood deathly still. Silent. Obviously, she had kindled his ire. Yet, she hadn't the slightest clue why.

She lowered her gaze, ambled to the breakfront, busied herself with untying a box. The realization that she had angered him deeply troubled her. She was the one who always soothed ruffled feathers, not stirred them. What should she do? Should she say she was sorry? But for what? A person couldn't apologize if she didn't know what infraction she had committed.

She heard his long strides crossing the kitchen and when she turned, he was holding out a brightly wrapped, rectangular-shaped parcel.

"For you," he said, handing her the parcel.

She looked up at him as she accepted it, guarded but wondering. The anger in his eyes was gone, she saw. That pleased her. Nonchalance replaced it. That perplexed her.

"It's fripperies," he said. "All women want fripperies." He turned, not waiting for her response, and made his way outside.

She sauntered back into the parlor and struck a dusty key on the piano, still clutching his package, still wondering, still fretting. Then she roused herself as she looked around the disheveled room.

She had no time for vexation of spirit. She would turn her vitality to more fruitful endeavors. She found herself galvanized by the labors that awaited her, ready to set this house aright, eager to work a cure, willing to double-march.

But she knew she must go slowly, proceed gently. Because of this man and his. . .cankerworm of crossness.

And two wee girls who desperately needed affection.

She turned and walked across the hardwood floors, anxious to explore her new home. Her heart stopped when she came to the first doorway on the left.

Could this be Mr. Parker's bedroom?

Their bedroom now?

The only thing she saw was the big bed, bigger than any bed she had ever seen. It was wide and long, and it was centered on the wall between two windows.

His bed.

Their bed now.

Her heart raced.

I take thee. . .a stranger. . . .

Chapter 4

After breakfast the next morning, with the food put away and the dishes done, with Mr. Parker in the fields and the children cutting out paper dolls, Corinn decided to finish unpacking before starting on the housework.

She made her way to the bedroom, off the kitchen, that Mr. Parker had led her to the night before, a good-sized room which looked as if it hadn't been occupied in a long while. Now, in the light of day, she noticed dusty cobwebs hanging in the corners and saw that the pastel-colored rug needed a good shaking. But the furniture was fine mahogany like the other pieces in the house.

She was thankful for the privacy he had granted her. She wondered how long that would last. After all, they were man and wife.

She drew items of clothing from her portmanteau and shook them out, then hung them in the tall wardrobe. Two skirts, one with a matching jacket. Five shirtwaists—three nearly threadbare. Two nightdresses.

"Oh, I'll take the high road, and you'll take the low road," she sang gustily as she worked. "And I'll get to Scotland a'fore ye."

She pulled out a framed sampler that Granny Jen had embroidered and stared down at it, wondering if she should hang it.

HASTE YE BACK TO SCOTLAND

As much as she loved Scotland, she was ready and willing to cut all ties with her motherland and start a new life. When she lived in Massachusetts, alongside many who had left their homelands and come to America, she had seen what she called "weepy women" who were pining away and useless to their families. She'd resolved that she would be strong and brave in this fine new world. And now, she would be a good wife to Mr. Parker, the best wife possible.

"Ach, dear Scotland," she said aloud. She ran her fingers over the fancy stitch work, then decided that it couldn't hurt to display a sentimental sampler in her bedroom. Within moments, the handicraft was hanging on the wall above her bed, and she stood back to admire it, then returned to her work.

She placed her carpetbag on the bed, then reached for the package Mr. Parker had given her last night.

Fripperies, he had called them. *All women want fripperies,* he'd said.

From the colorful wrapping paper, she pulled a pair of lace-trimmed gloves and a heavily embossed sterling silver glove box. She sighed. She'd never owned such niceties. Then she spotted the three bolts of fabric he'd also given her.

To make yourself some new clothing, he'd said. *In case*

you need them, he'd added.

She looked down at her drab brown skirt, the seams shiny from frequent ironings, and her brown print shirtwaist, the flowers blurred from fading. In all probability, Mr. Parker's uncle, Dr. Robbins, had written him about her dire circumstances. Though embarrassed when she accepted the fabric last night, deep down she felt grateful for her new husband's foresight and care.

She recalled the letter he had written Dr. Robbins, when he'd promised he would take good care of the woman who agreed to marry him. Surely Mr. Parker's gifts were an indication of how he would treat her in the days to come. The thought warmed her now.

"Oh, I'll take the high road, and you'll take the low road," she sang as she placed her stockings and underpinnings in the drawers of a mahogany dresser. "Or is it, I'll take the low road," she said, "and you'll take the high road? I always get those two mixed up."

From the corner of her eye, she saw the two wee girls standing in the doorway. She pirouetted around and swung into a low curtsy, holding her skirts out sideways. "Please come in," she bubbled, smiling broadly. "Welcome to my private abode."

"Yippee." Little Adeline skipped into the room and pounced onto the bed, but Edith held back.

"Scots are known for their hospitality. I'm honored that you chose to visit me today."

"What are you doing?" Little Adeline asked.

"Unpacking." She fastened the empty carpetbag and stowed it in the bottom of the armoire, then sat down beside Adeline. "Adeline, sweet Adeline. What a great big name for such a wee little girl."

Adeline giggled, her blue eyes dancing. "Will you play with uth?" she lisped. "My mama did. All the time. We played with the dolls in our dollhouse and we played dwess-up with her wed parasols and we—"

"Adeline," Edith snapped from the doorway. "You know Papa doesn't want us talking about that."

"Perhaps you can show me your dollhouse another time," Corinn said soothingly, "but this morning, work's awaiting. However, I have time for one song.

"Edith, would you care to join us?" She patted a spot on the bed, then pulled out her lap harp, and little Adeline's face shone with wonder. Edith sauntered into the room and sat down on the bed.

Corinn was pleased at Edith's response. She would win both girls' hearts if the task took every ounce of strength within her.

"What are me and Adeline going to call you?" Edith said in a grown-up voice, far too mature-sounding for her seven years. Her eyes were a brilliant blue; her hair white-blond and full of curls, just like little Adeline's. If they'd been closer in age, Corinn decided, they would be mistaken for twins.

"What are me and Adeline going to call you?" Edith repeated.

"You mean, *Adeline and I,*" Corinn gently corrected, looking across the bed at the two wee girls, her heart going out to them. Here were two lassies who'd recently lost their mother. Though they were sorely in need of a mother's love, she must first gain their trust.

Then she could bestow the abundance of affection begging to pour out of her. And she must measure every word she said to them. She glanced beseechingly upward. She needed divine wisdom.

"I called my mother 'Marmsie,'" she said brightly, "but my given name is Corinn. I'd be honored if you chose to call me that."

After she sang them a song, she was amused at Adeline's curiosity and answered the lassie's many questions.

She explained about the sampler.

She explained about the lap harp.

She explained about the sheepskin bagpipes that Galen was holding in the daguerreotype on the bedside table.

She explained about the plaid wedding coverlet on the bed.

"The coverlet symbolizes an old custom my clan adheres to." She caressed the plaid folds beside her. "Every lass is given a wedding coverlet before her marriage. She and her new husband sleep under it their first night as man and wife."

"Papa. Papa." Edith shrieked in delight as she hopped off the bed and ran toward the door where Mr. Parker stood. He dipped under the doorway and stepped into the room, giving Edith a brusque pat as he passed her and came to stand near the bed.

Corinn felt flustered in this tall man's presence, but she pushed her feelings aside. Did he need her assistance? She sprang to her feet, still clutching the lap harp with one hand, smoothing her skirts with the other, then her chignon. "Mr. Parker, are you in need of something?"

"Please keep your seat," he said in clipped tones.

She saw that he was drenched with perspiration. Perhaps the heat was making him irritable. But why had he come inside at midmorning? Something must have happened. "Was there a mishap in the fields?"

He shrugged. "Black Deuce threw a shoe. Had to be seen to. As I passed under the window—" he gestured at the curtains billowing in the breeze "—I heard. . . music."

She held out the lap harp. "It's a jolly thing to make merry. The lassies and I were singing. And having a good time, we were."

His features as still as glass, he didn't say a word.

"She talks funny, Papa," little Adeline piped up.

Corinn laughed, but he remained stoic.

"She says her r's like a whir," Edith said quietly.

"That's known as a Scottish burr." Corinn smiled. "The most identifiable feature of a Scot."

Still he didn't respond. He just stood there, twirling his hat around and around.

Corinn looked down at the floorboard, trying to hide her hurt. Nothing she said seemed to elicit a smile or even a friendly nod from this man. Earlier, she'd made a resolve to win the lassies' hearts if it took every ounce of her strength. She wasn't sure she had the strength to win Mr. Parker's affections.

Why was he so uncommunicative—this man who was now her husband? Yesterday afternoon, on the long ride to Sunny Acres, he'd uttered less than a handful of words. After their arrival last evening, he'd been silent. All through breakfast, his comments had been brief. Now, it was the same. Could she go a lifetime like this? In mournful silence? *I've jumped out of the kettle and into the flames.*

He stared into her eyes momentarily. Then his gaze inched away and came to rest on the sampler hanging above her bed.

She felt the color rush to her face, knew he was reading it, wished she had not hung it. "I–I—"

"No need to explain." He fixed her with another silent stare, then turned and strode toward the door. "I'll be in the fields until nightfall."

Chapter 5

Corinn finished her ablutions early one morning, a spark of joy welling up inside her. Today after breakfast, she was going to a quilting bee. A quilting bee was merry, from what she'd heard. There would be new friends to meet and get to know. That was a pleasant thought.

She pulled on her rose-dotted skirt and shirtwaist, then fastened the tiny buttons up the front. Last night, she'd finished making the matching set from one of the bolts of fabric Mr. Parker had given her when she'd arrived three weeks ago. She was grateful for new attire to wear this morning. Soon, she would have the blue calico and green silk dresses completed and hanging in the armoire.

But who knew when she would have another opportunity to sew? The workload seemed to be unending. Daily chores. Weekly chores. Chores that, for some reason, had not been done in. . .a year? Two? Like the awful task of scraping the muck out of the nickel-plated cookstove. Or the backbreaking job of clearing the thick viney undergrowth from the shrub beds surrounding the house so that she could plant flower seeds.

Standing before the mirror, she brushed her hair, pinning it into a chignon, then stared at the rose color of her blouse. Galen had loved this hue, had said it cheered him in the bleakness of their lives. In the tiny room they had occupied in his parents' stone cottage in Scotland, she'd hung ruffled rose-colored curtains—much to her mother-in-law's consternation.

"Abominable," the elderly woman had proclaimed at first sight of them. "Too fancy for poor people. You think you're a Stuart, Corinn? Well, you're not. A McCauley you are, and a McCauley you'll die."

"Enchanting," Galen had said, when they were snuggled in bed that night. "They remind me of dear Scotland's mauve and pink thistle beds that carpet the moors."

Abruptly, Corinn turned away from the dresser, wishing she had time to change her clothing, even if it meant she had to wear her dark blue walking skirt that bore three patches. Memories were harder to deal with than embarrassment. But she couldn't take any more time for herself. She must prepare breakfast for a hungry family.

Hurriedly, she began to tidy the room. She pulled the red plaid wedding coverlet up over the bed, smoothing the wrinkles lovingly, tucking in the corners at precise angles. Suddenly, as if she had stepped on a thistle, she cried out in pain—yet this pain emanated from deep within her.

"Galen, oh, Galen," she whispered as she stroked the plaid, then sat on the bed, wringing her hands.

"How I miss your tender words."

My Scottish lass, he had called her.

A tear plopped on her skirt.

My bonnie prince, she had called him.

Another tear plopped beside the first one.

Since the day she arrived, she had endured impenetrable silence from Mr. Parker.

She clasped, then unclasped her hands, felt her forehead forming into a scowl. A scowl like the one Mr. Parker sometimes wore. He was so drastically different from Galen. Like night and day. Like the Highlands and the Lowlands. Like Scotland and England.

Galen with his lightheartedness. . .

Galen with his laughter. . .

Galen with his. . .love.

She roused herself from her reverie, even reprimanded herself as she stood up and walked toward the door. This was fruitless thinking.

Galen was. . .gone.

Mr. Parker was. . .here.

❧

"Thank you for bringing me to the quilting bee this morning," Corinn said as Mr. Parker helped her down from his shiny new Empire buggy. "Adeline and I shall have a grand time today."

"I wish I could go with you," Edith mumbled from the black leather tufted seat.

"You know how much you love school." Corinn smoothed her full skirts with her right hand, then adjusted the brim of her hat as Mr. Parker climbed back up on the seat. In her left arm, she carried a pound cake she had just pulled from the oven, rich with sweet creamery butter and fresh eggs. She looked up at Edith. "You'll have a fine time at school today."

Edith nodded. "Teacher said we're going to cut autumn leaves out of colored paper."

"See? I told you." She patted Edith's leg, and the child did not pull away from her. Her heart did a little somersault of joy as love exuded out of her and into the girl.

Her hand cupped over her eyebrows, Corinn looked up at Mr. Parker through the brightness of the October sun. "You'll be back for us this afternoon? When the quilting bee is over?"

"As soon as I pick up Edith from the schoolhouse."

"Bye-bye, Papa," little Adeline said, standing in the identical position as Corinn, right hand cupped over her eyebrows.

"I'll look for you this afternoon, Mr. Parker." Corinn picked up her skirts and strode across the raked pathway, little Adeline following closely on her heels.

Standing in front of Mrs. Wallace's heavy oak door, Corinn noticed that the gingerbread fretwork on the porch was similar to the trim on Mr. Parker's house. She admired the colorful flowers in the shrub beds. *Soon,* she told herself, *my shrub beds will be profuse with flowers, too.* Snowdrops, wood violets, and hyacinths. She took note of the streak-free windows lining the porch and the white lace curtains that hung inside them. "Adeline, would you like to knock on the door for me?"

Before Adeline's tiny fist hit its target, the door swung open in front of them.

"So you're the new Mrs. Parker," said an ample-bosomed woman with a yellow-toothed grin. "I'm the one that's kept house for the Parkers. I'm Erma Henderson, and I've been dying to meet you."

"Now, now." Another woman bustled past the first one and drew Corinn and Adeline inside. "Welcome to my home. I'm Mrs. Wallace. We're so glad you came."

"Our pleasure," Corinn said, handing her the pound cake. "We've been looking forward to it."

"I can't help wondering if the new Mrs. Parker will fare better than the last one," Mrs. Henderson said, peering closely at Corinn. "Some women can take it; some can't."

Mrs. Wallace tsk-tsked, playfully wagging her finger at the first woman. "Erma Henderson, don't you go scaring off Mrs. Parker with your prattle, good-natured though it is."

"I'm speaking the truth, and you know it." Mrs. Henderson's tone was somber, but her eyes were genial.

Mrs. Wallace tsk-tsked again as she took Corinn by the elbow and ushered her into the parlor to introduce her to a host of women.

Corinn exchanged pleasantries with them. Some she had met at church, and some were new to her.

"Please have a seat beside Mrs. Ross," Mrs. Wallace offered, gesturing at a shiny-faced young girl and the empty chair beside her. "I'll show Adeline where the children are playing," she said over her shoulder as she took the child by the hand.

Corinn tried not to stare at the girl she was supposed to sit by. Had she heard correctly? Had Mrs. Wallace said *Mrs.* Ross? Why, the girl looked young enough to be in short skirts and braids.

Slowly, Corinn scanned the faces in the room again. Of the fifteen or so women present, nearly all of them had streaks of gray in their hair and a wrinkle or two. Three looked to be as old—or older—than Granny Jen. The only one anywhere near her age was the young Mrs. Ross. And she had to be a good eight or so years younger than her own twenty-three. Why, the lass was a mere child.

With a start, Corinn remembered the letter Mr. Parker had written to his uncle, when he was looking for a wife.

There are very few unattached females in this area of Florida, he had said.

With another glance at the young Mrs. Ross, she decided that some men in these parts robbed the cradles.

As she took her seat, the rest of the women sat down, too, around the wide quilting frame. They began stitching the colorful shapes, the wedding ring pattern it was called, intermittently chatting about a myriad of subjects, from husbands to children to school to church to vegetable gardens.

"Was that an orange tree I saw outside, Mrs. Wallace?" Corinn asked timidly, not wanting to be forward among her new acquaintances.

"My, yes. Mr. Wallace planted it when we first moved to Florida." She rolled her eyes. "He insisted that we needed an orange tree, but mostly, the fruit falls to the ground and rots. The children nor I can stand the slimy things. What a mess it makes in my yard."

Corinn tried to keep the look of surprise from her eyes.

"I'm the one who winds up gathering them," Mrs. Wallace said. "I have to haul them across the yard in heaps on a gunnysack and throw them into the woods. I tried giving them to the chickens once, but even *they* turned up their noses. Smart birds, if you ask me."

"May I come and gather your oranges?" Corinn asked.

Mrs. Wallace's eyebrows shot up. "Gather them, you say? Why would you want to do that? Forget the rotted ones. You may have as many as you want, straight from the tree."

"I may?" This time, Corinn smiled—brilliantly— and she didn't care if the women noted her unladylike exuberance. "Long may your chimney smoke, Mrs. Wallace," she added softly.

"What's that?"

"It's an old Scottish saying. It means I wish halcyon days for you."

"Why, thank you, Mrs. Parker. I'll claim prosperity and happiness anytime."

Corinn stared at a red calico quilt square, remembering when she had passed Mrs. Wallace's orange tree that morning, its branches laden to the ground. She looked up and smiled at Mrs. Wallace. "Oranges. . .all I want. . .just for the picking." *Free. I've certainly come into my own halcyon days.*

"Why, a person looking at you would think you had struck gold. What is it about oranges that you love?"

"Marmalade."

"Marmalade?" Mrs. Wallace said, wide-eyed.

"Marmalade?" Mrs. Henderson said, wrinkling her nose.

"Marmalade?" young Mrs. Ross said, pinching her nostrils.

"I cook them up as preserves, using plenty of sugar," Corinn explained. "How I love to make my marmalade."

"And where did you learn to do that?" Mrs. Henderson asked.

"My mother taught me. And her mother taught her. And her mother taught her. And so on. Many years ago, a Scottish woman from the port of Dundee came up with the idea of making marmalade." She moistened her lips, then smiled. "Eating my mother's recipe will make you think you've died and gone to heaven."

"If you can make marmalade like that," Mrs. Wallace said, "I'll pay you a dollar for one jar."

Corinn felt like jumping up and dancing a Scottish jig. Instead, she sat still, hearing her mother's words ringing in her ears. *I'm proud of you, my canny Scot. You're a clever and prudent lass.*

"I'll take the challenge," Corinn exclaimed.

"I'm glad it's you and not me," young Mrs. Ross remarked. "I'm not very good in the kitchen, I'll admit. But give me some knitting needles and yarn, and I can whip out a pair of socks in no time."

"You'll learn," Mrs. Wallace said. "Soon enough. Too soon, in fact. You know what I always say. Love. . . it starts when you sink in his arms. . .and ends with your arms in the sink."

The women cackled. Some even wiped tears from their eyes after their laughter had died down.

"It does my heart good to see these young brides here today," an elderly woman spoke up. "Makes me remember my early days of marriage." Her eyes twinkled.

"You know why we seated you and Mrs. Ross side by side, don't you, Mrs. Parker?" Mrs. Henderson had a mischievous grin on her ruddy face. "Most likely, two new brides have a heap of confidences to share." Guffawing loudly, she elbowed the woman at her side, and several of them followed suit.

Mrs. Henderson rose cumbersomely, her wide girth making it hard to maneuver the tight space around the frame as she bustled out of the room. "It's almost dinnertime. I'll get the food laid out on the trays, Mrs. Wallace. I know where everything is in your kitchen, if it's anything like mine. You all keep sewing. And exchanging confidences—" she let out another loud cackle "—till I call you."

Corinn didn't flinch a muscle, knowing without looking in a mirror that her cheeks were beet-red. Confidences, Mrs. Henderson had said? A heap of confidences, she had talked about?

She cleared her throat, feeling as if she had swallowed a ball of sheepdog hair. The only confidence she had. . .and could never share. . .was an aggrieved heart.

"That Erma," Mrs. Wallace clucked, swinging her head from side to side in exaggerated motions. "She's a sight." She turned to Corinn and touched her arm in a motherly gesture. "She doesn't mean any harm. She'll mind her p's and q's from here on out. I promise."

"There are so few women of marriageable age around here," one of the women spoke up. "New brides are few and far between. We can't let the occasion slip between our fingers without having a little fun with it."

"That's why Erma said what she did," Mrs. Wallace offered. "None of us meant any of this as an affront."

Corinn glanced at Mrs. Wallace, and she was sure she had found a new friend. For life. She looked around the quilting frame at all the women, and she was sure she had found many new friends. For life. Even Mrs. Henderson.

Inwardly, she smiled. Yes, even good-natured Mrs. Henderson. These women sang together in life's chorus —in perfect harmony. She sensed that they understood each other, pulled together, stood beside one another. They were acquainted with—no, akin to—each other's troubles. Surely they poured oil on each other's wounds. They were a sisterhood, a sodality. They were sympathetic, warmhearted, fellow-feeling.

They were just what she needed.

"We didn't mean it as an affront," Mrs. Wallace repeated.

"Affront?" she finally said. "Oh, no. To the contrary. You've endeared yourselves to me this day."

෴

When Mr. Parker arrived to pick up Corrin from the quilting bee, she noticed he had changed from his work attire to Sunday-go-to-meeting clothes. Had he done that for her? When he climbed down from the buggy, Mrs. Wallace insisted that he come in and chat awhile, and Corrin's heart swelled with pride at his impeccable manners and his genteel ways.

Later, on the way home, Corrin sat on the Empire buggy with Edith and Adeline sandwiched between them. When they passed through the pine forest, she didn't even join the wee ones as they counted the tall, skinny trees. Instead, her mind was on the quilting bee.

There are so few women of marriageable age around here, one of the women at the quilting bee had said. *New brides are few and far between,* she'd added.

Corinn drew in a sharp breath of pungent pine as a forceful thought hit her.

I understand Mr. Parker's reason for procuring a wife the way he did. If only I could understand *him.*

She glanced at the tall man across from her, saw the strong set of his handsome jaw, noticed the precise cut of his dress clothing, realized anew how capable he was, how hard he worked, how well-thought-of he was. What was it Dr. Robbins had said about him?

My nephew is Philadelphia-born and bred and well educated. He's hobnobbed with high society since he was a suckling. Whatever he puts his mind to do, he succeeds. Now, it appears he has put his mind to acquiring land in Florida. One day, he'll be an elected official, mark my words.

It didn't matter to Corinn whether Mr. Parker ever became an elected official. He was her husband, bound to her under God's solemn law in the holy estate of matrimony.

If his earthly estate never amounted to anything, she would still be loyal to him as her husband, no matter how unapproachable he seemed to be.

Chapter 6

The next day, Corinn accompanied Mr. Parker to town. They spent the morning running errands, him purchasing farm supplies, her buying household items with little Adeline tagging along at her skirts. She completed her duties and made her purchases, checking "to-dos" off her list, feeling a sense of accomplishment. She and Mr. Parker had agreed to meet at the wagon at noon. On their way home, they would eat the picnic dinner Corinn had prepared earlier that morning.

Now, in the mercantile, amidst bushel baskets of apples and cabbages and bins full of root vegetables, with the smell of coffee beans permeating the air, she gathered up her packages and hurried out the door, nearly colliding with Mr. Parker as he entered the store.

He personified politeness, expressing apologies at his lack of manners, but with a stiff reserve about him.

We may have bumped into each other, Corinn lamented to herself, *but we are as far apart as the North and South Poles.*

Why is this so? she questioned herself. Why were they still a division instead of a convergence? Was the late Mrs. Parker so beautiful that she—the present Mrs. Parker—didn't stand a chance of winning his affection?

"I need to pick up the mail," he said. "And I have a matter to tend to at the livery. Then we'll head for home."

She nodded as she fell into step beside his long strides, their feet making loud plunk-plunks on the boarded walk. "Adeline's been complaining for the longest time that she's hungry. I was on my way to the wagon to get her something out of the basket to tide her over—even though it's a half hour before noon."

"You mustn't spoil her."

Corinn bristled, the familiar chafe surfacing in her chest. Not only had he not greeted Adeline, he had been stern with the child, to her way of thinking. When Corinn was growing up, her father had frequently swung her high into the air, smothering her cheeks with kisses, and his bright laughter had rung out, creating memories that would last a lifetime. Did the Parker family never have any merriment? Was it all strictness and austerity?

She tightened her grip on Adeline's tiny hand. It would be easy to fall a sacrifice to resentment.

Mr. Parker pulled open the door of the mail office, then turned toward Corinn. "Why don't you get the mail, and I'll finish up my business?"

She nodded, then swept into the mail office, little Adeline at her skirt tails.

"Good morning," Corinn said. "I'm Mrs. Parker. May I pick up our mail?"

The postmistress stuck out a plump hand over the

tall counter. "Name's Mrs. Leah Hancock. Welcome to these parts."

"Thank you, Mrs. Hancock. It's a pleasure to meet you." Corinn returned her shake.

The postmistress turned toward the slots behind her, retrieved the mail, then walked back to the counter, and handed her a small stack of letters.

"Thank you again." Corinn stepped backwards, thumbing through the envelopes, studying each one, wondering if she had received any mail from Scotland.

"No mail for Mrs. Parker? Hmmm. That's unusual." The postmistress laughed. "Unusual—that's a good word choice, if I do say so myself." This time she let out a loud peal of laughter then slapped her thigh, like she was laughing at a private joke.

"Unusual? But I've only just moved here."

"The late Mrs. Parker received *lots* of mail." The postmistress put great emphasis on the word "lots," and there seemed to be an air of mystery about her.

"So she was a letter writer too?" Corinn asked cheerily. Perhaps she had something in common with the late Mrs. Parker. That would be nice. "She enjoyed corresponding with people—as I do?"

"I'll never tell." The postmistress paused. "And I wonder if Mr. Parker ever will."

Corinn looked at her, wondering, then said her good-byes and left, troubled over the woman's comments.

All the way to the wagon, the hammering of her footsteps echoed the hammering of her heart. Not only had she married a stranger, she had married one who appeared to be shrouded in secrets.

Chapter 7

As Corinn stirred the bubbling orange concoction in the large pot, she was glad for the warmth coming from the big black stove. For the two months she had lived in Florida, the weather had proved to be sunny and warm. This morning, the first day of November, it was rainy and chilly and had been since dawn, reminding her of the mists of Scotland.

She pulled the pot off the burner, pleased with the way her marmalade was setting up, and decided that this was a good time to take tea—her midmorning respite from her heavy workload.

With precision and care, she laid out a tea tray. First, a lace doily. Then, a china teapot with purple hyacinths and yellow butterflies banded in gilt. A matching footed cup and saucer. Piping hot scones on a cut-glass platter. Fresh-churned butter in a yellow-lustered compote. Warm-from-the-stove marmalade in a silver jam pot, complete with a miniature silver spoon.

She certainly was glad the late Mrs. Parker had been appreciative of fine things. The lovely appointments were a pleasure to behold.

She carried the tray to her favorite place. She remembered the evening she had arrived at Mr. Parker's house and first set eyes on the big double kitchen windows. She had known that this would be her special spot. Now, two cherrywood rocking chairs and a round table stood in front of the windows, softened by flowered pillows and throw rugs.

Every morning in this sunny alcove, she read her Bible. She loved this place, her sanctum of solace. Besides that, when Adeline ventured outside, Corinn could keep her eye on the child as she played on the oak-tree swing. Today, because of the rain, the wee one was in her room, playing with her dollhouse.

She lit a lamp on the table beside her, and the light dispelled the dreariness of the downpour. As she took a sip of her tea, she heard the back doorknob jiggle. Looking up, she was surprised to see Mr. Parker coming inside, his mackintosh dripping with water.

She jumped to her feet, smiling, at the ready to welcome him and help him. "If I didn't know better, I'd think we were in Scotland—rain, rain, and more rain. When you can see Ben Nevis on the horizon, it's going to rain. When you can't see it, it's raining already."

He didn't respond as he took off his rain gear and hung the heavy coat on a hook, then his hat.

She decided her friendliness would make up for his lack. "Ben Nevis is a mountain," she explained as she handed him a towel to dry his face. "We Scots try to make light of our unstable weather."

"I see," was all he said.

Why was he here? At midmorning? She had never

seen him idle. At all times, he labored tirelessly—in the fields, in the barns—wherever his farmwork took him.

He held up a harness. "Mind if I sit in here while I mend this?"

"It's a warm place, this kitchen. Indeed, I'm pleasured at your company. It's time for my morning tea. Would you care to join me?"

"You do this every day, don't you? I've seen you sitting at the window."

She felt like she had been slapped across the cheek. Was he saying that because she had time for tea that she was not working hard? Why, since coming to Florida, she had never worked so hard in all her life, not even when she and Galen had toiled so tediously to make a life for themselves in America.

She resisted the urge to let out a snort of disgust. At Sunny Acres, she had awakened each morning at dawn to prepare a sumptuous breakfast. She cleaned, scrubbed, polished, cooked, gardened, canned, washed, sewed, and ironed. And cleaned, scrubbed, polished, cooked, gardened, canned, washed, sewed, and ironed. Over and over again. Besides that, there had been the children to tend to, though that task had gladdened her heart.

But her labors—they were never-ending. Why, right now, the floors needed sweeping and mopping— a shaft of lamplight revealed a coating of dust—yet she'd just swept and mopped yesterday afternoon. The nerve of him—to criticize her.

"Yes, I'll take some tea." He strode to the washstand and scrubbed his hands, then walked back to the window spot. "My insides could use a touch of something warm."

I couldn't have said it better, Mr. Parker. She gestured at one of the rockers. "Please have a seat." She picked up a cup and saucer from the wall shelf as he sat down, then laid a place for him at the tea table and took her seat opposite him.

Why, oh why, she thought with a sad pang, *couldn't things be different?* This occasion—a husband and wife sitting together for a private moment—should be filled with cordial camaraderie. Instead, she knew from past experience it would be a soliloquy of stony silence. Why was he so unfathomable?

As she poured his tea, she heard the rain pelting the windows. But it was more than raindrops, she was sure. Hail, perhaps? A quick glance told her it was so. Then that meant the temperature had dropped. She glanced covertly at him. Temperature outside—cold. Temperature inside—cold too.

A moment ago, this line of thinking had saddened her. Now, it rankled her. Immediately, she chastened herself. She must not succumb to the legendary disagreeable temper of a Scot.

Scotland selected the thistle as our national emblem, her mother used to say, *because it reflects a Scot's rough character. Anybody who bumps into it gets pricked.*

Corinn felt like she was in a predicament with no glimmer of hope. Yet, she must display a Christlike attitude. She must. Hadn't she promised God that she would seek Him and His righteousness, and in turn, He would supply all of her needs?

Conjuring up her sweetest smile, she put two scones and generous helpings of marmalade and butter on a plate, then held it out to him.

"Thank you," he said, rather cheerily. "One reason I came inside is because of the weather. Another reason is because I wish to talk with you."

She took a sip of tea, trying hard not to rattle the cup when she returned it to the saucer. *Praise be.* Her patience had paid off. He was finally coming around. Then she remembered she wanted to tell him of *her* good news.

"You're a fine cook," he said, after he'd swallowed a bite of scone and wiped his lips in a mannerly gesture.

This is water to a dying plant, Mr. Parker. Surely the sun had come out. At least in her heart.

"You are to be commended for the fine care you've given my daughters."

Ah.

"They've come to think highly of you."

Her heart was pitter-pattering.

He finished his second scone and asked for a third. "I never liked marmalade until I tasted yours."

Oh, Mr. Parker. Then she remembered what she wanted to tell *him.* "I have customers who love it, too," she gushed, so happy she could burst, happy about the sales, but more than that, thrilled that he was conversing with her in a cheerful manner, elated that he was complimenting her. "I've made sixteen dollars thus far and—"

"That's what I want to talk to you about." His features seemed to darken. "It's come to my attention that you are. . .that you are. . .engaged in selling marmalade."

"Yes. Mrs. Wallace provides the oranges. And I don't

even have to use rotting ones. I have my pick of the tree. This isn't costing you a dime."

"That's not the point."

She stared into her tea that was now cold. "I see that you don't approve—"

"A correct assumption."

"I thought you would be proud of me. I thought you would—"

"This is a most embarrassing situation."

"Embarrassing? Any Scot worth his salt is frugal. In fact, thriftiness is lauded in Scotland."

"We're not in Scotland."

"No. . ."

"Neither are we down to cheese parings and candle ends. On the contrary, I am a—"

"Man of means," she said emphatically. She was hurt, wounded to the bone. She thought he'd be proud of her when he found out her marmalade was clamored for and bringing in goodly sums, money that could be put to worthy uses—even though he was a man whom fortune had smiled on.

Unlike her poor Galen.

"I must admit my resources are vast," he said. "I suppose it's time you knew more about my business dealings. . . ."

It's time I knew more about you, Mr. Parker, only you never seem to give me the chance.

"I've worked hard—very hard—to acquire all that I have. And for my efforts, an old saying has proven true for me. 'It never rains but that it pours.' "

She set her cup and saucer on the tea table. Yes, he

had spoken a truth. His resources were vast. He was as rich as Croesus. Galen had been as poor as Job's turkey on beam-ends.

She fought to keep her tears in check. She would not lower herself to weep in this man's presence.

He rocked in his chair as he drained his teacup, the runners making creak-creak noises, the only sounds in the room save the incessant pelting of the rain against the windows.

She gripped the arms of her rocker, her knuckles turning white. Then, like a bird in flight, she fairly flew across the kitchen.

"Here's something to add to your resources, Mr. Parker." From a high shelf, she pulled down a blue and white soup tureen, removed the lid, and scooped out a handful of money. "I promise not to sell any more marmalade." She walked back across the room and thrust the money toward him, her other hand on the rocker to steady herself.

"I can't accept that." He held his palm up in a stop signal.

"I wash my hands of the whole affair." She was so near weeping, she couldn't even look him in the eye.

He waved her away. "I insist that you keep it. You've worked hard for it, I'm sure." He paused, glancing at the cookstove. "Perhaps I need to give you more household money—"

"No. You've been quite generous." She kept staring through the window, holding the money out to him, hoping he wouldn't see her trembles, impatient for him to retrieve the filthy lucre.

"You take it and use it for something that will benefit you," he said.

Suddenly, a loud clap of thunder sounded, and streaks of lightning flashed, lighting up the room as bright as the noonday sun.

From the hallway, Corinn heard Adeline calling her name. The wee girl came racing into the kitchen crying and burrowed her face in Corinn's skirts.

"There, there," Corinn soothed. In one swift movement, she placed the money on the table, then knelt and gathered the tyke in her arms.

"I'm scared, Co-winn," Adeline lisped.

"There's nothing to be frightened of," Mr. Parker said, his chair abruptly stilled as he leaned forward. "You're a big girl, and big girls don't cry."

"Rain, rain, go away," Corinn sang softly, hoping to allay Adeline's fears, "come again some other day." She hugged her, then smoothed her corkscrew curls. "But truly, lassie, we don't want the rain to go away. Remember my flower garden?"

Adeline nodded, her bottom lip pooched out, tears still in her eyes.

"My anemone and wood violet and snowdrop seeds must have rain to make them grow. Just like you need food to make you grow." She smiled. "Which reminds me. How about a nice hot scone and some of my marmalade—"

She stopped, couldn't help wincing. She didn't want to think about marmalade right now. It had been the source of the disagreement between her and Mr. Parker. Then she continued. "I'll even allow you to have a lady's cup of tea today."

"Tea? I can have tea?" The lassie was all smiles. "Like a real lady drinks?"

"Laced with lots of milk. But yes, you can have your own cup of tea."

"Yippee."

"Mind your manners," Mr. Parker said. "Act like a lady if you want a lady's privileges." He stood.

From the corner of her eye, Corinn noticed that the rain had stopped.

"I'd best get back to work," he said.

A surge of strength hit her, and she turned to face him head-on, her gaze unwavering. "Mr. Parker, I'd like to have a word with you. . . ."

He looked puzzled.

"It's about—" She tipped her head sideways at Adeline. "Mr. Parker, if you'll wait here, I'll get her settled, and then we can talk for a few moments."

"For a few moments, then. That's all the time I have." He sat back down on the flowered cushion and began to rock. "I'll wait here."

❧

Corinn settled little Adeline in the parlor with her lady's cup of tea and scones, giving her permission to rewind the music box each time it wound down. "Enjoy the lively tunes, and I'll join you soon," Corinn promised the bright-eyed tyke.

Then she turned and made her way back to the kitchen, dreading her meeting with Mr. Parker. But the time had come for her to state her opinion on a very important matter.

She sat down in her chair, then looked over at him where he sat rocking steadily. She wouldn't bandy words. She would get right to the point. "I've a matter of grave import to discuss with you."

He crossed his arms, then turned his gaze on her, raising his eyebrows as he did so. "Please proceed."

Was he being smug? No matter. She must intervene. "Mr. Parker, I've no intent to show you disrespect. I've carefully weighed what I have to say for some time, and now is the time to say it." She squelched the case of nerves that threatened to overtake her. "I—I hope you'll take it the right way."

"I would very much like to hear what you've obviously thought long and hard about. You indicated you wish to talk to me about Adeline?"

"And Edith."

"Yes?"

"Sometimes you seem so. . .stern with the children."

"I was raised to believe that children should be seen and not heard."

"So was I. . .in certain settings." She took a deep breath and plunged on. "They need more from you as their father."

"I'm a good father," he countered.

"Yes. . ."

"I work hard to provide their food and clothes and baubles."

"They need more than that."

"And just what is it they need, pray tell?"

"They need your love—"

"I love them." He looked smitten, even contrite. "I

care for them beyond description."

"Second, they need your attention."

He stopped rocking and glanced at the floor. "There are only so many hours in the day," he said softly. "I want to do well by them, but I'm overwhelmed with the workload. . . ."

How well I know the feeling, Mr. Parker.

"I can only do so much," he said.

She remembered a father who greeted her with a boisterous hug after a long day's absence and made her laugh and told her stories.

He chewed on his bottom lip. "My father. . .was. . . stern."

"Third," she said, "they need their memories of their mother kept alive, perhaps a picture of her displayed. Every time they talk about her, you stop them."

He only glared at her, his brow furrowed, and she visualized Nessie, the mysterious monster in the dark waters of Loch Ness.

"Fourth, Mr. Parker, they need your affection."

Almost lazily, he reached down and picked up her lace-trimmed handkerchief.

She held her hand out. "I didn't realize I'd dropped it."

As if he was ignoring her, he stared down at it, then ran his fingers along the ruffled edging, not responding. When he reached the first corner, he turned the handkerchief and ran his fingers along the edging of the second side. When he reached the second corner, he turned it and ran his fingers along the third side. When he reached the third corner, he turned it and ran his fingers along the fourth side.

She tapped her toes inside her work shoe. She wiggled her foot. She smoothed her skirts. Wasn't he going to say anything? She was anxious to get this interchange over with. Why didn't he answer her? She wanted to say something but didn't know what to utter. No words came.

When he turned the handkerchief for what seemed like the tenth time, she thought she would burst. Instead, she tapped her toes inside her work shoe. She wiggled her foot. She smoothed her skirts.

"I thought we would marry and grow fond of each other," he whispered. "And then. And then. . ." He looked over at her, and she couldn't read the expression in his eyes.

"*Mrs.* Parker," he said, putting great emphasis on the word "Mrs.," his voice low and controlled. "You—" he paused "—are a wife in name only."

She was stunned. This conversation wasn't about them as man and wife. It was about two wee girls.

"And therefore, you're a mother in name only. You have no right to interfere." He drew out his last sentence, six short-clipped words stretched to a piercing allocution.

She squeezed her hands into tight balls. He was odious. Horrid. Execrable. He had forced her to quaff the bitter cup, and she detested him for doing so.

She absently touched her chignon, her fingers shaking, wondering what to do, what to say. She'd been talking about what the wee ones needed. Instead of addressing what had been placed before him, he had skirted the issue and then offended her. Highly.

She stiffened her shoulders. By offending her in this manner, she decided, he had thrown the red rag to the bull.

The Scots are descendants of the fierce, fighting Irish, she wanted to shout at him. *I have Irish blood in me. I'll not sit still and listen to your insults.*

Needs, they'd been talking about? She let out a snort of disgust. "Mr. Parker, all *you* need around here is a workwoman and a nursemaid," she stormed. "You don't need a wife. You don't know the meaning of the word."

"You don't need a husband. Your ghost gives you quite good company—"

"How dare you speak of Galen in that way?"

"Then you admit it? That he's the barrier between us?"

"You're the barrier, Mr. Parker. If you had ever approached me, just once, with tenderness. Or said a kind word. Or displayed a loving gesture toward me—anything. But no, you've stayed behind your stiff facade—"

"And if you'd ever given *me* a moment's notice," he spouted. "All you ever do is cook and clean and care for my daughters—"

"But it was all for you, Mr. Parker—"

"That's not what I need. I need. . .I need. . ." He looked toward the open door of her bedroom.

She followed his gaze and saw her bed, the red plaid wedding coverlet lying atop it.

"I'll tell you what I need. I need you to get rid of that. . . that thing." He pointed at her coverlet. "I overheard you when you told my daughters the meaning behind it."

"Never," she shrieked. Especially not now—after his insults and harshness.

"Never," she repeated, this time more calmly, knowing exactly what he meant, more determined than ever to keep Galen's sweet, tender memory alive. "All I've ever desired is the love of a good man, and the only man offering me such is now dead." She pushed back the tears that burned her eyes.

"For two months, every time I walked by this doorway, I saw that. . .that thing." His tone a snarl; he gestured at the wedding coverlet.

She was so hurt, she couldn't even make the nasty retort she was harboring.

"We'll make a deal, Mrs. Parker." He spat out the words in disgust. "I'll approach you with tenderness—" he paused, like he was formulating his words "—and say a kind word to you—" he paused again "—and what else was it you said *you* needed?"

He touched his temple. "Ah, yes, now I remember. You said if only I'd display a sweet gesture toward you. I'll tell you what, Mrs. Parker. I'll display a sweet gesture toward you—" he stood, then glared down at her and pointed once more toward her bedroom "—when you do away with that. . .that wedding coverlet."

Angrier than she had ever been, she jumped up and whisked from the room.

Chapter 8

"Today, in honor of our twenty-fifth anniversary," the parson announced from the pulpit, his wife at his side, "I'll be speaking on the topic of marriage."

Corinn sat beside Mr. Parker in his pew with Edith and Adeline to her right, wondering at the coincidental timing of their pastor's sermon. She clutched her Bible, running her fingers along the smooth leather surface. Coincidental? No. That was a misnomer. It was providential. For a week, ever since their tempestuous altercation, she had avoided Mr. Parker, and in turn, he had avoided her.

Perhaps it was time for a truce, though what the truce would be and how it would come about, she could not imagine. To her way of thinking, the rift would be healed when Mr. Parker made the first move. After all, he had been the one who had said such hurtful words.

" 'Husbands, love your wives,' " the parson quoted, " 'even as Christ also loved the church, and gave himself for it.' That Scripture is found in Ephesians. Another Scripture I wish to look at is, 'Wives, submit yourselves unto your own husbands, as unto the Lord'—also found in Ephesians. Let us pray."

After prayer, the parson smiled broadly at the congregation. "Lord Byron said, 'Man's love is of man's life a thing apart. 'Tis woman's whole existence.' In marriage, the man's responsibility is to show courtesy to his wife and make her feel cherished. He must initiate love and cause her to feel desired. What a lofty ideal—for a man to love his wife as Christ loved the church."

For close to forty-five minutes, Corinn listened in rapt attention as the parson preached to the congregation, telling them that ultimately, the husband was responsible to God for what the home became.

She sat there, enjoying the parson's command of the English language, feeling smug at how apropos the sermon was to Mr. Parker and his sad lack.

"As for women, dear ladies, you must give up any preconceived notions as to what men in general are like and discover what *your* man is like. Then you must seek to meet his needs, and in so doing, your needs will be met."

Corinn was dumbstruck. Needs? The parson was referring to needs? That's what she and Mr. Parker had talked about. Needs.

"About the role of a wife, Shakespeare wrote, 'Thy husband is thy lord, thy life, thy keeper, thy head, thy sovereign; one that cares for thee, and for thy maintenance! Commits his body to painful labor, both by sea and land; to watch the night in storms, the day in cold, while thou liest warm at home, secure and safe, and craves no other tribute at thy hands, but love, fair looks, and true obedience, too little payment for so great a debt. Such duty as the subject owes the prince; even such a woman owes her husband.'

"Husbands and wives, I prescribe to you today," the parson continued, "to join your hand and heart to that of your mate's and love each another with sacrificial love, for love is of God, and everyone that loveth is born of God and knoweth God. He that loveth not, knoweth not God, for God is love. Please stand for the closing prayer."

Shakily, Corinn arose, holding tightly to the pew in front of her to steady herself. The parson's words—straight from the Bible—had pierced to her marrow.

❧

On the way home from church, Corinn sat beside Mr. Parker with Edith and Adeline sandwiched between them as they always were when he drove his shiny new buggy. As they clip-clopped through the dense green forest on the warm December day, she felt heartened, thinking about the sermon.

Suddenly, a gust of wind blew the wide brim of her hat backward—causing her to laugh out loud—and a fresh burst of hope filled her being. As she righted her hat, she made a new resolve in her heart.

She would make every attempt to show kindness to this man.

She would make every attempt to get to know this man.

She would make every attempt to become acquainted with his needs.

And she would start now.

"When will Edith be out of school for the Christmas holidays, Mr. Parker?"

"December the nineteenth, I believe."

"Hmm. . .that's only two-and-a-half weeks away."

"I had the bestest day of school yesterday," Edith said.

"You mean, best," Corinn gently corrected, smiling, feeling the sunshine flooding her soul. "And it was Friday, not yesterday, that you last went to school."

"I want to go to 'cool," little Adeline piped up.

Corinn ran her finger up one of Adeline's corkscrew curls, then cupped her chin. "You will, lassie. The time will be here before you know it. And then one day, you'll be all grown-up, and handsome young men will come courting at our house."

Adeline's delightful giggles filled the air.

"Teacher said I'm to read out loud more," Edith said. "She told me I need to practice." She held out her Sunday school papers and pointed to a word. "What's that word, Papa?"

"Have her—" he tipped his head sideways at Corinn, his eyes on the road "—tell you."

Corinn looked at the paper. "The word is tenderhearted. It's from a Scripture in Ephesians."

"Read it to me," Edith said.

"Your teacher said you're the one who needs the practice." Corinn smiled down at her. "Read it for us."

" 'Be ye kind one to another, tenderhearted, forgiving one another,' " Edith slowly read, " 'even as God for Christ's sake hath forgiven you.' "

"That's a powerful verse." Mr. Parker looked over at Corinn.

She thought she detected a flicker of. . .something. . .

that crossed betwixt them—a knowing between them. That was the only way she could interpret it, and it thrilled her.

"It's a Scripture that should be memorized." He took another long look at Corinn, and there was kindness, even tenderness, in his eyes. Then he looked back at the road.

Her heart raced. Yes, she would make every attempt to get to know this man, her wedded husband.

" 'Be ye kind one to another,' " he quoted—with meaning—glancing at her again. " 'Tenderhearted, forgiving one another. . .' "

Forgive me? his eyes implored, *for hurting you with my caustic words?*

Even as God for Christ's sake hath forgiven you, her gaze conveyed. *And hath forgiven me.*

She drew in a slow, deep breath, her heart flip-flopping in her chest. *Oh, Mr. Parker.*

"Edith," Mr. Parker said, "tonight after supper, why don't you read aloud to us? In the parlor."

"I could pop some corn," Corinn offered, tapping on her chin for a moment. She could make it festive. *Yes, I will do that,* she decided. She would make it a grand occasion—to celebrate the fact that she and Mr. Parker had forgiven each other and made things right between them. She was glowing inside—so vibrantly she almost shouted out an Adeline yippee.

Instead, she patted Edith's shoulder. "Why don't we have a soiree tonight?"

"A soiree?" Edith chirped. "What's a soiree?"

"What's a soiree, Mr. Parker?" Corinn asked.

A long moment passed with him not saying a word, and Corinn was surprised that neither girl broke the silence.

"A soiree is an evening party," he finally said.

"A party?" Edith shrieked.

"A party?" Little Adeline squealed.

Corinn nodded, smiling again, enjoying the twinkles dancing in their eyes. "We'll tell stories, and Edith can read some things aloud to us. And we'll sing some songs and—" She stopped, thinking about what else they would do at their soiree. "And we'll have some party dainties to eat."

Both girls clapped their hands and shouted with glee. Adeline added, "Yippee."

"That sounds like a pleasant proposition," Mr. Parker said, a smile on his face.

Chapter 9

That afternoon, Corinn made preparations for their evening soiree. She decided which stories to tell, selected a few readings of Burns, chose a children's book for Edith to read aloud, and placed her lap harp in the parlor, at the ready to accompany them when they all sang together.

Then she went into the kitchen and put on her daisy-dotted apron. Social gatherings always had delectable food, and for this special occasion, she would make a few dainties. Scottish shortbread would be one of them. As lively folk tunes danced in her head, she laid out the makings.

She passed the double kitchen windows and saw Edith swinging on the oak-tree swing and little Adeline awaiting her turn nearby.

"Swinging on the oak-tree swing," Corinn sang. "Soaring where the bluebirds sing, oh, to be a girl with a headful of curls, swinging on the oak-tree swing."

Under the sprawling branches, she saw Mr. Parker sitting on a bench—a sight she had never seen—him in a state of inaction, his labors in abeyance, enjoying his daughters. Her heart swelled with emotion.

Again, as had happened on the way home from church, sunshine flooded her soul and hope for their future soared to new heights.

She took the flour canister down from the kitchen shelf, walked to the table, and measured two even cups into a mixing bowl. "Swinging on the oak-tree swing," she sang at the top of her voice, "soaring where the bluebirds sing—"

When she heard Edith scream, her heart stopped, and she jumped up, raced across the kitchen and out the door, frantic with worry.

As her feet flew over the back walkway, she saw Mr. Parker hovering over Edith who lay on the ground. Nearby lay the swing, one of its ropes severed and frayed.

Edith screamed again, and Corinn saw that Edith's arm was twisted in a grotesque angle. "Dear God. . ." Tears sprang to her eyes, but she forced them back. Edith needed her strength right now.

"Mr. Parker?" she said softly as she bent over him and touched his shoulder.

He looked up, a wide arc of sunlight lighting his worry-filled face. Corinn saw that he, too, had tears that apparently he was trying to keep at bay.

Edith screamed in agony, and Corinn fell to her knees in the dirt and put her mouth in the tyke's ear. "You're going to be all right, lassie," she crooned, seeing the twisted arm, not sure at all if Edith would be all right. Would she lose the use of her arm? The thought made Corinn sick to her stomach.

Adeline whimpered behind Corinn as she kept

crooning to Edith.

"It hurts so bad," Edith cried. "So bad."

"I know, my wee one. I know. But soon, we'll have you all righted, and—"

"I want Mama's Bible," Edith wailed.

"I'm going to try to move her into the house," Mr. Parker whispered to Corinn, "and then I'm going for Dr. Adams."

Corinn nodded. Why did a mishap have to happen—just when things were looking so bright? And why did a mishap have to involve one of the wee girls? If a tragedy had to occur, why couldn't she have taken the brunt?

Edith screamed out again, and the pain in Corinn's heart was so great, she wanted to cry out, too. Instead, she stroked Edith's cheek, then dabbed at the tyke's tears with the tail of her apron.

"Please let me have Mama's Bible," Edith begged, great heaving sobs shaking her little body. "If I can just hold Mama's Bible. . ."

"I'll get it," Corinn offered, willing to do anything to help Edith. "Where is it, Mr. Parker?"

A shadow crossed his face. "I'll get you a Bible, Edith. Mine is handy—"

"I want Mama's."

Corinn held Edith's shoulders to keep her from shaking so badly. "If she thrashes about too much," she whispered to Mr. Parker, "it might damage her arm further."

"Papa, please—"

"Let's get her into the house." His face was lined with deep distress.

Corinn nodded.

"You go pull down her bed, while I carry her in." Gently, with the finesse of a musician, taking great care with her twisted limb, he scooped Edith into his arms, then stood up.

"Papa, what about Mama's Bible—"

"After I leave for the doctor—" he looked down at Edith, his voice choked, his words halting "—Corinn will get your mama's Bible for you."

❧

With Edith settled in bed but moaning in pain, Corinn followed Mr. Parker into the kitchen at his bidding.

He stopped and faced her. . .

He peered into her eyes. . .

He grasped her hand. . .

He turned it palm side up.

For a moment, she thought her heart had ceased its beating.

His eyes seemed to search her soul as he placed a key in her hand. "This will open that door," he said softly, gesturing at the pantry. But his gaze never left her face. "Edith's mother's Bible is on the second shelf."

I trust you, his eyes told her.

I know, Mr. Parker, her eyes told him. *And I am glad. So very glad.*

"I'll be back as soon as I can," he said over his shoulder as he dashed out the door.

Chapter 10

As breathless as a burglar on the stealth, feeling like an interloper in this abode, Corinn approached the kitchen pantry with a sense of misgivings and trepidation. Somehow she knew that behind this door, she would find the answer to the many questions she had asked herself throughout the three months she had lived here.

She knew uncannily that, in past years, all had not been sunny at Sunny Acres. What would the pantry reveal? What would she find behind that locked door, besides the late Mrs. Parker's Bible?

She put the key in the lock and turned it, then pulled on the doorknob, but nothing happened. She turned the key again, but still, it would not open. Had Mr. Parker given her the wrong key? She pulled out the key and brushed a few specks of rust tracings from the lock, then thumped on it. Why wouldn't it release its hold?

She put the key in the lock a second time and turned it. Still nothing happened. Her heart lurched within her breast. She couldn't disappoint this tyke, especially in her pain-wracked state. She would rather take a beating than have to tell Edith she could not bring her the treasured Bible.

Edith called out, begging for her mama's Bible, and Corinn heard her—all the way in the kitchen.

"I'm coming, lassie," Corinn called back. "Hold tight."

Turning the key once again, then jiggling it, Corinn felt like shouting in glee when the lock gave way at last. Trembling, she yanked on the knob and swung open the door, its hinges squeaking from disuse.

Before her eyes, on the second shelf of the pantry, she saw stacks and stacks of china plates, cups, saucers, and platters—surely more than one family would ever have need of—all the pieces red-flowered and grotesque.

She stared at the third shelf, lined with exquisite porcelain figurines. Puzzled, she looked more closely at them.

Were there one. . .two. . .three. . .she kept counting . . .half a dozen of the same dancing lady in a tiered red gown? That was odd.

One. . .two. . .three. . .four. . .five of the same soldier in a red uniform blowing a bugle?

One. . .two. . .three. . .four of the same girl holding a red basket on her arm?

And parasols. She quickly counted eight of them, all identical, all bright red silk. And there were more behind the first bundle.

On the fourth shelf—she was squatting to be at eye level—she saw a towering stack of books—all with the same title—*The Day of the Red Haze*.

She inched back up, feeling dazed. Instinctively, she knew these items had been the late Mrs. Parker's.

On the very top shelf, higher than she was tall, she saw lovely music boxes, all with red bases. When she stood on the tips of her toes, she still couldn't see them all, so crowded were they against the wall.

Words popped into her mind. Eccentric. Unsound. The words kept coming. Delusional. Daft.

Daft? She grabbed hold of the doorknob, trying to summon the breath that had been knocked from her. For that's what she'd experienced—a blow—as surely as she was standing here.

She remembered the day she had arrived and Edith had said, *Florida means 'flowery land,'* and she had replied, *That must mean flowers are everywhere*. Mr. Parker had said, *Only where they're planted*, his features expressionless. By the thick viney undergrowth surrounding Sunny Acres, she had quickly determined that, indeed, no one had planted flowers in years.

She recalled him telling her that Mrs. Henderson had been cooking and cleaning for his family for several years and that a seamstress kept his daughters well clothed. *But I thought your wife passed away only months ago*, she had naively said. He hadn't responded, only given her a stony stare.

She remembered when Adeline had said, *Mama said I was her baby*, and Mr. Parker had commanded her to stop her chatter.

She recalled the sad disarray of the house.

She remembered Mr. Parker's harsh tone when she had tried to open the pantry door. *This door is always locked*, he had said.

She recalled the gift he had given her the night she

arrived. *It's fripperies,* he had told her. *All women want fripperies.*

Fripperies? She stared at the music boxes, at the stacks of china, at the dancing ladies and bugle-blowing soldiers and basket-carrying girls, at the red silk parasols, at the books, all with the same title.

The late Mrs. Parker had liked fripperies.

A hard shudder shook her, and she grasped the doorknob more firmly. Then she hugged her upper body, suddenly feeling cold to the bone, despite the heat from the cookstove.

She looked across the kitchen. Had she been standing at the stove only an hour ago? About to begin baking something for some occasion?

Her mind was fuzzy. Hadn't she been planning a special event for tonight? To celebrate something? She glanced back at the shelves in the pantry. Then her mind continued its journey down memory lane.

Edith snapping at Adeline, when she'd said her mother had played with them every day. *You know Papa doesn't want us talking about that.*

Mrs. Henderson's comment. *I can't help wondering if the new Mrs. Parker will fare better than the last one.*

The remarks the postmistress had made. *No mail for Mrs. Parker? Hmmm. That's unusual.*

That woeful word came to her mind again. *Daft.*

Poor Mrs. Parker had taken leave of her senses. Poor Mrs. Parker.

She was stunned. Poor *Mr.* Parker. She rubbed her temples, couldn't think anymore.

"Corinn," Edith wailed. "Are you coming?"

Was Edith calling her?

"Mama's Bible. Did you find Mama's Bible?"

Edith had fallen when the swing snapped.

Edith had broken her arm.

Edith had wanted her mama's Bible.

From the locked pantry.

Suddenly, thankfully, her mind grew clear, and she remembered Mr. Parker saying that the Bible was on the second shelf. She moved the footed teacups. She shifted the stacks of saucers. She pushed aside the china plates. There, shoved against the wall, was a black Bible.

The late Mrs. Parker's Bible.

Poor Mrs. Parker.

Poor *Mr.* Parker. What had all this meant for him?

Without any explanation, she knew.

He would never have to tell her about it. She just knew.

Yes, poor Mr. Parker.

No, *dear* Mr. Parker.

Chapter 11

Corinn carried a tray laden with refreshments into the parlor and set it down on the mahogany table, humming a hymn, thankful that Edith's arm was healing well.

She glanced about the large room, admiring the furnishings, enjoying the scene, absorbing the ambiance. The highly polished mahogany pieces shone in the lamplight, and the fragrance of freshly cut flowers filled the air. Over at the hearth, a fire burned in the grate, its yellow flames saying *welcome*. Next week, when Christmas came, a decorated pine tree would grace the corner.

She peered into the mirror above the mantel, fingering the delicate ruching around the neckline of her green silk dress. The flowing sleeves as well as the cupped-in waistline added a feminine touch, and she was glad she had decided on this pattern. The mirror revealed that her cheeks were glowing with color, and she sighed, knowing it was not from the warmth of the fire.

She strode back to the table and placed the platters of dainties on its polished surface. She had spent all afternoon preparing for an evening soiree, and she was looking forward to it as much as the wee ones. At first, when Edith had asked if they could have it, Mr. Parker said no, that it was only a week after her accident. But when he asked Dr. Evans about it, he had said it would do the child good. After that, Mr. Parker had readily agreed.

I want her to get well soon, Mr. Parker had told Corinn. *I have grand plans to spend more time with her, as well as Adeline.*

She looked at the clock in its handsome fine-grained casing just as the chime bonged out seven bright tones. At seven-thirty, she would usher the lassies into the parlor, as she had promised them, to begin the soiree. She envisioned them in their room this moment, getting dressed by themselves as they had begged to do. *Like ladies,* they had said.

The door to the hallway opened, and Mr. Parker walked in. With her seamstress's eye, she took in his finely cut apparel, from his burgundy waistcoat to his gray serge trousers to his white satin tie. *He looks dashing,* she decided, *as dashing as any man I've ever seen.*

"May I speak with you?" he asked. "I don't want to interrupt your preparations. Do you have a few moments?" Like the gentleman that he was, he stood near the door awaiting her response, as if he were ready to retreat if need be.

"Yes, of course. We've plenty of time." Corinn finished arranging a doily on the table, thinking about the night of Edith's accident, after the doctor had left.

As soon as possible, I'd like to talk with you, Mr. Parker had told her, his eyes troubled.

About the kitchen pantry, her look had said back.

But the entire week, she had run herself ragged tending to Edith as well as her other chores, and so had he. There had simply been no time for them to converse.

Now, as they seated themselves in the parlor, he on a rose damask chair that looked much too small for his tall frame, she on the matching settee, swallowed by the length of it, she couldn't help but feel fidgety, remembering the sight she'd beheld last week when she'd swung open the pantry door. She remembered grabbing hold of the knob, trying to summon the breath that had been knocked from her.

"Edith and Adeline are looking forward to the soiree this evening," he said brightly, smiling at her. "Perhaps there'll be many soirees in the future."

"That would be nice. . . ."

He crossed his right ankle over his left knee. He drummed his fingers on the upholstered chair arm. He stared into the flames.

She glanced at the clock. "You said you wished to speak with me?"

He glanced at the clock, too, then gripped both chair arms, his knuckles white. "Ten years ago, the late Mrs. Parker and I came to Florida. I'd heard about the reasonable land prices and the virgin timber and the rich soil."

He looked down at the hardwood floor. "I had high hopes for our lives in this beauteous new state. My goals were to acquire acreage, establish myself in the area, and do some land prospecting. After that, the sky was the limit, to my way of thinking. And that's exactly the way things turned out. I acquired acreage, established myself in the area, and did some land prospecting.

"And," he continued, "to put the icing on the cake, two beautiful daughters joined our family. They brought us great pleasure. Things couldn't have been sunnier at Sunny Acres."

He crossed his left ankle over his right knee. He drummed his fingers on the upholstered chair arm. He stared into the flames. "It was when Adeline was a year old that I began to notice—"

"You don't have to continue, Mr. Parker. I know."

"You know?" He looked in her direction, his eyebrows shooting up.

She returned his intense gaze with one of her own, a cognizance passing between them.

"Yes, you know," he said quietly. "You know. . .but I need to say a few things."

She nodded, folded her hands in her lap.

"Madeline began to order the. . .the. . ."

"Fripperies?"

"Yes. . .fripperies." He nodded only slightly. "Madeline chose them from catalogues. Red was a fixation with her. They began arriving almost daily. First, the parasols. Then the music boxes. Then the china. On and on it went. It was. . .it was mail-order mayhem."

He looked so pained Corinn wanted to run to his side and draw him into her arms, like she'd done with Edith and Adeline many a time when they were hurt or afraid.

"And there were other things she did. . .and did *not* do. . .many things."

Mail-order mayhem, he had said? She swung her chin up, then down, understanding flooding through her.

"The postmistress. . ." *The late Mrs. Parker received lots of mail,* the postmistress had said. Corinn clutched at her throat. "That's why the postmistress said what she did."

It was as if he hadn't heard her. He stared into the flames. "It was so hard, seeing Madeline like that. For as long as I'd known her, she'd been vibrant. . .beautiful . . .capable," he choked out. "I loved her dearly."

His face contorted in agony. "Madeline," he whispered. He sat forward, his elbows propped on his knees, his fingertips rubbing his temples. "I've asked myself a million times if there was anything I could've done. Should've done."

Corinn squirmed in her chair, feeling his misery, wanting to ease his pain, grieving with him over the demise of his beautiful wife. "Mr. Parker, surely you realize it wasn't your fault."

He didn't say anything for a long moment. "Then, I decided to remarry," he finally said, nearly whispering. He pulled his chair closer to her, so close their knees almost touched. "I knew I wanted to give my heart to my new bride—whomever she would be—but I also wanted to honor her tender sensibilities.

"When you arrived," he continued, "I provided a private place for you. I assumed affection would come to us eventually, and I also assumed that our fondness would run its natural course. But I was determined to be very careful. For the marriage ceremony, I even told the parson to skip the part about the kiss."

He looked directly at her, his eyes seeming to mesmerize hers. "I figured. . . ," his voice grew husky, his breathing ragged as his hands found hers and held them tightly, "I figured kisses would come when. . .when. . ."

"Co-winn," shouted little Adeline, running into the parlor, shattering the magical moment.

Neither Corinn nor Mr. Parker made a move, their hands still entwined.

"Co-winn, Co-winn." The tyke tugged on Corinn's skirts.

She stood up, smiled down at Adeline, touched her white-blond curls. "I thought you and Edith wanted to be ushered into the parlor like ladies."

"But Edith says it's—"

"Seven-forty," Edith said from the doorway, leaning against the doorjamb, her right arm cradled around a white sling on her left arm. "At least I think that's what the eight means. Isn't it time to start the soiree?"

"Yes, it's time," Corinn whispered to Edith, but her eyes were on Mr. Parker. "It's time."

❧

All evening, they enjoyed the soiree, telling stories, reading aloud, eating the dainties, and singing songs accompanied by Corinn on her lap harp. She even wound up the music box and tried to teach Edith and Adeline the steps to a Scottish reel, their shoes clacking on the hardwood floor. Over and over, she repeated the instructions until they caught on, stepping forward then backward, right then left, leaping in the air as they held up a knee.

As the music box played for the sixth time, Corinn and Edith, and then Corinn and Adeline, jigged the reel with near perfection. When it ended, the three of them were raucous with laughter.

After their merriment died down, Corinn settled

Edith on the settee, her arm propped on a pillow, then Adeline beside her. "One last piece of Scottish shortbread and one last cup of punch for the lassies." She handed the goodies to them.

"These are pretty cookies, Co-winn," little Adeline said, then popped hers in her mouth.

"Yes," Mr. Parker agreed. He picked up a shortbread cookie from the cut-glass platter Corinn held out to him. He studied the fancy edging on it. "It's evident you spent a lot of time making these."

Corinn reached for one too. "And I loved every moment." She ran her finger along the spiked edge. "This is called fluting."

"Fluting?"

She nodded. "It's an old Scottish symbol—the sun's rays. It represents hope for the return of spring."

"Hope?" he asked, his eyes searching hers.

"Hope," she said softly.

"I—I appreciate all that you do for our family," he stammered.

Our family, he'd said? Hope surged through her being. Surely spring was on its way to this household that had been awry for a long winter.

As she sipped a cup of punch, she couldn't help but smile to herself. In nature, spring was a time of growth and development. She thought of the spring beauties she would soon plant, pictured the two-leafed stems bursting forth bearing delicate pink flowers, emerging from the hard-packed dirt though their seeds had long been dormant.

She touched the purple wood violets in the tall vase

on the side table. Yes, here in Mr. Parker's household, beauty was emerging, though its seed had long been dormant.

When the clock chimed on the half hour past nine, Mr. Parker announced bedtime.

"Papa, please let Corinn teach you the reel," Edith begged. "Like she taught us."

"Yeth, Papa," little Adeline lisped.

"It's growing late." His voice held concern. "You two need your rest, particularly Edith."

"It's so much fun, Papa," Edith said. "Please? I promise to go to sleep as soon as my head touches the pillow."

Corinn looked over at him, and there were smiles in his eyes. "Sir?" she questioned, her heart racing.

"I'd be honored." With a flourish, he stood up and strode to the middle of the floor.

Corinn wound the music box and set it down, the lively tune filling the air, then walked toward him, feeling awkward and nervous, but tingly too.

They came together face-to-face, and neither said a word.

"Put your hand on her back, Papa," Edith said, suddenly at his side. She picked up his hand and placed it on Corinn's waistline. "There." Then she moved back to her spot on the settee.

"Yes. . .there." Corinn could feel the color rushing into her face. "We'll go slowly at first, Mr. Parker, so you can learn the steps."

"And hold her fingers with your other hand, Papa," Edith said.

"Like this?" He took Corinn's hand and held it out in midair, his gaze never leaving her face—as if his eyes were memorizing her every nuance.

As if his eyes were. . .feasting on her? She sighed. Was she going to swoon?

"Like this?" he repeated, squeezing her fingers.

She didn't even nod in agreement. She didn't have to. For his thoughts were her thoughts, and her thoughts were his thoughts.

"Start with your left foot," she whispered. "Move one step to the right, then move back in place."

He did as she said, tightening his hold on her waist and squeezing her hand more firmly.

If she had been in a cocoon, she would have burst forth as a brightly colored butterfly. The room was filled with kindness and affection and tenderhearted-ness, and she warmed to it, embraced it. This. . .was the abode of love.

"Move one step to the right, Mr. Parker," she said softly, "then, move back into place." She paused as they completed the action. "Then raise your left knee while I raise my right one and hop in the air."

As they hopped, not a spot touching save for his light graze on the small of her back and their fingers in midair, their eyes locked for what seemed like all time.

" 'Whoso findeth a wife findeth a good thing,' " he whispered, " 'and obtaineth favour of the LORD.' "

She willed herself not to go weak-kneed. *Oh Mr. Parker. My dear Mr. Parker. My beloved Trevor.*

The music ended abruptly, and Edith and Adeline raced toward them, Adeline burying her face in Corinn's skirts, Mr. Parker scooping Edith up and giving her a hug. "Wasn't that fun, Papa? Wasn't it?" she shrieked, laughing. "See? I told you it would be fun. Corinn's my favored friend."

"Hmm," he said, looking contemplative. "By favor, Edith, do you mean you regard her highly?"

In answer, Edith did as Adeline was doing and buried *her* face in Corinn's skirts, and Corinn thought her soul would burst with happiness.

"Favor also means to win approval." With a thankful heart, Corinn hugged Edith to her. She had finally won the tyke's approval and affection.

She took a deep breath. She had finally won Mr. Parker's approval. . .and affection.

"I'm glad I won yours, Corinn," he said. In his eyes was that familiar knowing again, and she knew exactly what he was referring to.

Chapter 12

Christmas Eve

Corinn left her bedroom and walked into the kitchen, wondering when Mr. Parker would come inside. She lifted the yellow ruffle at the window and peered into the night, dark except for the light shining from the lantern beside the back door.

Earlier, they'd had their Christmas Eve supper. Then, while Mr. Parker had checked on something in the barn—she knew not what—she bedded the lassies. But Edith and Adeline had repeatedly risen, too excited to sleep because of the prospects of Christmas surprises. Now, it appeared they were in dream world, judging by the fact that not a noise had come from their room for a full fifteen minutes.

She sat down in her kitchen rocker, wondering what Mr. Parker would say about her Christmas gift to him. She felt her face grow hot, fanned it with her handkerchief, sighed. Then she settled back against the slats, her heart thumping hard in eager anticipation.

She remembered when Edith had asked her if it was

time to start the soiree. *Yes, it's time,* she had whispered to Edith, but her eyes had been on Mr. Parker. *It's time,* she had repeated, knowing full well what she meant.

She fiddled with her chignon, her hands shaking. Was tonight the right time? To—

The doorknob jiggled, and she jumped.

"Are the girls asleep?" he asked as he came inside, then took off his coat and hung it on a hook.

"As far as I can tell." She fingered her buttons as the runners of the rocker *ker-plunked* on the hardwood floor.

He walked over to her. "Mind if I sit?"

"I'd be delighted. Would you like some tea? Coffee?" She made a movement to stand, but he waved her down as he sat beside her.

"No, thank you. Your Christmas Eve meal. . .I don't believe I've ever tasted better cooking."

"You already told me."

He crossed his left ankle over his right knee. He drummed his fingers on the wooden chair arm. He stared at the far side of the room.

She continued her ker-plunking.

He jumped up and dashed across the kitchen, then peered down the hall.

"What is it, Mr. Parker?" she asked.

"I thought I heard the girls, but I guess I didn't." He strode toward her, then stopped midstride in front of her bedroom door.

From where she was sitting, she could clearly see what was happening. She knew why Mr. Parker had stopped in front of her bedroom door. She knew what he had seen. He had discovered one portion of her

Christmas gift to him, and her breathing became ragged.

"The wedding coverlet. . .you removed it." He looked at her questioningly.

"Yes," she said shyly.

He rushed to her, drew her up from the rocker, crushed her in his embrace. "My darling. . .Corinn Parker." He kissed her. "Say *my* name."

She looked up at him, wondering.

"Please?" he said.

"Mr. Parker."

"And my given name with it."

"Trevor Parker," she said timidly.

"I'm glad my name's Trevor Parker instead of John Smith," he said with a twinkle in his eye.

"Why?"

"If my name were John Smith, I wouldn't be able to enjoy your Scottish burr."

She smiled.

"I love the way you roll those r's."

"Yes, Mr. Trevor-r-r Par-r-r-ker-r-r, your-r-r name gives my tongue quite a wor-r-r-k-out."

He leaned over and kissed her, squeezing her to him.

When she was able, she murmured, "The rest of your Christmas gift is in *your* bedroom."

He drew back. "My bedroom?"

"Go see."

"Come with me." He took her hand, and they walked to his bedroom.

There, on his bed was a plaid wedding coverlet, only it was blue plaid, not red like the other one.

He smiled from ear to ear, then drew her into a tight embrace as he kept smiling. "You've been sewing it for weeks, haven't you?" He didn't wait for her answer. "I thought you were sewing Christmas things for the girls."

"I did that too. But I've been working on our wedding coverlet since—"

"Since the sermon?"

She smiled, dipped her chin demurely, nodded. "I bought the fabric in town. . .with the money from the marmalade. . .the money you told me to keep."

He lifted her chin with his finger, forcing her to meet his sensuous gaze. "The money I told you to use for yourself." Now *he* was smiling, and his eyebrows were going up and down, and he tipped his head in the direction of the wedding coverlet.

She knew her cheeks were flaming as she caught his meaning. She felt her heart racing. Encircled in his arms, she felt *his* heart racing. Love had finally come— to both of them—and she let out a little sigh.

He pointed to the framed sampler she had just completed and hung on the wall above his bed.

FLORIDA, MY HOPE AND HOME

He read it aloud, then repeated it, his voice husky. "Oh, Corinn. . .my darling."

She saw the two of them down through time, husband and wife—*certainly* not in name only—happily rearing a large family in this young, prosperity-filled state. Then a sad thought gnawed at her. If only she were a beautiful woman to grace the side of this tall, handsome gentleman who would one day be a person of public prominence.

"I'm plain." She tucked an errant lock of hair behind her ear, so thin it brushed back into her face.

"You're pretty."

"I'm uncomely."

"You're uncommonly lovely." He kissed the lock of her hair, then her lips, then drew back slightly. "I'll never forget the first moment I laid eyes on you. You were standing on the gangplank with that little beret on your head and your plaid about your shoulders."

"I stood there, trying to summon my courage to meet you. I prayed that you would love me as Isaac loved Rebekah."

"I do."

She giggled an Adeline giggle, couldn't help herself. "Yippee," she exclaimed, and Mr. Parker grinned.

" 'For sweet is thy voice, and thy countenance is comely,' " he quoted. "That's from Song of Solomon."

She gazed adoringly up at him. "Oh, Mr. Parker. My dear Mr. Parker. My beloved Trevor."

Chapter 13

Edith crept back into bed beside Adeline and adjusted her nightcap with her good arm. Then she snuggled down under the covers, gently elbowing her sister. "Marmsie is sleeping in Papa's bedroom tonight."

"Mawm-sie?"

"Yes. Marmsie. And I heard her say, 'Yippee.'"

Adeline giggled her delightful giggle.

"And there's a picture of Mama in the parlor."

Adeline giggled again.

"'Night, Adeline."

"'Night, Edith."

"Sleep tight, and don't let the bedbugs bite."

KRISTY DYKES

Kristy lives in sunny central Florida with her hero husband Milton, and she's a native Floridian as are generations of her forebears. She's had hundreds of articles published in such publications as two *New York Times* subsidiaries, *Guideposts's Angels*, *Leadership*, etc. For one *Times* subsidiary, she wrote a weekly cooking column, "Kristy's Kitchen," which generated more reader mail than the letters to the editor page! Kristy is also a public speaker, and one of her favorite topics is "How to Love Your Husband." Her goal in writing is to "make them laugh, make them cry, and make them wait" (a Charles Dickens's quote). In all her endeavors, her motto is, "Whatever your hand finds to do, do it with your might" (Ecclesiastes 9:10).

Blessed Land

by Nancy J. Farrier

Dedication

To Anne who had so much fun
plotting the story with me.
To Dell and Audrey who read it in a hurry.
For John, with whom I am blessed.

In that I command thee this day to
love the LORD thy God,
to walk in his ways,
and to keep his commandments
and his statutes and his judgments,
that thou mayest live and mutliply:
and the LORD thy God shall bless thee
in the land whither thou goest to possess it.

DEUTERONOMY 30:16

Chapter 1

Spring 1854

The big dun horse whickered softly and stomped his foot. Antonio Escobar grinned and rubbed Grande's neck. "Sorry, amigo. You must be the most jealous horse in all of Tucson. I'm only looking at the senorita, not asking her to marry me."

Antonio continued to brush Grande as he looked back down the stable aisle where his cousin, Chico, talked to a young woman at the entrance of the building. Chico lifted his horse's leg off his knee and stood slowly, like someone whose back has been bent in an awkward position for too long.

Smiling, Antonio watched his handsome cousin at work. Chico, with his silver tongue. Chico, the man at whom all the women flashed their eyes as he swaggered down the street. A chuckle welled up, threatening to burst forth. For once, Chico had met his match. This young woman refused to buy his sweet talk.

The quirt in her hand snapped rhythmically against her skirt. The tip of her long braid swung slightly, showing beneath the scarf she wore over her head. From the cut of her clothing and her proud stance, Antonio gathered she came from a wealthy family. Although he couldn't see her face clearly, he knew she was a stranger to their small pueblo. He watched all the senoritas who came to visit Chico, and this one was new. Perhaps she would be the answer to Antonio's prayers. Despite his assurance to Grande, he hoped that someday the Lord would answer his prayer for a wife and family.

Chico moved around the horse closer to the girl. She lifted the quirt like a weapon and stepped back. Chico flashed his infamous grin, the one designed to set hearts thumping and fans whirring. But to no avail. The girl continued to gesture toward the small adobe house in front of the stables, where Antonio lived and had his workshop.

Grande nickered again and nudged his shoulder. Antonio patted him absently on the neck. "I think I will have to finish you later, amigo. It looks to me like this lady in distress needs rescuing." Antonio nodded his head toward the pair near the door. "Or, perhaps, this time it's Chico who needs help." He laughed softly and sauntered down the aisle, past horses boarded in stalls and others waiting to be shod. Yes, this just might be the one time Chico would lose and he, Antonio, would win.

He could see the young woman more clearly now, even if the view was from the side. He noted the tilt of her head, her slender neck, the smooth dusky cheek that made him long to run a finger across it. She lifted a slim hand, gesturing once more as if trying to make Chico understand the importance of her mission. Antonio couldn't take his eyes off her. A longing to help and protect her nearly overwhelmed him.

Her hand ached from the desperate grip she had on her quirt. Paloma Rivera forced herself to loosen her fingers, trying at the same time to rid herself of the longing to use the small whip to wipe the idiotic grin from this hombre's face. She could feel the anger starting at the pit of her stomach and working its way throughout her body like a living thing. Why wouldn't he help her? Instead, the imbecile seemed to think he could wink at her, and she would swoon at his feet like some empty-headed buffoon.

"Rosita Lopez. I'm looking for my sister, Rosita Lopez," Paloma repeated for what seemed like the hundredth time. "Her husband's name is Pablo. Have you seen them?"

"Is there a problem, Chico?"

Paloma swiveled around to face the newcomer now sauntering down the stable walkway. Her breath caught in her throat. For a moment, she forgot her mission. Gunmetal black eyes, glinting with humor, captured hers. She noted the stranger's strong arms. Muscular arms. Probably strengthened from his hours of physical labor running the blacksmith shop. His hair, combed straight back, fell in raven waves that dipped and shone in the afternoon light. Paloma gave herself a mental shake, trying to remember why she was here.

Standing straight and as tall as she could at five-one, Paloma blurted, "I explained to this mor. . .um, this man that I'm looking for my sister, Rosita Lopez. Do you know where I can find her?"

She didn't miss the fleeting glance directed toward

Chico or Chico's answering shrug. What was going on here?

He bowed slightly to her and said, "Allow me to introduce myself. I'm Antonio Escobar, owner of this establishment."

She nodded in greeting. "Paloma Rivera. As I said, I'm looking for my sister. I must find her."

"And why do you think you will find your sister in a stable?" Antonio grinned, and she noted the slight gap between his front teeth. Why did he have to be so handsome?

She sighed, allowing her gaze to wander over the walls lined with tools and tack for use with the horses. "This was the last address that my sister gave when she wrote home."

"And may I ask how long ago she wrote?"

Paloma shifted uncomfortably. "We haven't heard from her in three years."

"Three years?" Antonio's eyes widened. "And you think that after three years she might still live here—at this address?"

Clenching her jaw, Paloma fought back the tears of frustration. Nothing was working out right. She had ridden to the small pueblo of Tucson, hoping to convince her sister to come back home to Mexico. When Rosita and Pablo moved up here, Tucson was still a part of Mexico. Now, with the Gadsden Purchase signed and the ratification nearly finished, Tucson would soon become a part of the United States of America instead of the United States of Mexico. Hatred welled up inside. She couldn't bear for Rosita to be a citizen of

America. She had to bring her back home to Mexico where she belonged.

"Please, Senor Escobar, it's the only place I had to begin my search. I didn't think I would have any trouble finding her. I know she hasn't written, but sometimes the mail is very slow making its way to us."

Antonio's gaze softened as if in sympathy for her plight. "Your sister and her husband aren't here. Perhaps they chose to move on. Many people have trouble making a living in Tucson."

"But Pablo was always good with horses. I thought maybe he worked for you."

Antonio shook his head. "The only one who helps me here is my cousin, Chico." He indicated the young man leaning on the partially shod horse. Chico flashed his idiotic grin at her.

"What did your sister say in her letter to you?" asked Antonio.

"She said they were doing fine, described the town, and mentioned Pablo either getting work at a stable or at a ranch as a blacksmith."

Antonio gestured outdoors with his hand. "There's your answer. Perhaps he's working for one of the big ranchos down south of here."

Paloma felt as if the wind had been knocked from her. How would she ever find Rosita? How many ranches were there to search?

"How long have you lived here?" she asked. "Do you remember Pablo and Rosita at all?"

Antonio smiled softly. "I've only lived here four years, but Chico has lived in Tucson all his life. Do you remember her sister, Chico?"

Paloma turned hopefully to Antonio's cousin. Chico frowned, as if deep in thought.

"Some of the women might have known your sister. Have you asked them?"

With a sigh of resignation, Paloma shook her head. "No, I came here first, hoping she would be here. I'm staying with Senora Fernandez. Perhaps she will know something. Thank you for your help."

Paloma stepped out into the late afternoon sunlight. Its warmth wrapped around her, giving some slight comfort. Where should she go now? She trudged slowly down the dusty street, lost in thought. A dog slinked out from the side of a building to nose at her skirt, tentatively waving its tail. She smiled and patted the dog, its tail now wagging enthusiastically.

Wait a minute! She straightened so fast the dog scurried off, tucking his tail between his legs. Antonio and Chico had to know something about Rosita and Pablo. She remembered seeing a saddle and blanket at one side of the stable. Yes, she was certain. They belonged to Rosita. They had been a gift from her father when Rosita and Pablo married. The saddle had been hand-tooled by one of the men who worked for her father. There couldn't be another one like it.

Paloma swiveled around, retracing her steps to the stable. Chico still leaned against the horse's haunch. Antonio's back was toward her, and the two men were apparently having a heated discussion. Chico noticed her and nodded in her direction. Antonio turned.

Paloma strode into the stable, angry at their deception.

"I believe you do know my sister," she blurted. "I want to know where she is."

Chico moved to the far side of the horse, as if hoping to escape her anger. Antonio studied her, then spoke quietly, "What makes you think we know of your sister?"

"This saddle," Paloma hissed, gesturing to the saddle not quite covered by the red and gray blanket. "This was a gift to Rosita from my father on her wedding day. I recognize the pattern. The blanket is hers, too. Now, where is she?" Paloma moved to the saddle and jerked the blanket off. She ran her hand lovingly over the roses and leaves carved into the leather.

"I, too, am a maker of saddles," Antonio said softly. "What makes you think I didn't see the pattern somewhere and copy it?"

Unwanted tears burned Paloma's eyes. "This is Rosita's. See these initials carved in the rose petal? I did that the day she left for Tucson. I told her that way she would always remember me."

She wanted to bury her face in the saddle blanket and weep. Where was Rosita? What had happened to her? Why was her saddle here, when these men denied ever knowing her?

"Please," she begged. "You have to tell me where she is."

Antonio studied her for a long moment without speaking. He rubbed the back of his neck. Chico picked up the horse's hoof again and began to scrape away at embedded dirt.

"You will have to ask some of the women around town about your sister." Antonio's eyes reflected an inner sadness. "I can't tell you where this saddle came from. I can only tell you that your sister and her husband aren't here."

Resignation overwhelmed her. She knew she wouldn't get any answers here. Suddenly, exhaustion from the long trip north drained her of strength. Her whole body relaxed, and the daylight faded to darkness. Paloma tried to stop herself from falling, but her muscles refused to respond. She barely felt the strong arms that caught her and lowered her gently to the ground.

As if from a great distance, Paloma heard Antonio and Chico talking.

"Is the senorita all right?" Chico asked.

"I think she's just fainted. Bring some water and we'll see if we can revive her."

"What will you tell her about Rosita and Pablo?"

"I'll tell her nothing. You won't say anything either, Chico. Understand?"

"But she seems very determined."

Paloma felt a hand gently brush the hair from her face. A finger traced a path down her cheek. She felt a tingle run throughout her body and struggled not to move. She didn't want them to know she could hear what they were saying. She nearly cried out at Antonio's next words.

"We'll just have to be *more* determined, then." Antonio sounded angry. "Rosita's life depends on it."

Chapter 2

Antonio tightened his arms around Paloma. What a beautiful name, Paloma. This young woman appeared as graceful as the dove—her namesake. Although small in stature, she carried herself with a dignity that spoke of determination.

He studied her, noting the gentle curve of her round cheeks. Her full lips were slightly parted, giving a glimpse of small, even teeth. Delicate eyebrows framed what he knew to be large, expressive eyes the color of well-worn leather. Her scarf slipped slowly back on her head. A wisp of nut-brown hair drifted down across her cheek. Tenderly, he smoothed the wayward tendril back into place.

Paloma stirred and groaned.

"Where's the water, Chico? I think she's starting to come around." Taking the dipper full of cool water, Antonio lifted Paloma up and slowly dribbled water into her mouth. He handed the dipper back to Chico and gently wiped the water from her chin. When he looked up, her eyes were open. An unreadable expression clouded their depths.

"Are you feeling better?" In a way, he wished that she

would faint again. He could go on holding her all day and never tire.

As if suddenly realizing her whereabouts, Paloma sat up. She gasped and grabbed her head, covering her eyes. For a moment, she leaned once more against his chest, then slowly straightened.

"I'm fine." She sounded disoriented. "My weariness from my long journey has just caught up with me. I need to get back to Senora Fernandez."

"Let me help you up." Antonio slowly lifted her to her feet. She swayed slightly; he hoped, in vain, to catch her again. "I'll walk you to the Senora's house."

The fact that she agreed told him she still wasn't herself. He tucked her arm into his and set off at a leisurely pace.

"I'm sure you know where my sister is." Paloma's soft words barely reached him. "I have to find her. You don't understand how important this is."

He studied her, seeing for the first time the dark circles under her eyes. Her face seemed paler than when she had first walked into the stable. Perhaps she did have a good reason for finding Rosita. Maybe he should listen to her. Try to understand.

"Why don't you tell me the reason it's so important for you to find your sister? You must have traveled a long way to get here. I hope you didn't travel alone."

She shook her head, wincing as if it hurt. "I came with my brother, Berto. He dropped me off at my mother's cousin's, Senora Fernandez. He and some of my father's vaqueros continued on to a friend's rancho to purchase some horses."

For a moment she walked in silence. In the distance, Antonio could see the walls of the *presidio* where the Mexican soldiers kept watch for raiding parties of Apaches. Although Tucson was relatively safe, many of the surrounding ranches had been abandoned due to the fierce attacks.

"Did you live in Tucson during the war?" Paloma asked.

Antonio frowned. "No, I moved here after the end of the war in 1848. Chico and my uncle and aunt were glad to have me come."

"Then perhaps you can understand my reason for needing to find Rosita." Paloma looked up at him, her eyes sparkling as some of her passionate fire returned. "You see, my family lived near the Nueces River, in the territory disputed by the two governments. The Americans," she nearly spat out the words, "wanted the land between the Nueces and the Rio Grande for themselves even though the Mexican government refused to sell to them. The Americans decided to fight for that land. They stole it from us and killed many fine Mexican men."

She stopped, obviously struggling to get her emotions under control. Antonio wanted to wrap his arms around her and take away the pain that must be tearing her apart. He put his hand over hers and tightened his arm.

Her eyes brimmed with tears. "My brother died in the war. Our beautiful home was taken from us. Of course, the American government promised that we could keep our homes, but they lied. They used trickery to swindle us out of our lands and our homes."

"Where do you live now?" Antonio asked.

"We live in Mexico." She raised her head and stared at him. "I wouldn't live anywhere else. My mother's health was ruined by the hardships of the war and the aftermath. My father struggled to rebuild what we had in a different location. Only by the grace of God do we have food to eat and a place to live."

"Then perhaps the grace of God should be enough." Antonio stopped as she turned to him, jerking her hand free from his arm. Anger sparked in her eyes.

"How can you say that? Is the death of my brother, the ruin of countless families, and stolen lands nothing to you? Don't you care about what the Americans have done? I will never live in America, and I won't stand for my sister living here either. This is now American territory. I will find Rosita, and I will bring her home."

Antonio watched Paloma stride across the street to Senora Fernandez's small adobe house. The riding crop that had dangled from her wrist moments before, she now used to hammer an angry tattoo against her skirt. He smiled. This was the woman for him. He had always longed for a woman with passion, one with intelligence who would challenge him at every turn. Paloma Rivera was that woman.

❧

Paloma stepped through the thick doorway of the small adobe house. She leaned back against the wall, closing her eyes, fighting back tears of frustration. She had hoped that, by appearing to be a little disoriented, she could trick Antonio into telling her what he knew about

Rosita and Pablo. Instead, she had lost her temper and ruined everything. Now, he would never talk to her. How would she ever find her sister before her brother returned to take her back to their home in Mexico? She didn't have much time, two to three weeks at the most.

A wave of anger swept through her again. How dare Antonio suggest that God's grace be enough? Didn't he understand the hurt and destruction Mexico had suffered? He probably lived in some remote area unaffected by the war. But she had seen the devastation firsthand. She'd heard the cannons. She'd seen the bloodied fields. She remembered the graves visited by weeping mothers, widows, and orphans. These haughty Americans had much to answer for. She couldn't wait to get Rosita and escape from here.

"Senora Fernandez?" Paloma walked through the main room to the kitchen where she could hear the rattle of dishes.

"Si, *mija,* please call me *'tia.'* I know you aren't really my niece, but your mother and I were as close as sisters when we were young." Elena Fernandez smiled, her eyes crinkling into mere slits. "Come sit down. How do you like our little pueblo Tucson? You haven't even told me what you went to find. Did you just want to walk around?"

Paloma smiled as she sat down. Her mother had told her that Elena could talk the legs off a donkey. That was why she hadn't questioned her before setting out on her search for Rosita. She'd been so sure of where to find her sister, she didn't want to be detained by a lot of useless conversation.

"Tucson seems very nice, *tia*." Paloma paused, not wanting to offend. "I only wish it would stay a part of Mexico."

Elena patted a ball of corn *masa* between her fingers, flattening the dough into a rounded tortilla. "I think it will not be so bad to be in America. If it's God's will, then He will make it right." She tossed the small tortilla on the hot stove, flipping it quickly to brown both sides. "Will you stay here, *mija?* There are many fine young men here who would make good husbands for you. I can ask my friends and we will introduce you. Maybe we can have a small fiesta just so you can meet someone."

Paloma sighed. "I don't want to live here. I want to live in Mexico. It's where I belong. It's where all Mexicans belong. I wouldn't marry someone who is willing to live as an American."

Elena's eyebrows arched and her eyes widened. She picked up another ball and began to shape it. "But, what of God's will? Didn't He even lead the Israelites to other lands? Those who were faithful to Him were blessed no matter where they lived."

"They were slaves for the most part." Paloma was having trouble keeping her temper. "I don't want to be a slave to the Americans."

Elena stared out the window, a dreamy expression on her face. "I would think to have God's blessings one would be willing to endure anything. Even America might be a blessed land."

Her quiet words pierced Paloma's heart. Was her anger against the Americans keeping her from God's blessings? She shook her head, forcing the thought from her mind.

"*Tia* Elena, I came here to find my sister, Rosita. I thought I knew right where she lived, but she isn't there anymore. The man who lives there says I have to ask the women in town about her. Do you know where I can find Rosita?"

Elena grabbed at the bubbling tortilla, preparing to turn it. Her fingers missed, and she jerked them back from the hot stove, a look of pain on her face. Quickly, she recovered, plucked the tortilla, and flipped it.

"Are you all right?" Paloma jumped up from her chair and grabbed her aunt's hand. The tips of her fingers showed the red marks of a burn that would probably blister.

"It's nothing, *mija*." Elena pulled her hand away and lifted the finished tortilla from the stove. "It happens all the time when I'm cooking."

Paloma once more caught her aunt's plump hand firmly in hers, stopping her from picking up another ball from the pile. Elena fidgeted nervously for a moment, then looked up.

"*Tia*, do you know where Rosita is?" Paloma tried to speak softly. But she really wanted to shake someone and get the answers she needed.

"If Antonio said you should talk to some of the women, then that is what you should do." Elena spoke as if the matter were settled. "Some of my friends get together to do embroidery. Maybe we could take a few minutes to drop by and talk with them before I finish our supper." She pulled her hand from Paloma's and covered the balls of *masa* with a damp cloth, then led the way out the door.

An hour later, Paloma followed *Tia* Elena back into the dim interior of the house. Silently, she watched as her aunt lit a lantern in the kitchen and added wood to the fire in the stove. The last hour had been a lesson in frustration. All of the women had been very polite and eager to talk with her until they found out her real reason for being there. They longed for news of Mexico, but when it came to Rosita and Pablo they refused to talk.

She didn't know so many women at once could have an unspoken agreement to stop talking or change the subject. Every time she mentioned her sister, one of the women would totally ignore her and begin talking about a certain young man courting a young lady. . .or how soon the newest senora would become a mother. . . or some other subject that had nothing to do with Rosita. They only talked to her when she willingly told them about the people she knew in Mexico.

She hadn't missed the furtively exchanged glances when they must have thought she wasn't looking. The quick shake of the head here and a glare of warning there told her more than their words could have. These women knew something about Rosita, and Paloma had to find out what.

In the midst of stirring beans for supper, Paloma stopped her spoon in midair. Poised above the pot, the utensil dripped bean juice in a steady rhythm. She swiveled around to where *Tia* Elena was just cooking the last of the corn tortillas.

"*Tia?*" Paloma let out the breath she'd been holding unconsciously. "You knew where Rosita lived. If you didn't know about Rosita, how did you know Antonio was the one I talked to?"

Chapter 3

Paloma grasped both of her *tia's* hands in hers. "*Tia*, please, you must tell me what you know about Rosita."

She watched as her aunt began to tremble. A look of pure fright crossed Elena's face. Tiny beads of sweat dotted her forehead.

"Oh, *mija,* don't make me say this. If you love your sister, don't make me say things I shouldn't."

The acrid scent of burning corn filled the air. Elena tugged her hands free and whirled around to the stove to toss the scorched tortilla away from the heat. Her hands shook so bad Paloma feared she might burn herself again.

"I just want to find my sister. Is that too much to ask?" Paloma fought to keep the frustration from her voice.

Tia Elena turned back to her, tears filling her eyes. "Yes, *mija.* I know you don't understand right now, but you must trust me. Your mother and I were best of friends. I would never mislead you. But, right now, you have to listen when I tell you to give up your search for Rosita."

Paloma began to stir the beans again. Before her trip to Tucson, her mother had insisted that she stay with her old friend Elena. Had her mother known something she hadn't known? At the time, she only thought her mother wanted to learn how her childhood friend was doing. No matter what, Paloma knew her *tia* Elena could be trusted. Still, she had to find Rosita. How could she vanish like this? Why would it hurt to look for her?

Tomorrow she would return to the stable. Antonio wouldn't give her the information, but perhaps, if he wasn't there, she could convince Chico to help her. With his empty-headed ways, all she had to do was smile at him, and he would tell her anything she wanted to hear. She frowned and shrugged away the thought that such a move would be deceptive. Hopefully, he would tell her the truth.

❦

The next morning Paloma helped her *tia* clean the dishes. "The morning is a fine one for a walk, *Tia* Elena. Do you mind if I go for a stroll after we finish here?"

Elena smiled broadly. "Not at all, *mija*. Just remember not to go outside the edge of Tucson by yourself. The Apaches and banditos can be dangerous."

"I'll just look around close to home." Paloma assured her.

A few minutes later she slipped out the door and strolled slowly until she couldn't see the small adobe anymore. Then she quickened her pace. With purpose in her stride, she headed directly for Antonio's stable. Her full skirt swished softly, dancing with the swirls of dust raised by her feet. The ever-present quirt brushed softly against her side.

She stopped just outside the open doors of the stable. The steady bang of a hammer told her that Chico must be working on a horseshoe. The quiet murmur of voices from the side of the building stirred her hope that Antonio was discussing business with someone and wouldn't notice her. If so, this might be the right time to corner Chico and get some information from him.

She stepped from the bright sunlight into the dim interior. Standing still, she allowed a few moments for her eyes to adjust. Chico, his back to the stable door, pounded a red-hot horseshoe on an anvil. A sweet-faced sorrel mare tied nearby, turned to stare at her. She couldn't see Antonio anywhere.

The sharp clangs of the hammer beating the horseshoe stopped suddenly, and quiet enveloped Paloma. She wiped her sweaty palms against her skirt. As Chico turned her way, she forced a smile on her face.

"Good morning, Chico." She hoped he couldn't read her intense dislike of him in her eyes.

"Paloma, you look so beautiful this morning." He picked up the horseshoe with a set of tongs, then dropped the hot metal into a bucket of water. His idiotic grin showed through the steam that boiled up in a cloud. He stepped closer to her, and she fought the urge to back away.

"Your eyes could make a man's heart melt." Chico reached out to touch her. She flinched and he dropped his hand. His grin wavered only slightly. "I love the challenge of taming a wild mare," he spoke softly, swaggering over to stroke the sorrel mare. "Perhaps you would accompany me to dinner this evening. I can show you a wonderful time."

Repressing a shudder, Paloma knew she couldn't carry out this ruse. How could she even pretend to like this man when he was so full of himself? Comparing her to a horse. Indeed! Anger boiled up and she resisted to no avail.

"I want you to tell me where Rosita and Pablo are," she snapped, her quirt slapping rapidly against her leg. "I won't give up, and I'm sure you know something. Now, tell me before I lose my temper completely." She glared at him. "Remember, sometimes a mare can pack a mighty kick."

Chico tried to laugh, but it came out more like a strangled squawk. "I think Antonio told you to talk to the women, my pretty."

"I'm not your pretty," she hissed, "and I have talked to the women. They refused to say anything." Paloma closed her eyes, fighting for a modicum of self-control. "Why won't anyone tell me about my sister? Is there some dark secret about her? I'm beginning to wonder if the whole town has done something shameful. Maybe you've all decided to lie to protect one another."

Chico lost his grin as she spoke. He looked wary and perhaps a little afraid. "I have to get back to work." He headed toward the water bucket and the now-cooled horseshoe.

"No." Even she was surprised by the forceful tone with which she spoke. "You have to help me."

"Perhaps I can help you instead, Senorita Rivera."

Antonio's voice sounded close behind her, stopping her from saying more.

Paloma spun around. Antonio stood with the sunlight at his back, his face mostly in the shadows. Still, she couldn't help but notice her response to him. It wasn't just his good looks or the way his broad shoulders complemented his narrow hips. There was something else that attracted her to him. She just couldn't quite figure out what. She found herself wanting to stand here, simply looking at him. She loved the way his homespun shirt hung loosely over his muscular frame. The accent of the bright red sash he wore heightened the effect. She couldn't look away.

"How can I help you, Paloma?" Antonio sounded amused, as if he had read her thoughts.

"I—uh. I—" Paloma stuttered. Then, forcing herself to look away, she managed to regain control of her thoughts. "Tell me where to find Rosita. I'm sure you know where she is. No one I've met seems to want me to find her, but I have to. I won't quit until I do. I explained to you yesterday why." She stopped, knowing she was rambling on without making much sense.

Antonio stepped closer. She could see his dark eyes flashing.

"Have you prayed about all this?" He spoke so softly, she might have thought she imagined his words if she hadn't seen his lips move.

"Of course, I prayed," she retorted. "I prayed with my mother before I even began my journey to Tucson. We prayed that I would find my sister and get her safely back to Mexico where she belongs."

He studied her silently. "I guess what I'm asking is, did you pray about God's will in finding your sister?"

She stood straight, clenching her fists at her sides. "And why wouldn't it be God's will? Doesn't He want her to be where she belongs? How dare you question whether I'm seeking to do what God wants?"

"I'm sorry, Paloma. There are circumstances you don't understand. But I will help you look for your sister."

Paloma swallowed the fresh tirade of angry words forming on her lips. "You what?"

"I said, I will help you look."

As he spoke, she studied his face before nodding her acceptance of his offer. "All right; where shall we start?"

"Why don't you accompany me to a couple of the ranches near Tucson? We could ask if Pablo is working there."

She nodded. "That's fine. Maybe on the way you can tell me these circumstances I don't understand."

He smiled and her heart fluttered. "I'm sure there are many things we can find to discuss."

∽

Antonio secretly watched Paloma as she rode. She sat astride the horse in an easy manner—one that only came with hours of time in the saddle. For an instant, he wished her horse would become lame so that he could insist on her riding with him. He longed to hold her again. All afternoon, she had pummeled him with questions about her sister and the circumstances he had so foolishly mentioned. It had taken his every effort to dodge her inquires.

He hated leading her on. Hated making her think

that he was helping her when he really wasn't. He knew Pablo and Rosita weren't at the ranches they visited. But he couldn't let Paloma know that. He had to keep up the pretense of a search until her brother returned to take her home to Mexico. After all, he'd given his promise to a dying man. He couldn't reveal what he knew.

Moving his horse, Grande, closer to her mare, Antonio noted that Paloma's long-legged horse was nearly as tall as his. As slight as Paloma was, it would take no effort at all to scoop her out of the saddle and deposit her in front of him. He smiled, wondering what her reaction would be.

Earlier he had asked her if she had prayed about finding her sister. Now, his conscience pricked and reminded him that he hadn't really prayed about Paloma. He just assumed God had answered his prayer for a wife, but he hadn't checked to be sure. What if she wasn't the right one? After all, she insisted she wouldn't marry a man who lived in the United States of America. And he didn't intend to move back to Mexico. Too many bad memories were there for him. He wanted to stay right where he felt the Lord had placed him.

Oh, Lord, I don't talk with You enough. I'm just like I believe Paloma is. I assume I know what You want and rush ahead with it. I'm afraid I follow my will sometimes instead of Yours. Please, show me Your will clearly. Help me to walk in faith and to trust You with my every step.

"I think this was a wasted effort." Paloma's velvety voice cut through his thoughts.

Antonio looked into her doelike eyes and could find nothing to say. She had thrown him off guard again and he couldn't afford that. Finally, he managed to ask, "Why is that?"

"Since we left the Hidalgo ranch, I've been thinking. You don't want me to find Rosita and Pablo. None of the women in the pueblo want me to find them either. Even Chico is being secretive. So, why would you suddenly agree to help me look for them?"

"You tell me." Antonio hoped she didn't notice the strain in his voice.

"I think it's because you knew they wouldn't be there. You knew no one at the ranchos would have heard of them. You only did it to pass the time until my brother comes back. You hope that, by then, I will concede defeat and return to Mexico."

Antonio held his breath and stared into her beautiful eyes. Could this woman read his thoughts?

Paloma leaned across the narrow space that separated them and put her hand on top of his. "Listen to me," she spoke slowly and forcefully, "I will never give up. Never."

Chapter 4

The interior of the small chapel wrapped Paloma with a welcome coolness. The weather had turned very warm today. Walking around the small pueblo of Tucson and inquiring after her sister had caused her to perspire in a most unladylike fashion. Now, sinking into the narrow pew felt like a piece of heaven. The quiet helped her to relax for the first time in the week since she'd arrived here.

"God, I don't know what's happening here. I have tried to find Rosita, but no one will talk. I think I've asked every one of the people who live here. Yet, they either deny knowing her or they tell me to ask someone else. Why, Lord?" Tears traced a path down her cheeks.

What more could she do? Every day she had tried to get Chico to talk. He acted as though she only wanted to see him because he was so wonderful. Ridiculous! Antonio had been of no help, either. He hadn't even offered to search with her since taking their visits to the two ranchos near town. Of course, he was always polite, always acted like he hoped she found her sister. But deep down, she knew he was doing everything he could to ensure that she didn't find her. After all, she had heard him tell Chico that first day that he wouldn't tell her anything. Perhaps if she had confronted him right away, he would have said something, but she doubted it. The man was mule-stubborn.

Despite that, she couldn't help but like him. He worked so hard. He loved the Lord. He seemed honest and was obviously well-loved in town. Plus, every time she saw him, her heart skipped a beat. She found herself longing to touch him, to feel his arms around her as she had on the day she fainted. She cherished that memory.

"God." Her whisper echoed in the quiet building. "This afternoon, I'm going with *Tia* Elena to visit with some of the women. I know they're keeping something from me. Please, help me to convince them to tell me what it is. You brought me here for a reason, and I'm sure it's to find Rosita and bring her back home. Time is running out. I have to know today."

Paloma stalked from the small church, trying to ignore the fact that she was angry with God over His obvious reluctance to do what she wanted. Determination gave a spring to her step. This afternoon, God would show her everything.

After a light lunch, Paloma hurried to wash up the dirty dishes. *Tia* Elena was gathering her things, then they were leaving for Mrs. Garcia's house. There they would meet the same women she had questioned earlier. Only this time, she wouldn't do the asking. God would make them talk. She was sure they knew something.

"Ready, *mija?*" *Tia* Elena clutched her embroidery

under one arm as she fastened her scarf.

"I'm just finished." Paloma smiled. She had come to love this friend of her mother's. *Tia* Elena would do almost anything for anyone. She visited the sick and took them food. She helped the young mothers with their children, and the children loved the sweets she gave them.

After a short walk in the heat, Elena and Paloma were welcomed into Mrs. Garcia's adobe house. Paloma loved the way the thick earthen walls kept out the heat. It felt like walking into a cave.

Settling into a chair, she watched as the women pulled out their embroidery and began stitching. She tried to fade into the background, hoping Rosita's name would come up. As she relaxed, the tension and stress of the last few days began to catch up to her. She struggled to keep her eyes open. She *must* remain alert. Gradually, the light chatter of the women faded to a drone. Then silence, as sleep overtook her.

Paloma didn't know how much time had elapsed, but she woke slowly to soft, murmured whisperings. Keeping her eyes closed, she pretended to still sleep. Breathing deeply and slowly, so as not to alert the women that she was awake, she slowly opened one eye just enough to see. The women had abandoned their chairs and were huddled together on the opposite side of the room. She longed to lean forward to catch more of their conversation, but knew that would give her away. Instead, she sat quietly, straining to hear something.

". . .sister. . . Does she know. . .Franco. . .Pablo?"

". . .sees the gravestone. . .keep her away."

Paloma leaned slightly forward, frustrated at only catching a few words here and there. What were they saying about Pablo? Who was Franco? She'd never heard of anyone by that name.

The material she'd been stitching earlier now shifted, and her scissors clattered to the floor. The talk ceased abruptly. Paloma opened her eyes, knowing the women realized she was awake. She yawned and stretched, trying to make it appear as if she'd just woke up.

"Ah, Paloma," *Tia* Elena's light laugh sounded strained. "You had a little siesta. Come here and see Mrs. Garcia's scarf. We were all admiring it."

Paloma walked over and pretended interest in the intricately embroidered cloth, but she really wanted to leave. She needed to think about the words she'd overheard. Somewhere there was a clue to finding Rosita. She was certain.

❧

"Antonio, we have to talk." Chico's serious tone cut through the haze that surrounded Antonio. He hadn't been able to concentrate on the saddle he was tooling. The rancher who had placed the order wanted the work finished before his son's birthday in two weeks. Antonio knew time was growing short, but he couldn't get his mind off of a certain pretty senorita.

"What is it, amigo?" Antonio beckoned to a seat across from him, and Chico sat down.

"I can't do this anymore." Chico kneaded his work-blackened hands as if thoroughly agitated.

"You are tired of shoeing horses?" Antonio looked at him in surprise.

"No. You know I love working with the horses."

"What is it, then, that you can't do?"

"I can't continue to deceive Paloma. Is it so wrong to let her see her sister? What would their meeting hurt?"

Antonio studied the saddle beside him, polishing it gently with a cloth. "I, too, am having trouble with all this deception, amigo. But you know what happened to Pablo. He was my best friend. I can't go back on the promise I gave him when he was dying."

"But would he want Paloma and Rosita kept apart?"

"I don't know." Antonio felt miserable. He didn't know what was right anymore. "On one hand, I feel that I should take Paloma to Rosita. But you saw what that monster did to Pablo. What if he does the same to Rosita—or Paloma? I can't let that happen."

He paused, studying the forlorn expression on Chico's face. He leaned forward, placing his elbows on his knees, wishing God would show him a clear way to do the right thing.

"Chico, you know I can't take back what I said to Pablo. He died in my arms." Antonio fought to swallow around the lump in his throat. "I still have his bloodstains on my shirt."

"But Paloma is Rosita's sister. They're family." Chico protested. "Maybe Rosita needs family right now."

Antonio began to pace, his hands knotted behind his back. He wanted to kick something. Why all these questions? He felt as if he were being torn in two. On one hand was a promise to his best friend, and on the other was the need of a sister looking for her sister. What was the right thing to do?

"Chico, I'm not doing this out of cruelty." He hoped his passionate plea wouldn't go unheeded. "That killer promised to find Rosita. You know we can't let that happen. I have to protect her. I know he's watching me, and he's watching everyone who knows me. We have to wait a little longer."

Chico's shoulder slumped as he leaned back against the wall. "All right; I'll wait, but I want you to know, I don't like it."

"I know, amigo. I don't like it either. I just don't want to see Rosita dead like Pablo." Antonio whirled around to look out the window. "Did you hear something?"

"No." Chico stood and crossed to look out. He groaned. "It's Paloma. This time you have to talk to her. I can't stand her prying for answers again."

"Wait here." Antonio clapped him on the shoulder as he headed for the door. He squinted as he stepped out into the brilliant afternoon sunshine. Paloma stood near the stable door, her back to him. Something was wrong. Could she have heard them talking? *Lord, please don't let her have heard,* he prayed.

"Paloma?"

She turned slowly. She wiped her eyes with the edge of her scarf.

"Is something wrong?"

She shrugged, not meeting his eyes. "You know how the dust can be." Her voice sounded choked.

"Can I help you with something?" He had to fight back the urge to sweep her into his arms. The desire to protect her nearly overwhelmed him.

"No; I. . .I wanted to ask you something, but I'm not

feeling so good right now. I think I'll head home." Paloma turned and nearly ran toward the street.

"Would you like me to walk with you?"

"No." Her sharp retort held a note of desperation. "I need to be alone."

❧

Paloma halted her headlong flight and leaned against the shady side of a building. Her knees shook so badly, she didn't think she could stand much longer. She had wanted to scream at Antonio. How could he deceive her about something so important? Now she understood the snatches of conversation she had overheard from the women. They had mentioned a gravestone. Surely, it was Pablo's.

She covered her mouth, fighting for control. *Oh, God, how can Pablo be dead? He was always so kind. He loved to laugh and have fun. I've never known him to get in a fight. Who killed him? Why?*

She made her way slowly back to the church where she had prayed that morning. She remembered a small courtyard beside the church with several headstones. Maybe she would find her answer there.

The streets were deserted as she passed through the gate into the small graveyard. Her heart pounded. *Please don't let this be true, Lord. But, if it is true—keep Rosita safe.* She walked slowly through the yard, reading those small crosses that bore inscriptions. As she neared the far side, she noticed a grave with freshly mounded dirt. Her tight fists causing her knuckles to turn white, she dragged herself closer.

"Pablo Lopez, 1854." She sank to the ground next

to the cross. A sob shook her as her fingers traced the name. "Oh, Pablo, what happened? I remember the day you left to come here. You were so happy and full of dreams. You loved Rosita so much. How could you be dead? What's happened to Rosita?"

She could no longer hold the tears at bay. Covering her face with the loose end of her scarf, Paloma cried for what had been and would never be again. She barely heard the footsteps approaching. Strong arms lifted her from the ground, and she found herself held in a powerful embrace. The familiar smell of leather and horses surrounded her.

"Palomita, my little dove." Antonio's soft words warmed her. "I'm so sorry. I thought, perhaps, you heard us talking. I loved him, too." He softly rubbed her back. Slowly, her tears subsided. She wanted to stay close to him, to feel the solid strength he gave her. Reluctantly she pushed away, wondering at these feelings she was experiencing for someone she barely knew.

Brushing the tears from her cheeks, she stepped back. "Now I am even more convinced—I must find Rosita. I told you America is bad. See, already I have lost someone I loved here."

Chapter 5

The first fingers of rose-colored dawn stained the cotton clouds in the eastern sky as Paloma slipped from the house the next morning. *Tia* Elena still slept. Paloma didn't want to waken her and face all the questions about where she was going, alone, so early in the morning. After a sleepless night, she couldn't face the thought of answering questions from anyone.

Hurrying down the deserted streets, she pulled her shawl snugly around her shoulders. Although the days were warm, the nights cooled drastically. Only a couple hours of sunshine could chase the chill from the air. Paloma shivered. She didn't think even direct sunlight could warm the cold that had settled deep in her heart and soul.

"God, I hate this place," she whispered as she walked. "I know *Tia* Elena is wrong. You couldn't possibly bless such a cruel land as this. Please help me find the answers that I need. Quickly."

The dry, crisp air brushed like a cool cloth against her face as she passed through the shadows of the church. The gate to the churchyard stood slightly ajar. She slipped through and slowed her pace, trudging past the row of crosses that led to Pablo's grave. She stared at the ground, hating the thought of seeing the rectangle of disturbed ground, which now covered her brother-in-law's body.

"Good morning, Paloma."

She jumped and clamped a hand over her mouth to stifle a shriek. Antonio rose from where he had been squatting next to Pablo's grave. Her heart pounded—she didn't know if from fright or from the strange attraction she had for Antonio.

He smiled. "I didn't mean to startle you."

She fought the urge to run as he moved closer. "What are you doing here?" Paloma bit her lip and looked away, wishing her words had sounded less demanding.

"I come here for a few minutes every morning."

"Why would you do such a thing?" she asked, meeting his eyes again. She immediately regretted that. The memory of being held in his strong embrace was too fresh. It took an iron will to keep from flinging herself at him, begging him to hold her and help ease her hurt.

The smile left Antonio's face. He turned back to the grave, running his fingertips along the top of the small cross. "Pablo was like a brother to me. I loved him."

"Then you lied to me." She wanted to scream at him.

"I didn't lie to you. I said Pablo isn't here and he isn't. Neither is Rosita."

"But you led me to believe that you didn't know Pablo or Rosita."

He studied her before he nodded. "I suppose I did.

Perhaps I was wrong, but I made a promise to Pablo."

"A promise that includes refusing to tell Rosita's sister of her whereabouts?"

A sad smile flickered across his lips, then faded. "I suppose, in a way, yes."

Clenching her fist, Paloma wished she had brought her quirt so she could take out her frustrations with it. "I have no idea why you're doing this, but I do know you don't understand the pain my family has been through already. The war was cruel. So many we knew died. My brother suffered a horrible death. It took him hours to die from his wounds. If the Americans hadn't been so greedy in their lust for land, those fine young men would be alive today. All the Americans could say was, they had a 'Manifest Destiny' to own the land. As if they're the only ones who count."

She turned away, blinking back tears of anger and frustration. "I'm sorry for being so passionate about this. I don't believe anyone understands unless they've been through such trauma."

His hands, warm on her shoulders, startled her. He gently, but firmly, turned her to face him. His palm, smooth from hours of working with leather, cupped her cheek. He wiped a tear from the corner of her eye.

"Look at me, Palomita." His voice was soft, undemanding. She looked into his serious eyes. "I understand. Believe me; I do understand."

"How can you understand?" she barely managed to choke out the question around the lump in her throat. With his touch, her anger fled and was replaced by a longing to stay close to him.

"Sit with me for a few minutes." Antonio beckoned to a bench near the fence that surrounded the graveyard.

Paloma sat nervously on the edge of the stone bench, trying to put some distance between them. For some reason, this man had an effect on her unlike any other man. He frightened her, in a way. She didn't know whether she should run toward him or away from him as fast as possible.

"I, too, lived in Mexico when the war broke out." Antonio's statement surprised her and grabbed her attention.

"Did you fight in the war?" she asked.

Antonio shook his head and leaned forward to put his elbows on his knees. "I begged my father to let me fight with the army. He said no. Said he needed me at the ranch. Said I was too young. I scoffed at his words. I was fifteen and thought I was already a man. Others younger than I were fighting."

He paused and rubbed his face with his hands. When he glanced at Paloma, she could see the pain etched in his expression. She wanted to reach out and comfort him. Instead, she forced herself to sit still.

"I knew my father needed me. I was the only boy in a family full of girls. My sisters were all younger than I. My father had been injured in a fall from a horse. He couldn't do many of the necessary chores around the ranch. As the only son, I helped him with the work."

He stopped as if battling with strong emotions. When he continued, his voice had a raspy quality that wasn't there before. "At sixteen, I ran away to join the army. Selfishly, I thought my family could do without me, but my country couldn't. I had to fight against the Americans who were trying to take away our beloved Mexico. For days, I wandered through the hills looking for the army so I could join. I had no idea how to do it, just a determination to do so. Finally, God showed me I shouldn't have left my father when he needed me. As I was heading home, I got my wish. But the war found me, not the other way around."

"Did you join the army?" Paloma wanted to reach out to him but couldn't.

"No; I entered the city of Monterrey as the Americans were battling to take it over. The sight of the bloodshed in the streets sickened and frightened me. You see, in order for the American army to reach Monterrey they had to pass very close to our ranch."

"What did you do?"

"When the fighting ended, I slipped out of town and hurried home as fast as I could. Although the main army had passed by without going to my hacienda, a group of renegade soldiers couldn't resist. I watched helplessly as they burned our house. My family lay in the yard, murdered. I knew the old musket I carried would never stand up to those killers, and my family was beyond my help."

Antonio bowed his head, burying his face in his hands. Paloma touched his shoulder lightly, wanting to ease his pain with a desperation borne of sorrow. "I'm so sorry, Antonio. I had no idea."

When he looked up, the sheen of unshed tears brightened his eyes. He nodded. "I left for Tucson that day. I buried my sisters and my parents, then I rode away and never looked back. The bitterness and anger in my heart took years for God to erase. I had to learn to forgive, which wasn't easy."

"Forgive?" Paloma jerked her hand from his shoulder. "How can you possibly forgive something so horrible?"

"My mother always told me that if I kept anger and hatred in me it would turn to bitterness. 'Bitterness is a root that will dig down into your very soul and ruin you,' she would say. I didn't want those murderers to kill me too, because of a root of bitterness that I allowed to grow. Paloma, you need to ask God to help you get rid of your bitterness against the Americans."

A wave of anger washed over her. "I am not bitter; I'm angry at what they've had the gall to do. They deserve my anger. I don't know how you can forget your family so easily. They died for their country. Maybe it would have been better if you had tried to defend your home when you had the chance." Paloma practically ran from the churchyard, tears streaming down her face. *How dare he suggest I should act like they did nothing wrong?* she fumed, trying to ignore the voice in her heart that said Antonio was right.

❧

For the rest of the day, Antonio fought a battle with himself. Had he been too hard on Paloma? Had he been out of place to tell her she needed to forgive the Americans for what they had done to her family and all the others she had known? Should he go to her and apologize, or should he give her some time to think about it?

All day as he worked, he watched the door, hoping

she would come to the shop so they could talk. *Oh, God, give me wisdom in this,* he prayed over and over. But, no matter how much he prayed, he didn't feel any wiser. He still didn't have the answers.

Lord, You know I'm falling in love with her. I feel she's the one You've sent to me, but how can that be when we can't even agree on where we would live? I'm sure she has feelings for me, but she won't admit them for fear she would have to stay in America with me. What am I to do? And, Lord, I want so much to take her to Rosita. Please show me what's right to do. As always, I pray for Rosita's safety.

The last golden glow of the sun was fading from the sky when Antonio closed up the shop and headed toward the Fernandez home. He had to talk to Paloma. His footsteps were nearly silent on the dirt road. Rounding a corner, he saw Paloma step out into the twilight. She didn't look his direction but turned the other way and set off at a brisk pace.

Antonio opened his mouth to call out to her, but something stopped him. What if she had seen him and deliberately turned the other way to avoid him? Maybe she was still mad and refused to talk to him. He stood watching as the distance between them grew. Well, he would follow her and if he got the chance, he could apologize for offending her this morning.

Hurrying to catch up, Antonio nearly missed the turn Paloma made. When he reached the corner, he could only see the white of her shawl as the darkness swallowed her. Loud laughter rang out through the evening as a door across from Paloma burst open, bathing her in golden lamplight. A man stumbled out, almost knocking her over. He grabbed her, and they both staggered to one side to keep from falling.

Antonio began to run, wishing he had stayed closer to her. He could see Paloma pushing the man away, but he seemed to be pulling her closer. Paloma's scarf drifted from her head into the dirt of the road. Both appeared unaware of him rushing toward them.

"Rosita, my sweet. I've missed you. I knew you would come back to me."

The man's slurred words reached Antonio's ears, filling him with fear. *Oh, God, it's Franco. Please help Paloma. Help me protect her, Lord.* He felt utterly powerless as he watched the outlaw drag Paloma into the alleyway beside the house.

Chapter 6

Paloma could barely breathe. The only good thing about the hand clamped over her face was that it blocked some of the odor of alcohol that surrounded this man. Who was he? What did he want with her? Why did he think she was Rosita?

God, why, when I finally find someone who will talk about Rosita, is it like this? What is happening here? she prayed.

She pulled at the sinewy arm, trying to loosen his hold, but he laughed. Grabbing her dangling quirt, she tried to swing the whip around. He wrenched it out of her hand and threw it in the dirt.

"I always loved your spirit, my little Rosita. Only you would pretend to fight against Franco." He pulled her close against him, dragging her around the corner of the house. "You know, my sweet, the other women are so jealous of you."

Panic gave way to desperation. Paloma kicked back hard. She heard the man's grunt of pain as her heel connected with his shin. His grip tightened, squeezing the breath from her lungs. His hiss of anger sounded loud in her ear. She knew she could never defeat him on her own.

Twisting to one side, Paloma tried to remove his hand from her mouth. She had to find out what he wanted. How did this vile excuse for a man know her sister?

"Easy, Rosita." His hoarse whisper in her ear sent a shudder rippling through her. "I love the way you act like you don't want me, when you really do."

Paloma managed to open her mouth slightly. The fleshy part of his palm pressed close, and she clamped her teeth into his skin as hard as she could. He let out a grunt of pain and jerked his hand away, then slapped her across the mouth. Stunned, she stood mute for the precious few seconds when she could have talked. Once more, his hand covered her mouth.

"If you bite me again, my sweet, I'll give you more than a little love tap."

She closed her eyes, fighting the fear that threatened to overwhelm her. *Oh, God, I need help. I don't know what's happening. Please send someone.* As she flung her silent prayer toward God, a picture of Antonio came to mind. How she longed for him right now.

"Franco, let her go."

Paloma's heart skipped a beat. Could God have answered her prayer so quickly? Was Antonio really here to rescue her?

Franco whirled around to face Antonio. He turned Paloma sideways, shoving her face against his chest. "She's mine," he snarled. "I won her fair and square. All you've done is try to interfere in my business. This time I won't allow it."

Pushing away from Franco, Paloma tried to turn far

enough to look at Antonio. For some reason she had to see him. She knew the sight of his solid presence would comfort her.

In answer to her twisting, Franco whipped her around, pulling her back against him. He removed his hand from her mouth but wrapped an iron-muscled arm tight around her neck. Breathing became a chore. She still couldn't speak.

"What's this, Franco? Hiding behind a woman? I thought you were more of a man than that."

Paloma drank in the welcome sight of Antonio as he stood splay-legged, his back to the street. Shadows made his face a black mask, but she knew every feature by heart. An overwhelming urge to touch him made her lift her hand, reaching out to him.

Franco jerked his arm tighter around her neck, forcing her to instinctively claw at the obstruction to her breathing.

"Forget it, little Rosita. Your coward of a husband couldn't stand up to me and neither can this lily-livered hombre."

"You're so sure that's Rosita in your grasp." Antonio's mocking voice cut through Franco's tirade. "I'm telling you that isn't who you're hiding behind."

Like a feral animal, a growl of protest ripped through Franco. "I think I should know the woman who loves me."

"Well, I know the woman I love and that's her. You don't think I would bring Rosita out of hiding this soon, do you?"

Paloma's heart pounded so hard she didn't think she

would hear anything else. What had Antonio said? Had he really referred to her as the woman he loved? And, what did he mean about bringing Rosita out of hiding? If only this baboon would loosen his hold on her so she could talk.

"Don't think you can trick me, Antonio. You thought I left town for California like I said I would. Well, I lied, and now Rosita is mine."

Antonio's hands were clenching and unclenching. Paloma wondered if he longed to get them around this Franco's neck. At this point, that would be fine with her.

"Look at her, Franco. This is Rosita's sister, Paloma, not Rosita."

Franco's arm tightened more. Paloma's vision dimmed. *Please, God, don't let me faint. Help Antonio, Lord.*

Muttering an oath, Franco twisted Paloma around, his grip loosening enough for her to gasp some air. Before she could cry out, she found herself staring into a shadowed, ruggedly handsome face. A heavy mustache drooped past his chin, giving Franco a sinister appearance. A shaft of fear pierced through Paloma. This man would show mercy to no one. She felt as if she were staring evil in the face.

"Who are you?" Franco shook her until her teeth rattled. "Where is Rosita?"

"I don't know." Paloma couldn't keep her voice from shaking. "I've been looking for her, too."

"Are you her sister?" he demanded.

She could only nod.

"Then you're lying," he roared. Grabbing her neck,

he nearly lifted her from the ground. She felt her eyes strain and blackness begin to descend again. "Tell me where she is before I kill you."

Something seized her from behind, pulling her from Franco's hold. She fell back, stumbling slightly. The next thing she knew, familiar arms were around her. She clung to Antonio, praying this Franco would leave her alone.

"She isn't lying, Franco. Rosita is beyond your reach. Now, get out of here. Why don't you just leave for California like you said before."

Franco snarled a reply, but Paloma heard little of it as she buried her face against Antonio's chest. Footsteps retreated, and she fought to still the trembling in her limbs.

"Ah, Palomita, my little dove." Antonio gently stroked his hand over her hair. His arms tightened around her comfortingly. "I'm sorry you had to meet Franco. Everything is all right now."

"Who is he?" Paloma wanted to scream, but instead her question could barely be heard. She looked up at Antonio. The moon, now peeking through the branches of a nearby Palo Verde tree, lit his face. His loving expression took her breath away. "I have to know," she whispered.

"I gave my promise to Pablo, my sweet. I can't tell you, but I will pray about taking you to someone who will tell you what has happened."

"What about *Tia* Elena? Why hasn't she told me? Did the whole town make the same promise?"

"Your *tia* Elena and many of the other people of

the town don't know all of what happened." Antonio frowned as if considering his answer. "They only know they must carefully protect Rosita."

Paloma gripped the front of his shirt in her fists. "Don't you see, Antonio? If Rosita needs protecting, what better way than to get her out of here and back to her home in Mexico? My father has many vaqueros. Each one would lay down his life for my sister or me. She must return with me. Now."

Antonio's smile glinted in the moonlight. "Palomita, I love your spirit. You never give up on an idea." He lifted a finger and traced a path down the side of her face.

Paloma knew she should move away from him and the feelings he stirred inside of her. After all, she had to stick with her plan, the plan to find Rosita and be ready to ride for Mexico as soon as her brother returned. She couldn't let her feelings for Antonio interfere.

❧

Antonio watched the moonlight play across Paloma's perfect features. He'd been so afraid that Franco would hurt her. *Thank You, God. I know You protected Paloma from that rogue. I've never known him to give up so easily. Please help me to protect her from him should he try to hurt her again.*

Paloma's doe-eyes reflected a shaft of light. Her full lips, darkened in the evening light, proved irresistible. Antonio bent his head, pulled her close, and gave her a slow, soft kiss. Fire raced through his veins. He longed to draw her close and kiss her again. Instead, he cautioned himself to retreat. He didn't want to frighten her.

"I love you, Palomita." He couldn't believe he blurted

those words out when he had just determined to restrain himself. "I've prayed so long for a wife, and I believe you are the answer to my prayers." He desperately wanted her to understand his serious feelings for her.

"No, Antonio." She pushed away from him. "I have to get back to *Tia* Elena's. I have to go now."

"Wait." He grasped her arm, turning her back toward him. "I'm sorry. I didn't mean to upset you. I can't help how I feel. Let me walk you home. I don't trust Franco."

She glanced fearfully around the shadowed streets then nodded her ascent.

He grinned and extended his arm to her. "I promise I'll be the perfect gentleman."

The walk to her aunt's house proved peaceful. No one bothered them. Paloma appeared lost in thought. She didn't speak again until they reached the Fernandez house. Antonio simply enjoyed watching the play of shadows and moonlight wash across Paloma's face.

"Thank you for rescuing me." Paloma tilted her head to one side as she looked up at him. She lifted a hand and softly cupped his cheek. He fought to keep from grabbing her and covering her face with kisses. He didn't want to frighten her again.

"It was my pleasure, Palomita." He turned to leave.

"Wait, Antonio."

He stopped.

"You promised to take me to someone who would tell me about Rosita."

He glanced around the seemingly deserted streets. "Tomorrow," he spoke softly, hoping the words wouldn't carry far. "I will take you to my *tia* Isabel tomorrow.

She will tell you what you want to know. Then you will understand why you need to leave without Rosita."

"I'll never leave without my sister." Paloma disappeared inside the house, her words echoing through his head and his heart. No matter how he felt about her, she still planned to leave. In fact, she acted as though she couldn't get away from there fast enough.

Antonio trudged through the streets to the little adobe that served as his house and workshop, his heart heavy. He felt sure she cared for him, but then she pulled away and wanted to leave. Would life in the United States of America be so awful?

Inside the house, he sank onto his bed and buried his head in his hands. *Dear God, help me to accept this if it is Your will. Lord, You know how I feel about Paloma. I feel sure she's the one You have for me—the one for whom I've prayed. Please, help me to have faith if she isn't, Lord. And, if she is the one, I trust You to work things out.*

As he prayed in the dark, Antonio remembered his *tia* Isabel talking about his uncle's favorite Scripture passage. He loved to hear about the Israelites going to the Promised Land. *Tia* Isabel always said the Promised Land could be anywhere, as long as you were there with God.

His voice far from steady, Antonio began to quote aloud the verse his *tia* had helped him memorize. "In that I command thee this day to love the LORD thy God, to walk in his ways, and to keep his commandments and his statutes and his judgments, that thou mayest live and multiply: and the LORD thy God shall bless thee in the land whither thou goest to possess it."

Lord, help Paloma to see that, as long as she walks with You, the land where she lives will be a blessed land. It's knowing You and following Your ways that makes our homes a blessing. And, Lord, please work out what's right concerning Rosita. Thank You, Lord.

Contentment surrounded him and for the first time since meeting Paloma, he slept peacefully through the night.

Chapter 7

Paloma rose early the next morning. She had slept fitfully. Memories of Franco's near-abduction haunted her dreams. She would wake in a cold sweat, but the thought of Antonio's loving protection comforted her each time.

She gazed out her window at the mountains standing tall in the distance. The sun barely peeked over the tops of them, but it held the promise of a warm, beautiful day. The dark, scary night faded.

A low, buzzing sound startled her. She jumped back, then laughed lightly as she watched a hummingbird thrust its long beak into the bright orange flower of a trumpet vine near her window. She hoped she didn't jump at every little sound today. Humming to herself, she headed for the kitchen.

"Good morning, *tia*." She leaned over to give her *tia* Elena a quick kiss on the cheek as she entered the kitchen.

"My, you are cheery this morning." *Tia* Elena smiled and stirred the meat sizzling in the skillet. "Is there a reason for all these smiles?"

"Antonio promised to take me to meet his *tia* Isabel.

She will tell me all about Rosita." Paloma paused, seeing a frown cross her aunt's face. "What? What is it?"

Tia Elena sighed and shook her head. "Nothing, *mija*. I just pray you don't have your hopes up for nothing. There may be nothing you can do for Rosita."

"I know she is having trouble here, *tia*. I can take her back to Mexico. There, she will not have trouble." Paloma sensed her aunt's scrutiny as she stirred eggs into the spicy Mexican sausage.

"Are there no bad people in Mexico, *mija*?" Paloma turned to look into the frowning face of her *tia* Elena as she spoke. "Does everything always run smoothly? I seem to remember a government that has trouble running the country. I've seen the poor get poorer and the rich get richer. Is this the best way?"

Paloma stalked across the kitchen and stared out the window. She breathed deeply, wishing people would understand. "At least in Mexico we don't try to take what is someone else's. We only want to hold onto what we have. The Americans see something they want, and they take—without thought of whose it really is. They're greedy and evil."

"In some ways that's true," *Tia* Elena agreed. "Or, at least, for some of the people. I don't believe all Americans are like that, just like I don't believe that all Mexicans are power hungry. You, *mija*, have been blessed with a family who has much. Think of all the poor of Mexico who struggle. Do the wealthy give up their riches to help them?"

"Do the Americans do that?" Paloma shot back.

Tia Elena tipped the skillet, scooping some of the

chorizo and egg mixture onto two plates. "No, *mija*, I'm not saying they do." She handed Paloma a plate and beamed a smile at her. "All I want you to think about is this: Maybe Americans and Mexicans aren't so different. We all have faults. God doesn't say that only Americans are sinners, *mija*. We have all sinned and need to ask His forgiveness."

Paloma scooted her breakfast around on her plate. Was *Tia* Elena right? Could it be that Mexicans were just as bad, in their own way, as Americans were in theirs? Had she been judging when she shouldn't?

A picture of the bloody street of Monterrey, Mexico, came to mind. She shuddered at the forever-etched mental image. That day, September 23, 1846, the Americans and Mexicans had fought the final full day of the Battle of Monterrey. She and her family had taken refuge with some of their extended family members in that small town, hoping to escape. Instead, the war had hit them full force. For two days, the battle had raged outside of town. Then, the hated Americans had come into the city and begun to force their way into homes, looking for Mexican resisters.

Paloma remembered her brother fighting bravely to defend their family. As the only male left in a house full of women and children, he had considered it his duty to protect the family. The Americans brutally shot him, ran him through with their bayonets, then threw him into the street to die. She would never forget her mother's sobbing as she held her dying son, his blood covering her hands. For years now, her brother had been the hero of the family. She wouldn't allow anything to change that or to detract from his sacrifice.

No, Paloma thought to herself as she resolutely began to eat her breakfast, *the Americans are much worse than the Mexicans. I will never live among the people who stole my home and killed my brother. And Rosita won't either.*

A knock at the door startled Paloma from her reverie. She could hear the husky rumble of Antonio's voice as *Tia* Elena greeted him. Her hands trembled slightly, causing the eggs to tumble from her fork. She pushed the plate aside, excitement taking away her appetite. Was it Antonio or the thought of hearing what his *tia* Isabel would say that affected her this way?

"Good morning, Palomita." Antonio's smile lit the room. His gunmetal black eyes glinted with laughter. Everything else faded into the distance, and Paloma found she couldn't look away from his warm gaze.

"Sit down, Antonio." *Tia* Elena's order broke the spell. "Let me give you some breakfast."

"I never turn down your good food. I could smell your cooking long before I arrived at your door." His words were for her *tia*, but his eyes told Paloma how much he had missed her.

Paloma turned away and busied herself with cleanup. She couldn't help but remember the sweet kiss he had given her last night. She found that, once again, she wanted him to hold her in his strong arms. She wanted to lean against his broad chest and feel protected from whatever might come. She wanted him to kiss her again.

Stop this, she scolded herself. *You can't fall in love with Antonio. He'll break your heart. He'll never leave Tucson, and you must never agree to live here. Wait and find some-one who is willing to live with you in Mexico. Perhaps when you get back home Father and Mother can suggest the perfect husband.* She determined to speak with her parents as soon as she got back to Mexico. It shouldn't be too hard to forget Antonio and his declaration of love for her.

❧

Pretending interest in the food Elena Fernandez set before him, Antonio couldn't take his eyes off Paloma. She hadn't braided her hair yet this morning, and it hung free in a glorious mass falling below her waist. He longed to run his fingers through her hair and feel its softness on his arms as he held her in his embrace. He loved the way the light glinted and sparkled in her silky locks.

From time to time he caught her glancing at him. His heart soared with hope. *God, are You working on her heart? Lord, I pray that You are. I will try to wait patiently, even though I want the answer now.* He sighed, longing to know quickly if Paloma would be his. He knew waiting patiently would not be easy for him.

"Are you ready to meet my *tia* Isabel?" He watched Paloma's eyes light with excitement as he asked the question.

"Yes." She grinned at him. "I'll be ready in a moment."

She rushed from the room, and Elena frowned at him. "Are you sure this is wise, *mijo?* You will be careful to protect Rosita, won't you?"

"I gave my word." Antonio reminded her. "Did Paloma tell you what happened last night?" Elena looked fearful as he continued, telling her all about Franco. "He may be getting close to finding Rosita. Please pray that I will know how to protect her. I wish that sending her back to Mexico were the answer." He stood and gave Elena a quick kiss on the cheek. "I'll be careful with them both," he assured her.

On the walk to *Tia* Isabel's house, Paloma constantly tugged at his arm. He wanted to stroll slowly, extending his time with her. Yet, she seemed to want to race like the wind.

"Easy, Palomita." He laughed, tugging on her hand to slow her down. "We'll both be so out of breath when we get there that we won't be able to talk."

She slowed and slipped her hand into the crook of his arm. "I'm sorry." Her smile dazzled him. "I have looked for Rosita for the last week and a half. Now, I feel she is very close. I want the answers, and I guess I want them now."

"I understand," Antonio agreed.

"I want you to know, I appreciate your willingness to keep your word to Pablo." She spoke so softly, he had to lean close to hear. "At first I was angry with you for keeping things from me. Now, I think I understand a little. A man should always keep his word. I believe that is a good quality about you."

Antonio tugged on her arm and pulled her slightly closer. "So, you have been thinking about my good qualities," he joked. "Have you found any more?"

She grinned. "Not that I would tell you about. Obviously, you are already full of yourself. Perhaps I should make a list of your bad qualities and read them to you."

"Ah, but that list would be very short, indeed."

Antonio laughed as Paloma rolled her eyes. "Here we are, Palomita. This is my *tia's* house."

In a short time, they were inside the cool adobe house and seated around the kitchen table. *Tia* Isabel, a short, rotund, motherly figure, sang softly to herself as she fixed a plate of sweet breads for Paloma and Antonio. Antonio smiled, seeing the frustration on Paloma's face. He knew she would rather talk than eat.

"*Tia* Isabel, I told Paloma that you would talk to her about Rosita and Pablo. She met Franco last night, and I believe she needs to know everything."

Isabel slipped into a chair across from Paloma, clutching her hand. "My Chico and Antonio have talked to me about your search for Rosita. For reasons you will soon understand, we had hoped you would tire of your search and leave. We have done this for Rosita's sake. I hope you will forgive us."

Paloma nodded and Isabel continued. "When Rosita and Pablo came to Tucson, we all fell in love with them. Rosita has such a love for God and is always looking for ways to help others. Pablo had a quiet strength and a love for people. He worked hard to support, not only themselves, but also the others Rosita wanted to help. They were such a blessing to our small pueblo."

Isabel bowed her head for a moment then began talking again. "Rosita, in the goodness of her heart, didn't see the bad in others. She has always been very trusting. That is what got her in trouble."

Antonio watched Paloma. He ached to hold her, knowing what she would hear next would be painful for her.

"That bandito, Franco, came to town a year ago." Isabel spoke softly. "He and his men caused much trouble. They always fought, either ganging up on someone else or bickering amongst themselves. Anyway, one day, they were fighting and Franco was shot several times. He nearly died. But Rosita decided she should save him. She talked Pablo into bringing Franco to their home where she could nurse him back to health. She assured Pablo that if she did this, it would give her a chance to tell the outlaw about Jesus. Perhaps lives would be saved."

Isabel shook her head. "There was never any good in Franco. He did recover, thanks to your sister. And, in doing so, he fell in love with her. For months he pursued her, trying to get her to leave Pablo and run away with him. Rosita couldn't leave her house without Franco finding her."

A tear traced a path down Isabel's cheek. "Finally, Pablo could take no more. He tried talking to Franco, telling him he must stop bothering Rosita. Franco laughed and said Pablo was the only thing standing between him and his love. That despicable killer pulled out his gun and shot Pablo. Then, he laughed as he kicked him around and told him to die fast so he could have Rosita for himself."

Paloma began to sob. Antonio scooted his chair close to hers and put his arm around her, cradling her close.

"Antonio and Chico ran to help, but they were too late. Pablo died in Antonio's arms. My nephew promised to protect Rosita no matter what. That is why he hasn't told you anything. In fact, that is why the whole town is silent about Rosita. If we let Franco know where she is, he will kidnap her and she will be lost—his to do with as he pleases."

Isabel paused until Paloma looked up at her. "Now, you see why you must go back to Mexico and leave Rosita alone. Only by forgetting about her can you help her."

"No!" Paloma exploded. "Don't you see? Only in Mexico will she be safe. America is wrong for her."

Chapter 8

A ntonio, you've got to listen to me." Paloma turned away from Isabel to face him, placing her hands on his chest, fighting a desire to grab his shirt and shake him. "I've got to get Rosita away from here. My father has many vaqueros who work for him. All of them would lay down their lives to protect Rosita. There is nothing Franco could do to her in Mexico."

Gazing into her moist brown eyes, Antonio longed to give Paloma whatever she wanted. If only he could. "You don't understand, Palomita. I'm sure your father and his men could protect Rosita once she got to them, but what about before then? He would follow you. How many men does your brother have with him? Think. They will be spread thin watching the horses they are buying. Rosita wouldn't have the protection she needs."

"I can use a gun. I'll protect her."

Antonio wanted to hug Paloma close for her determination to care for her sister. Instead he explained slowly, "Franco has many men, my sweet. He will promise them anything—your horses, your father's wealth—" he hesitated before adding "—you. It doesn't matter that they fight among themselves; they are very loyal to Franco. They will lay down their lives to get what he wants."

"But there must be a way," Paloma's tearful whisper tore at his heart.

"The best way is to keep her in hiding until Franco gives up," Isabel interrupted. "Perhaps, if we pray, that villain will lose interest. Maybe something will make him forget."

"It's up to you, Palomita. Will you do *anything* to help Rosita? Even if it means leaving her here?"

Paloma's fingers wrapped tightly around the soft folds of Antonio's shirtfront. She leaned her head against his solid chest, and he leaned his cheek against her hair. He could feel her shaking as if a battle was raging inside her. *Please, God, help her make the right decision,* he pleaded.

Lifting her head, Paloma looked up at him. "I have to see her." The quiet force of her statement startled him.

"But it isn't safe."

"There has to be a way. Please?" she pleaded.

Antonio glanced over at *Tia* Isabel, who nodded. "I think she has the right to see her sister before going back home, Antonio. We'll work out a way. I'll talk to the other women, and we'll work out a distraction. Then, you can spirit her away for a short visit."

"We'll have to do it soon, *tia*. Her brother is due back to pick her up anytime. He may not be willing to wait."

❧

Paloma nervously smoothed her skirt for what seemed

like the hundredth time. She glanced over at *Tia* Elena and *Tia* Isabel and then around at the other ladies from the sewing group. They were all in on the plot to get her safely to where she could visit with Rosita. Two of the ladies, who were almost as small as she, were dressed exactly like her. Hopefully, the dim evening light and matching clothes would fool Franco.

In a group, the ladies began walking toward the church. To anyone watching, it would appear as if they were off for a time of prayer and worship. As the chattering women turned into the church, Paloma slipped into the churchyard. Antonio pulled her into the shadow of the wall. They waited breathlessly until the rest of the women passed. At Antonio's gesture, Paloma followed him through a back gate. In the shade of a mesquite grove, Chico waited with horses for them.

"Here you are cousin," Chico handed them the reins and helped Paloma into the saddle. For once, she wanted to kiss him, despite the silly grin on his face. "My mother and the other ladies will pray long and hard. I think they will also visit long and hard."

"Thanks, amigo." Antonio leaned over to shake Chico's hand. "We'll take the back way and try to stay out of sight. For Rosita's sake, I hope this works."

Paloma allowed her horse to follow Antonio's. The clop of the horses' hooves was muffled in the soft dirt of the side streets. Glancing from side to side, Paloma tried to watch everywhere at once. Every little noise caused her to jump. What if Franco hadn't been fooled? Although some people were in the streets, she couldn't see anyone who looked suspicious. Perhaps all would be safe.

Full dark had turned everything to shadows by the time Antonio stopped his horse in front of a long low adobe ranch house. Paloma anxiously fidgeted, not at all tired after the long ride. Lantern light flickered in the windows. A slight breeze rustled the branches of the trees. When Paloma's horse turned to look behind them and nickered softly, she knew there must be other horses nearby.

Antonio swung down from his horse. He reached up to help her down. Her heart pounded, and she couldn't decide if it was the excitement of finally getting to see Rosita or Antonio's nearness. He pulled her close and whispered in her ear.

"Follow this walkway to the end of the house. There's a separate small house there. That's where Rosita is staying. I'll take the horses to the stable and let the rancher and his wife know we're here."

Clenching her quirt tightly, Paloma eased along the semivisible path. A break in the wall told her that she'd reached the end of the main house. A small house stood close by, joined to the main house by only a section of roof. She knocked at the door, holding her breath in anticipation of seeing her sister.

"Come in, Carmelita; the door is open."

Paloma pushed the door open. "Rosita? Rosita, is that you?"

A slight, dark-haired woman jumped up from a chair, her sewing scattering over the floor. "Paloma?"

She rushed forward, and suddenly, Paloma had her arms around the sister she had missed so much. "Oh, Rosita, I missed you so much. I've tried so hard to find you. Are you all right?"

Rosita backed away a step, holding on to Paloma's arms. Her dark eyes searched Paloma's face.

"What are you doing here? How did you find me?"

"Berto brought me to find you and take you home to Mexico. When I found out you'd disappeared, I didn't know what to do. Antonio finally agreed to lead me here." Paloma grinned. "I have to admit, I almost met my match. You have more friends than you know in Tucson. They all want to protect you."

"Paloma, you must go back home and forget about me. There is an evil man who is trying to capture me. If you stay, he might get you, too."

"I've met Franco." Paloma watched the look of horror cross Rosita's face. "Sit down, Rosita, and I'll tell you all about it."

Rosita picked up the piece of material she had been stitching and sank back into her chair. She clutched the bit of cloth in her shaking hands.

"I have come to bring you back to Mexico, my sister. You know how I hate America and all it stands for. When I heard that Tucson was to become a part of America with the Gadsden Purchase, I knew I must bring you home. Now that I know of your troubles with Franco and about Pablo being killed, I know this is the best thing. You must come back to Mexico. We will return with Berto in a few days. When we are home, Papa won't let anything happen to you."

Slipping to the floor beside Rosita, Paloma took her sister's trembling hands in her own. "Please say you'll come back," she begged.

"I can't come back with you." Rosita freed one hand and reached to smooth the hair from Paloma's forehead. "This is my home now. This is where God wants me to be. Pablo is buried here. I can't leave."

"But you can't possibly want to be a part of America," Paloma protested. "Think of our brother who died in the war. The Americans killed him. They're evil people."

"Paloma." Rosita lifted Paloma's chin. "There are evil people everywhere. American's aren't the only bad ones."

"But look at Franco. Tucson has barely become a part of America, and already the wickedness is spreading. If you stay here, he will find you and take you for his, no matter what you want, just like the Americans took part of Mexico because they wanted it."

"Hush, sister." Rosita's calm pierced through Paloma's panic. "Franco isn't an American. He is Mexican. And he has always been evil, even before Tucson belonged to America. He comes up from Mexico on raids with his band of men. You know, Paloma, that there are wicked people everywhere. Although not all of us are like Franco, still we all sin against God. Only by believing in Jesus are we made clean."

Paloma buried her face in Rosita's lap. *Oh, God, help me convince her,* she prayed. *I have to take her back with me. I know You want that.*

"I have another reason for not going back with you," Rosita said.

Paloma lifted her head and wiped a tear from her cheek. "What else is keeping you here?"

"This." Rosita spread her sewing on her lap. There

lay a tiny nightgown, embroidered with bright flowers. Each stitch showed a mother's love waiting for a child.

"Rosita, you're going to make me an aunt? When?"

Eyes glowing, Rosita held the tiny bit of fabric against her breast. Tears glittered in her eyes. "Six months," she replied. "Pablo didn't even know before he died."

"But you must come home to have the baby. Mama and Papa will be so happy. This will be their first grandchild."

"No." Rosita shook her head. "You didn't know that I've already lost two babies. I can't take any chances with this one." She leaned close, holding Paloma's face in her hands. "Don't you realize? This is all I have left of Pablo. I want to have this baby."

Paloma rose up on her knees and folded Rosita in her arms. "I do understand. I can't make you return to Mexico and run the risk that you would lose the baby on the way. But I will stay with you," Paloma insisted. "Then, as soon as the baby is born and you are able, we will go home to Mexico. I'll have Berto come back for us."

"Sister of mine." Rosita laughed. "I'm glad to know you haven't changed at all. You always were determined to have your way. Do you even tell God what to do?"

Although she smiled at her sister's joke, Paloma felt a check in her soul. Did she tell God what to do? When she had asked Jesus to come into her heart and guide her life, she'd wanted so much to live as He directed. But somehow she had simply continued to run her own life and tell Him what she planned.

No, she thought, *I'm sure God wants me to get Rosita away from here as soon as possible.* The only problem would be spending another six to eight months around Antonio. How would she ever tear herself away from him then?

Muffled sounds scraped against the door. Paloma's heart skipped a beat as she turned to greet Antonio. Instead, in one swift motion, Franco slipped into the room and closed the door.

"So, my sweet, I've found you at last." His devilishly handsome face broke into a villainous grin.

Chapter 9

Paloma jumped to her feet, standing in front of Rosita. She raised her quirt in a vain attempt to stop Franco. "Stay away from my sister," she snarled. "If you don't, I'll scream and Antonio will come running to help us."

"No, Paloma." Rosita gently pushed her aside and stood up. "This is between Franco and me."

A shiver ran down Paloma's spine at Franco's sinister laugh. He sauntered toward Rosita. "So, my sweet, you're ready to go with me? I knew you would admit how much you love me as soon as I got that no-good coyote, Pablo, out of the way."

Rosita paled. Paloma feared she would tear her skirt; her fingers gripped it so tightly.

"My husband was an honorable man, not a villain like you. He loved me enough to die defending me. That's more than you would ever do for anyone."

Twining his fingers in Rosita's hair, Franco jerked her to him. "Don't make me mad, my sweet. I worked long and hard to find you. Why don't you show some appreciation? I know you've been waiting for me."

"Leave her alone," Paloma demanded. "She wants

no part of you."

Franco's maddened eyes raked over Paloma. "So the sister has more fire than you, my Rosita. Maybe I'll take you both. After all, she is the one who so obligingly led me to you."

"We were very secretive," Paloma gasped. "I don't know how you could have followed us."

Franco leaned closer and grinned wickedly. "I didn't watch you, sassy one. I had men watching all the exits from the pueblo. You see, I knew Antonio left Tucson with Rosita. When you rode out tonight, one of my men followed you while another came back to get me—just like a fox catching chickens." His maniacal laugh chilled Paloma.

She thrust herself between Franco and Rosita. "Get out of here," she warned. "I won't let you hurt my sister. I'm taking her back to Mexico."

Still holding a fistful of Rosita's hair, Franco seized Paloma under the chin. His large hand encompassing half of her face, he squeezed hard. "So, my sweet, your sister is in competition for my affections. Apparently, she wants to come with us, too. Now, I'll have two women instead of one."

Without thinking, Paloma raised her quirt and slashed the outlaw across the face. Franco let out a roar. He freed her chin only to backhand her, knocking her across the room. Rosita began to sob.

"Please, Franco, don't hurt her. I'll go with you. Just leave Paloma alone."

"I knew you were looking for an excuse to go with me, sweet Rosita. You long for the exciting life of the outlaw. We'll ride together. What a team we'll make."

Paloma lay on the floor trying to get her breath back. Her head hurt where she had slammed against the wall. Her cheek stung from the blow. When she touched it, she could feel the welt that Franco had raised. She looked up to see Franco, once more clutching Rosita close to him. The tiny embroidered nightgown still dangled from Rosita's fingers as a pathetic reminder of the small life that depended on the outcome of this confrontation.

Pushing up from the floor, Paloma stifled a groan. She knew every muscle in her body would be sore tomorrow. Steadying herself against the wall, she called on all her determination to do what she knew she must do.

"Franco, take me instead of Rosita. I'm a good shot with a gun. I can ride a horse as good as anyone. I can help you with many things."

The outlaw paused in his attempts to kiss Rosita. "You see, my sweet. Your sister can't resist me. All women find me attractive."

"Don't fool yourself," Rosita retorted. "She just wants to protect me. There isn't a decent woman alive who would have anything to do with the likes of you."

With one hand, Franco picked Rosita off the floor. Like a wounded animal he snarled, "Enough of your talk. You say, 'I won't die for you.' How would you feel about dying for me? If you don't start pleasing me, this just might be the end of you."

Rosita's face turned dark as the villain's hand closed tightly about her neck, cutting off her air.

"No!" Paloma screamed. "Let her go! You're killing

her!" She leaped across the room toward the pair as the door crashed open.

"Franco," Antonio roared.

Franco dropped Rosita and whirled to face his opponent. Paloma slipped to the floor next to her sister, throwing her arms around Rosita to protect her from the violence she knew would erupt.

Crouched in a fighting stance, Franco began to circle toward Antonio. Antonio glanced at Paloma, then Rosita, as though trying to determine if they were all right. Before Paloma could call out a warning, Franco picked up a chair and brought it crashing down on Antonio's head. Paloma gasped as Antonio slumped to the floor. She tried to run to him, but Franco grabbed her, flinging her back to where Rosita huddled. He bent over Antonio, now lying motionless on the floor.

"Leave him alone," Franco thundered. "He can't help you. Now, we're getting out of here."

Paloma fought back tears as Franco herded the two sisters out the door. Antonio lay so still. Was he hurt bad? Maybe even dead? *God, where are You now?* she cried from deep within her soul. *Every time I try to make things right, they only get worse. Don't You care?*

❧

The drone of a hundred bees echoed through the room as Antonio tried to open his eyes. Even the dim flickering lamplight burned his eyes, and he let his lids drop closed. The droning sound grew louder, and he realized that a steady moan was coming from him. His head ached. He lifted a hand and traced his fingers across his temple. A tender spot indicated where Franco had hit him with the chair.

He opened his eyes again. This time, the light didn't hurt as much. From what he could see, the room was empty. How long had he been unconscious? Had Franco taken both Paloma and Rosita? Where had they gone? He forced himself to sit up, but the room spun in nauseating circles.

Dragging himself to his feet, he tried to reach the door. The room whirled and a veil of darkness descended. He woke to find himself stretched out on the floor, his hand touching the partially open door. How long had he been unconscious this time? Gritting his teeth, he pulled himself to the wall next to the door and sat up, leaning against the wall for support.

Oh, God, how will I ever help Rosita and Paloma if I can't even stand up. Father, all I ever wanted to do was to protect them. I don't want them to end up dead like my family. I couldn't help my mother and sisters. But, please! Let me help Paloma and Rosita.

Tears burned his eyes as he remembered the helpless feeling of watching his home being burned, seeing his family dead in the yard. Now, he felt just as helpless. He had no idea where to look for Franco and his captives. He didn't know how much of a head start they had on him.

God, I can't be everything to Paloma, even though I want to be. I have to trust You with her life, Lord. I think I haven't fully trusted You since my family died. I guess I blamed You, when I know You had a purpose. Lord, forgive me. Whatever happens with Paloma and Rosita, I want to trust You.

Resting his head back against the wall, Antonio pressed his fingers against his eyes. One of *Tia* Isabel's favorite verses from the prophet Isaiah echoed through his mind. "Thou wilt keep him in perfect peace, whose mind is stayed on thee: because he trusteth in thee."

"I do trust You, Lord. I trust You with Paloma and Rosita. And I trust You with my love for Paloma. I know You will work everything out according to Your will. Thank You, Father." A feeling of complete peace washed through Antonio. Despite everything being in a mess, he knew God was in charge. He need not worry.

The night air had turned cool. Antonio eased his way along the path leading to the stables. He planned to get Grande and follow Franco to the ends of the earth, if necessary, to rescue Paloma and Rosita. He could still see their frightened faces—Rosita huddling on the floor, Paloma standing over her, ready to protect her to the end. He smiled. He loved the way Paloma stood up for herself and what she believed. He loved her spirit. He loved her beauty. In fact, he couldn't think of anything he didn't love about her.

Approaching the stable, Antonio slowly shook his head, glad to find the dizziness gone. The spot on his temple would be sore for a few days, but he could live with that. Now, he had to be ready to go where the Lord would lead him. That would be the only way he could rescue his love.

A shout rang out from the stable. Lantern light cast a dim eerie glow. Two figures were struggling and the horses next to them danced nervously. Antonio slipped quietly up to the door, sensing that he had come across Franco and the sisters.

"You will get on that horse, or I will kill you," Franco's voice grated harshly.

"You can't make us go." Paloma crouched like a fighter, ready to defend Rosita, who was already seated on a horse.

Rosita leaned forward, trying to soothe the horse and get Paloma's attention at the same time. Paloma pointedly ignored her and continued to face Franco.

As if by magic, a long-bladed knife appeared in Franco's hand. He waved the dagger in front of him, its point coming ever closer to Paloma. "We'll see how much fight you have when I carve up your pretty face." His handsome features twisted into a mask of hate.

Paloma backed against her sister's horse. Her dark eyes glittered in the lamplight. She watched Franco as if trying to judge what he would do next.

"First you hide behind women and now you're fighting them. And I thought you were a rough sort." Antonio stepped into the light as he spoke. Franco swiveled around to face him.

"I thought you were dead," he snarled. "I guess I'll have to make sure this time."

Paloma reached to help Rosita from the horse. They slipped into an empty stall. Antonio sighed with relief, knowing he could concentrate more on Franco with them out of the way.

"You won't catch me off guard this time, Franco. I know you don't fight fair, but I'm not letting you take Paloma and Rosita with you, either."

Franco leaped forward, his knife blade flashing in the light. Antonio dropped and rolled to the side, coming up behind Franco as he rushed past. In one swift motion, Antonio grabbed Franco around the neck, jerking him nearly off his feet. With his other hand, he caught hold of the wrist of the hand holding the knife and squeezed. Hours of working with his hands had given Antonio a strong grip. Franco's knife clattered to the stable floor.

Throwing himself to one side, Franco knocked them both to the floor. Antonio refused to let go, and the two fighters rolled under Franco's horse. The stallion whinnied loudly and reared high above them. Antonio looked up at the flashing hooves, released his hold, and dove out from under the terrified animal. Franco began to turn over as the horse's hooves descended. Antonio knew he would never forget the sickening crunch as the horse's hoof connected with Franco's skull.

"Antonio!" Paloma screamed.

He tried to block her view of Franco, but she rushed to him before he could position himself. She glanced past him at the blood pooling on the floor and covered her mouth with her hand. When she buried her head against his chest, Antonio wrapped his arms around her trembling shoulders.

"It's all over with, Palomita. Rosita will be safe now."

Rosita slipped out of the stall, staring out at the night as if avoiding the gruesome sight on the stable floor. Antonio rested his cheek against the top of Paloma's head. "You'll be fine now, Rosita. If you want, I'll take you to your *tia* Elena's. You won't have to hide anymore." His hand slowly stroked Paloma's back.

Paloma pushed away from Antonio. Her small hand caressed his cheek. "Thank you for saving us." She gave him a watery smile then turned to Rosita. "I've decided I'll leave you at *Tia* Elena's until the baby comes. Then I'll come back for you and bring you both home to Mexico. You'll be much happier at home where you belong."

Chapter 10

The overcast sky, with its heavy gray clouds and chilly wind, matched Paloma's spirits. Yesterday, Berto and the vaqueros arrived with the herd of horses purchased from a ranch up north. Today, Paloma would join them on the long ride back to Mexico and her home. This was what she had longed for, so why did her heart feel like a lump of lead sitting in her chest?

For the past week, since Franco's death and their rescue, both sisters had spent hours talking about their lives, their expectations, and their faith. Antonio dropped by nearly every day with some excuse or another. Every time Paloma stepped out of the house, he would "accidentally" show up to escort her around. Each encounter only made her fall more deeply in love with him.

She had tried her best to convince him to move back to Mexico with her. Her father would welcome him, and a leather worker and blacksmith would always be needed on a ranch. But Antonio insisted that Tucson was the place God put him, and here he had to stay until God said otherwise. She respected his willingness to do God's will but thought he might pray a little harder about going with her. Had he even asked God?

Rosita firmly stated that, while Paloma was welcome to come and visit after the baby came, she wouldn't return to Mexico. Rosita wanted to be here in Tucson because Pablo rested here and this had been the home he had chosen for them. Here, a town full of people loved her and would watch over her.

Packing her few belongings, Paloma struggled to swallow the lump in her throat. Her eyes burned with unshed tears. *God, why didn't You work this out better? I thanked You for saving our lives and for Antonio's help. But, Lord, I don't know how I can live without him. I love him. Please, help him to realize that he needs to come to Mexico to live. That's where we belong.*

"Paloma, Berto is ready to go. He's asking if your bag is packed."

Forcing a shaky smile, Paloma turned toward the doorway. "I just finished packing." Her voice quivered from pent-up emotion. She hoped Rosita hadn't heard.

Rosita crossed the room and took Paloma's hands in hers. "Are you sure you're doing the right thing by going back to Mexico?"

"I have to." Paloma fought back the tears. "I can't live here in America. Not after what they did to our people."

"Paloma, remember what I said? The Bible tells us that God is in charge of the governments."

Paloma nodded and Rosita continued. "That means God allowed the war between America and Mexico. He knew what would happen. But He didn't do it to punish us. God loves us."

"So He allowed us to be beaten by a country that

only thinks of itself. The Americans demand what they want and don't consider anyone else. Is that for our good?"

Rosita smiled and cupped Paloma's cheek in her hand. "Isn't that a human trait?" she asked softly. "Follow God, my sister, and He will lead you in the right way. Wherever you go, you will be blessed by Him."

"I know He wants me to be in Mexico, not America," Paloma said stubbornly. "I'm certain."

An hour later, Paloma gripped her horse's reins tightly, determined not to cry as she followed her brother toward the edge of Tucson. Antonio hadn't even come to say good-bye. She would return in six months to convince Rosita to come to Mexico. By then, her heart would be healed. For now, her very soul was breaking in two.

God, I asked You to help with this and You haven't. Why am I hurting so much?

"When did you ask?"

Paloma glanced quickly about, wondering where the voice had come from. Then she knew. God had spoken to her soul and He was right. Her shoulders bowed with the weight of the realization.

"You're right, Lord," she whispered. "I never asked You; I told You. I promised to give You my life, but I've only given You what I want to give. I allowed a root of bitterness to sway my thinking. Please forgive me."

The desert at the outskirts of Tucson opened its wide arms to welcome her. The vaqueros herding the horses were slightly ahead and to one side, waiting for Paloma and Berto to come.

Jesus, I see how wrong I've been. Just like the Americans, I hate. I've demanded my own way. I didn't think of what Antonio or Rosita wanted. I thought I was right and I didn't consider anyone else, not even You, Lord.

Paloma bowed her head and closed her eyes, allowing her horse its head. *Show me what You want me to do. Lead me, Lord.* The steady clop of the horses' hooves and the yells and whistles of the vaqueros faded in the distance as the Lord spoke to her heart, showing her His will for her life.

❧

Despite the heaviness in his heart, Antonio relished the peace deep inside him. He had watched Paloma ride from town with her brother, but he couldn't bring himself to talk to her. Staying in the shadows, he knew a part of him went with her this morning.

I guess this wasn't Your will, Lord, he prayed. *I tried for the last week to convince her how much I love her and would care for her as my wife. She couldn't see that for her vision of returning to Mexico. I'm trusting You to heal this hurt, Father. Thank You for allowing me to know Paloma. Perhaps, when she returns in six months to see Rosita, I can convince her of my love.*

Absentmindedly rubbing at the same piece of leather he'd been polishing for the last hour, he sighed and pressed his fingers against his eyes. He hadn't slept at all last night, choosing to spend the night praying for Paloma instead. He'd prayed for wisdom, but he still didn't feel very wise—only saddened by his loss.

A beam of sunlight broke through the cloud covering and streamed through the open door. Antonio looked up at the brightness and blinked. Paloma's silhouette stood quietly outlined in the golden sunrays. He started to rise then realized it could only be a vision. Paloma was riding toward Mexico at this very moment. He'd seen her leave. Antonio sank back in his chair, but he couldn't take his eyes from the realistic image.

"Antonio."

The vision spoke. He staggered to his feet, and suddenly she was flying across the room, flinging herself into his arms. This was the most lifelike illusion he'd ever experienced. He pulled her tightly to him, breathing in the scent of fresh rain-laden air. *Thank You, God; she's come back.*

"Why are you here, Palomita?" He feared to ask.

She smiled up at him, her cheeks tearstained and dusty. "I'm following God's desire for my life. He showed me that you are His will for me and He'll bless us both if we follow Him."

Antonio cupped her cheek and kissed her. He looked into her sparkling eyes filled with love and peace and couldn't resist another long kiss. "I'm truly blessed," he whispered.

NANCY J. FARRIER

Nancy resides in Arizona with her husband, son, and four daughters. She is the author of numerous articles and short stories. She also is a monitor at the small Christian school her daughters attend and home-schools part-time. Nancy feels called to share her faith with others through her writing. Her first novella, *Wall of Stone*, appeared in the Barbour anthology *Getaways*.

Promises Kept

by Sally Laity

Chapter 1

1905—New York—Spring

If she lived to be a hundred, the briny smell of the ocean would forever bring joy and pleasure to Kiera MacPherson. The rolling gray-green waves had borne her all the way from northern Ireland to the eastern shores of this glorious new world, all the way to Sean O'Rourke. And if paved city streets, a veritable sea of tall buildings and stately residences, and the incessant cacophony of noises seemed a stark contrast to the verdant peace of their homeland, it was of little consequence. The two interminable years of separation had finally ended. Kiera and the second cousin to whom she had pledged her heart and her love would marry at long last. The very thought all but stole her breath.

She lost herself in fascinating new sights and sounds as a hired driver threaded his carriage through the thoroughfare clogged with pedestrians, horse-drawn trolleys, street peddlers, private conveyances, and chugging motor cars. Just inside her bodice, close to her heart, she had tucked Sean's last letter. She loosened the knitted shawl she wore over her best travel dress, recalling the words forever imprinted on her memory: *We'll have a wonderful life in this new land, I promise. Hurry to me, my love.*

Anticipating those jaunty eyes of his, to say nothing of his all-encompassing smile and manly bearing, Kiera felt her heart contract in exquisite pain. There was so much to tell her beloved. Details of her journey, news of mutual friends back home, the drawn-out humiliations at Ellis Island, and how thankful she was to have actually arrived here in Brooklyn to begin their life together. Within her bags, she had tucked her mother's wedding dress, hoping to wear it as she spoke her vows. Perhaps the gown would ensure her at least a portion of her late parents' happiness, rest their souls.

"We're here, lass," the gangly, black-bedecked driver announced, drawing in on the reins and halting his old mare. He hopped down and offered a hand.

Kiera's pulse raced, causing her fingers to tremble as she accepted his assistance and stepped out. She dug into her reticule for money while he set her bags on the curb. "I thank ye."

"My pleasure." His bony hand closing around the fare, he tipped his head politely and got back into his rig.

Kiera turned and perused the row of two-story brownstone townhomes, verifying the house number before taking a bag in either hand and going up the walkway. Placing her burdens on the stoop, she lifted the wrought-iron doorknocker and rapped lightly, nibbling her lip in anticipation of her betrothed's surprised and delighted expression.

The door opened to reveal a stranger.

"Yes?"

Kiera regarded the rumpled white shirt and dark suit, the thinning hair, the faded blue eyes behind rimless eyeglasses. " 'Tis the wrong address I have, to be sure," she mumbled, her flagging spirit plummeting to her worn button-top shoes. " 'Twas Sean O'Rourke I was expectin' to find."

The aging man offered a smile. "Of course. You must be the cousin. Mrs. O'Rourke mentioned you might be arriving one of these days. Do come in, miss. I'm Dr. Browning." Reaching past her for her bags, he set them inside while she entered.

Her eyes made a swift circuit of the modest but tidy room with its overstuffed furniture draped with Irish linen scarves and fine lace curtains at the windows. Pleasant, familiar sights. Then, the manner in which the gentleman had referred to himself dawned on her. "A doctor, ye say? Is someone ill?"

He nodded, a grim smile deepening the grooves in his already-lined face. "Your cousin has been ailing for some time now. Especially since—" Clearing his throat uneasily, he gestured for her to precede him up the narrow staircase. "Her room's the first one to the right."

Kiera looped her shawl over the banister at the end of the railing and set her straw bonnet atop it, a strange foreboding creeping into her as she climbed the steps.

The bedchamber seemed close and stale as she entered, but Dr. Browning crossed the room and opened the heavy curtains. Immediately, sunlight flooded over the rather ordinary furnishings. The cheery colors of a worn, handmade quilt, turned down to the foot of the bed, seemed somehow out of place.

"Auntie Kathleen," Kiera said softly, using the affectionate title she had adopted since early childhood because of their difference in age. Approaching the still form lying under a sheet and light blanket, her heart ached at the realization of how old and frail her relative appeared in comparison to when they'd bid one another farewell on the quay behind Guildhall two years prior. Hair that once had been bright red and as thick as her son's had thinned and faded to pale blond. Her formerly plump frame had diminished to little more than a collection of angles and hollows.

"Kiera? You've come, lass?" she whispered. Her small, tired eyes swam with tears as she reached weakly toward Kiera.

"Aye, 'tis me." A wave of affection flowed through Kiera as she bent to hug the older woman. "And a fine way to be greetin' your favorite cousin this is," she said lightly, reverting to the easy way they once had of speaking to each other. "And where's that wild son of yours, I ask? I thought 'twould be his merry face greetin' me at the door."

At this, her cousin's breath caught on a sob. Her lips moved, but no sound emerged as she reached out for the doctor before again meeting Kiera's gaze.

The physician stepped nearer and put a hand on Kiera's shoulder. "I'm afraid we have some bad news to convey, miss."

"Oh." She straightened. "So he's still off at his job, is he? The barge canal he wrote about in his letters. Well, after two long years, I'll not mind waitin' another day or so."

But the kindly gentleman remained silent, his expression grave. Grave. . .and something worse.

Dread crept up Kiera's spine as she looked from him to Auntie Kathleen and back again. "Sure and you're not tellin' me he's gone off and married some other girl, now, are ye?"

"There's been an accident," the doctor began.

Alarm weakened Kiera's legs. "Sean's in a hospital, then. Just tell me where he is. I'll go visit—"

A slow shake of the graying head.

Her knees buckled. She sank to the bed. "But you're not sayin'—I mean, he isn't—" Hopelessly she latched onto her cousin's limp hand resting beside hers. "Auntie, please tell me Sean is just sick somewhere. Or hurt, even. I can stand that, if only—"

But the grim faces she searched only confirmed her worst fears. Her head grew light, making the doctor's voice, as he spoke the appalling words, sound fuzzy and far away.

"He was killed, Miss MacPherson. Two weeks ago. I. . .can't tell you how terribly sorry I am."

Two weeks ago. . .while she endured the tedious and meticulous processing at Ellis Island. She had been detained without visitors until a nagging lung inflammation cleared up. Those precious last days they might have been together—now forever wasted.

Kiera saw a huge tear roll from the corner of Kathleen's eye. A lump clogged her own throat, closing her air passage. She couldn't possibly utter a word, even if her very life depended upon it. This was all a horrid nightmare. Surely. Nothing could have happened to Sean, her redheaded giant. He was big and strong, the hardiest of all the young men she had known back home. Why, at any moment he would stride through the door and sweep her off her feet in an exuberant hug.

But as the dire realization slowly permeated her consciousness, she felt the hopes and dreams of a lifetime shrivel and die within her. Along with all of Sean's beautiful promises. And in their place loomed an unspeakable void. Dark. Cold. Far too deep for tears. Numbly, Kiera forced her legs to stand. She had to get out of this room. Go someplace where she could breathe. Think.

A place where she could reconcile herself to the senseless cruelty of fate and decide what in the world she would do now.

❧

The longest fortnight of Kiera's life drew slowly to a close. Sleepless nights of weeping had taken their toll. Utterly spent and emotionally drained, she trudged home after work, her hands still gummy from mounting photographs in the dim confines of the photographer's back room. Each sepia-toned picture she had studied served as a sad reminder. Her mental picture of Sean was already an ever-fading shadow of the once-sharp image. And, thoughts of the week's pitiful wages now stashed in her reticule brought a bitter grimace in the fading light of day.

Not one of the glowing reports about life in the New World that she had read in her "America letters" from Sean or heard from the emigrant agents who roamed

Londonderry and the surrounding villages had prepared Kiera for reality. Here in New York she had seen so many "No Irish need apply" notices posted alongside employment opportunities that she was teetering on the verge of despair. Finally, she stumbled upon the photographer's establishment. The position consisted of only half days and paid very little. But from what she gathered, women typically earned a mere fraction of what men were paid for similar work anyway.

Not that such things mattered. Nothing mattered anymore. If only Sean had sent her more funds, she would have bought passage on the first ship back to Ireland. But that was out of the question. Auntie Kathleen needed her now. Somehow, Kiera must take care of them both. She had no other recourse.

Reaching their street, she tried to manufacture some semblance of cheerfulness for the moment when she would greet Auntie Kathleen. The older woman had taken her son's death extremely hard, and her health, already poor, had steadily declined ever since. She needed whatever gaiety Kiera could muster.

Oddly enough, she found the front door closed. Normally it stood ajar to permit freshening breezes to waft through the house, as well as to allow their kind neighbor free access to look in on Kathleen. But, Kiera attributed the closed state to the growing darkness, and she quietly slipped inside to start supper.

Just then, Dr. Browning came down the stairs.

He did not need to say a word. Kiera could tell from his expression. "Auntie is. . ."

A nod.

In slender currents comes good luck; in rolling torrents comes misfortune. Never had the old proverb seemed so true. First Sean. Now cousin Kathleen. Wordlessly, Kiera sank to the nearest chair and covered her face in her hands.

Almost immediately she felt the doctor's empathetic hand on her shoulder, but it was a long moment until he spoke, his tones gentle. "I'll help you with the arrangements. And afterward, when you are able to consider it, I may have a new position for you, caring for another patient of mine. I've noticed how good you were with Mrs. O'Rourke, and I think this particular opportunity would be to your advantage."

Completely numb inside, Kiera barely listened, hearing the details only on the fringes, as if they were being related to someone else. But slowly they sunk in. A place to live. A prominent family. Better wages. She could only nod, and the doctor squeezed her shoulder.

Days later, after Kathleen O'Rourke's ravaged body had been laid to its final rest, Kiera forced herself to deal with the wrenching chore of sorting through the belongings that her cousin and her son had left behind. So many items still bore lingering traces of their owners' scents. She could only hug them and sob until there were no tears left inside.

Coming upon Sean's bank deposit book, she discovered the revelation of a tidy, growing sum. He had obviously been setting aside funds for their marriage. . . until the last large withdrawal for an investment that, according to his mother, had turned out to be a fraudulent scheme. Too late to rue his foolhardiness now.

But other items brought tender memories, thoughts of their former life in Ireland. A treasured pocket watch that had belonged to Sean's now-deceased father, Padraic, still bore the chain Kiera had scrimped and saved months to buy as a parting gift before Sean sailed for America. Not even bothering to dry her cheeks as she wrapped the object in an intricately embroidered linen scarf, she placed the treasure in a trunk containing the other mementos with which she could not part. Others, unfamiliar and meaningless, she would leave to cover the funeral and burial. Then she packed her own possessions and walked out of the rented house without looking back.

❦

"Thank you, Kingsley. This way, miss." Excusing the loyal household servant with a tip of his head, Devon Hamilton led the newly hired Irish girl upstairs to her quarters. Petite, with skin like porcelain and a head full of glorious light brown curls bent on escaping the prim bun at the nape of her neck, she seemed somewhat aloof, at loose ends. She had barely even smiled. He wondered if such a somber individual would really fit in here with his family, but she came with Doc Browning's highest recommendations. Perhaps all she needed was a chance. "You'll find this room, being next to Mother's, quite handy. If she needs you, you'll easily hear her bell."

With little more than a cursory glance around the comfortably furnished bedroom, she looked up at him. He started at the vacant quality within the blue-green depths of her eyes.

"I thank ye, sir. 'Tis fine enough."

He nodded. "Well, I see Kingsley has already retrieved your luggage, so I'll leave you to unpack. If there is anything else you need, just let him know. We trust you shall enjoy working here. When Mother awakens from her nap, one of us will escort you to her room and introduce you."

Kiera gave another dutiful nod. "When I've put away me things, I'll go down and help with supper, then."

"That won't be necessary, Miss MacPherson. You shall have your own duties to tend. Mother needs someone to keep her company and run for things. With the rest of the staff busy elsewhere, she's certain to find you a blessing."

"Indeed." The word came out on a caustic note. "I'll do me best, sir."

Captivated by her lilting voice, Devon did not miss the sag of her fragile shoulder or the droop of her head as she turned away and started toward the bags left at the foot of her bed. It was almost as if she lacked any spirit at all. Well, whatever the reasons for her melancholy, perhaps she would soon overcome them. If nothing else, he must make it a matter of prayer. Perhaps the reason the Lord had brought her here was as much for her to *find* help as to be a help.

Devon took one last look at the fetching lass then quietly closed the door.

Chapter 2

At the faint click of the latch, Kiera released a ragged breath and took a closer look at her new living quarters. The Hamilton mansion, situated on Madison Avenue within strolling distance of beautiful Central Park, had to be the most elegant she had ever seen. Certainly a far cry from either the cramped stone cottage of her childhood or Cousin Kathleen's rented row house in Brooklyn. Were it not for the empty ache inside, she might have thought this all a dream.

Decidedly feminine rose-printed paper adorned the walls, and lush floral-patterned rugs cushioned the polished wood floor. And what hired help would have expected a lace canopy intertwined with a garland of pink roses to crown the cherrywood bed, or a mattress so thick it would likely be soft as heaven's own clouds? Her tattered travel case seemed almost a desecration atop the immaculate satin coverlet—like a dingy blot on the shiny rose and ivory splendor. But aware that she could be summoned at any time to meet the mistress of the house, she sighed and began unpacking her meager belongings.

Her unpacking chore completed, she closed the ornate carved doors of the wardrobe. Moving to the open window, she parted the Belgian lace panels. Her breath caught at the broad expanse of manicured grounds below. Myriad flowers and sculptured shrubbery added to the grandeur of a marble fountain flanked by curved benches. Truly, this place was fit for a king.

If only Sean could have seen it.

But before that thought could render its usual bout of anguish, Kiera took a deep breath and focused her concentration on identifying the blooms whose fragrance perfumed the mild breeze even now stirring the curtains.

A light knock carried through the door, and she went at once to answer.

"Mother has awakened," Devon Hamilton announced with a polite smile. "She'll be having tea shortly. I thought you might take some with her." Wide-set sable eyes the identical shade of his wavy hair and tailored pinstriped suit twinkled as he awaited her response.

"Thank ye, sir." Now that he mentioned it, a cup of tea sounded more than appealing. But following her employer's long strides across the portrait-lined hallway, she felt a nervous chill and shivered, despite the day's warm temperature. What would the lady of the house be like? Hopefully as pleasant as her son, with some of the same handsome, patrician features. Still, Kiera wished she had asked Dr. Browning for his address, just in case this position was unsatisfactory.

Mr. Hamilton paused in the partially open doorway. "I've brought someone to meet you, Mother." He gestured for Kiera to precede him.

Tamping down her apprehension, Kiera schooled her expression into one she hoped appeared calm as she crossed the threshold.

A world of variegated greens enveloped her. Wallpaper, curtains, bedclothes, even the rich Persian carpet—all bore varying shades of the hue, made all the more lovely by an occasional touch of peach and burgundy. Occupying the center of a massive bedstead, a dignified lady in a satin bed jacket reclined against a mountain of pillows. Wisps of silver hair from two thin braids stuck out in disarray around her pasty, lined face, evidence of restless sleep.

"Mother," Mr. Hamilton began, "this is Kiera Mac-Pherson, referred to us by Doc Browning to be your companion."

"Companion!" the well-modulated voice echoed. "With a houseful of loyal servants already, I fail to see the need to take on new help." Her thin lips pursed as she crossed her arms over her bosom.

Feeling like an unwelcome intruder, Kiera flinched.

"Nevertheless," he went on, "Kiera is now part of the household. Let's give her a chance, shall we?"

"As if I have a choice in the matter," the invalid returned. "I still say the very idea is redundant. If you and Alexandria would simply get married, I'd have plenty of. . .genteel company." Then she switched her focus to Kiera. "Well, come closer, girl. Let me have a look at you."

"Mistress," Kiera murmured. And with each dutiful step across the room, she felt keenly aware of the matriarch's critical assessment. Only with the greatest effort could she meet those probing hazel eyes, particularly considering the grim expression on the regal face.

"I trust you possess more presentable clothes." She flicked a glance of distaste toward her son before eyeing Kiera once more. "What is your name again?"

Still smarting from the lady's outright rudeness, it was difficult to answer. "Kiera, madam."

"Irish, no less."

"Aye."

"And as such, it's doubtful you can read."

Rather offended by the queenly attitude, Kiera raised her own chin. "My father was a respected schoolmaster who insisted that I gain an education, mum." At the mention of her dear parent, one of his favorite quotations came to mind, *Character is better than wealth,* but she wisely left the saying unspoken.

The presumptuous mistress gave a grudging nod. "Ah. So you've one point in your favor."

"And likely not to be the only one, Mother," her son declared. "You'll see."

"Humph. I insist you dismiss the girl at once. Companion, indeed."

'Tis fine with me, Kiera nearly blurted. Cutting a glance toward the man of the house, she surmised this to be as good a time as any to bolt.

But the arrival of the tea tray blocked her escape route.

Staying Kiera with a hand on her shoulder, Devon Hamilton didn't seem put off in the least by his mother's ill manners. In fact, he did not even respond to her last remarks. "Thank you, Louella." He took the refreshments from the slim, auburn-haired servant and placed them on the bedside table. "I'm afraid I have other matters to attend just now." He offered Kiera an encouraging smile. "I'll leave you two to get acquainted over your tea, if you don't mind pouring."

She looked at him in confusion. "As ye wish, sir." Having noted a bed tray resting on its side against the wall, Kiera picked it up and positioned it carefully over the invalid's lap. She tried to ignore the disgruntled expression leveled at her in the wake of Mr. Hamilton's departure. Then, willing her fingers to remain steady, she filled a china cup with the steaming liquid and set it before the lady, along with a linen napkin and a spoon. "Will ye be takin' cream or sugar, mistress?"

A grunt. A pause.

Kiera handed the embellishments one at a time to the older woman, paying close attention to the amounts she used. "And there are some lovely biscuits and stewed apricots, as well."

"The kitchen staff is bent upon fattening me up," Mrs. Hamilton said tartly.

"Or perhaps tryin' to restore roses to your cheeks," Kiera ventured. As she served a little of both delicacies, one of her grandmother's proverbs flitted through her thoughts. *Soft words butter no parsnips, but they won't harden the heart of the cabbage either.*

Not even the hint of a smile gentled the woman's features.

Whether a show of good humor might bestow a greater resemblance to her son remained to be seen,

Kiera decided. But since her charge had been tended to, she filled the remaining cup and helped herself to a sweet biscuit before claiming the emerald velvet chair nearby. There she sat, prim and stiff, gazing at anything and everything except her mistress. Given the choice, she would have gladly taken her leave from this position, this woman, and even this house, fine as it was. What could the kind doctor have been thinking, to send her here, of all places?

Endless minutes ticked by before Mrs. Hamilton's voice punctured the stillness. "Have you been long in America?"

"No, mum. I've only recently arrived."

"You've no family?"

Kiera swallowed so quickly, she all but scalded her throat. "Not anymore, mum." *And don't be askin' me to explain,* she pleaded inwardly.

A few moments of silence followed, during which the invalid continued to appraise her between sips of tea. "Well, if I'm to be stuck with you, I should like to hear you read."

"Certainly, madam." She returned her now-empty cup to the refreshment tray. Then, noting that Mrs. Hamilton had also consumed her tea, she removed the tray while the woman reclined against the pillows. "Is there somethin' special you'd be havin' me read, then? A book you've started, perhaps?"

"Something from the Psalms. The ninety-first."

"The Psalms, mum?"

A nod. "The Bible is there on the table."

Not exactly acquainted with the Holy Book, Kiera

wondered how she might conceal that fact. To her utmost relief, she discovered a list of its contents inside the front cover. She quickly found the correct section and turned to Psalm 91:

" 'He that dwelleth in the secret place of the most High shall abide under the shadow of the Almighty. I will say of the LORD, He is my refuge and my fortress: my God; in him will I trust. . . .' "

Even as she continued reading the unfamiliar passage, Kiera wondered at the meaning concealed in the verses. It was not hard to imagine Almighty God living in some secret and lofty place unattainable by mere man. But how could someone call Him a refuge, much less actually place trust in an unknown Being? Those thoughts kept her from concentrating on what else she was reading, until she noticed the end looming near:

" 'Because he hath set his love upon me, therefore will I deliver him: I will set him on high, because he hath known my name. He shall call upon me, and I will answer him: I will be with him in trouble; I will deliver him, and honour him. With long life will I satisfy him, and shew him my salvation.' "

These verses further confused Kiera. Who was speaking? And to whom? But having reached the last verse of the psalm, she hesitated and glanced at Mrs. Hamilton.

"You read quite well." The pronouncement offered mild gratification. "But that is enough for now. You may return to your room."

"Aye, mistress." With a bow of her head, Kiera set the Bible back in its place and picked up the tray of soiled dishes. At least returning them downstairs would occupy some of this strangely long day. . .made all the more uncomfortable as Kiera sensed the woman's stare until she stepped out of her line of vision.

Even while she descended the wide staircase to the main floor, Kiera imagined herself wandering the grand manse in search of the kitchen, but fortunately Kingsley approached her at the landing.

"May I be of service, miss?" The friendly sparkle in the old gentleman's eyes complemented his smile, one incredibly white against his immaculate black suit.

Noting his amiable expression, Kiera liked him immediately. From the top of his snowy-white hair to the soles of his polished shoes, everything about the man exuded an air of pleasant confidence. "The kitchen, if ye please."

He gave a polite tip of his head. "Right this way." He led her down the hall past the drawing room and library to another corridor hung with staid ancestral portraits. At last they reached the kitchen, yet another showplace filled with the very latest in modern advancements.

Kiera tried not to gawk at the wondrous delights gleaming at her from cupboards and walls, where iron hooks held polished copper and tinware pots within easy reach. And, oh, such a stove.

"Halloo everyone," Kingsley said in a booming voice.

The hustle and bustle in the busy room ceased as two women looked up from their food preparations. Both of them wore crisp uniforms of dove gray with crisp white collars, aprons, and cuffs.

If this is how the servants of the household usually

dress, Kiera thought, wincing inwardly, *'tis no wonder the mistress looks with scorn upon someone whose very best attire leaves much to be desired.*

"This is madam's new companion, Miss Kiera MacPherson," Kingsley said. Relieving her of the tray, he took it to the drain board as he gestured with his head toward the stocky, gray-haired cook. "My good wife, Cora, and over at the worktable is Louella. She has her cap set for the butcher man, but we can still claim her for a spell yet."

"Pleased to meet you," slender, freckle-faced Louella said, a flush pinking her cheeks. Her knife remained poised above the fresh carrots she had been chopping.

"Aren't we now," the cook said, beaming. She dried her hands on her apron and crossed the room. "You'll save the lot of us a few steps, I'd say. Welcome to the house, Miss MacPherson."

"Kiera. Please," she urged, smiling and offering a hand.

Immediately her fingers were grasped by ones pudgy and warm. "I trust the mistress was in good humor today," Cora said, and a conspiratorial grin made the rounds at Kiera's silence. "Oh, she does have a good heart inside her. Give her time."

Kiera nodded, hoping they weren't merely being kind.

"Are you hungry, child? We were just about to have some supper. Here, take this seat and tell us all about yourself while we finish up." Even as Cora spoke, her husband yanked a chair out from the already-set table and nudged Kiera down with gentle pressure on her shoulder while his wife brought another place setting.

⌦

By the time she reached the quiet solitude of her own bedchamber after supper, Kiera felt as if she had made some new friends. She truly liked the other staff members and looked forward to the warm relationship that would surely follow. Perhaps one day she would even share her recent sorrows with them.

But Mrs. Hamilton had not rung for her again. Even once. Was the woman so adamant about not needing a companion that Kiera would find herself dismissed on the morrow? And if so, what then?

With Sean gone, was there any point in remaining in America, this land of empty promises? Everything was strange here. Strange and foreign.

Kiera had no living relatives back in Londonderry. Still, the town within those great seventeenth-century walls was achingly familiar. She missed the main thoroughfare of Shipsquay Street and the narrow streets that fingered out from it. She missed the craft village behind O'Doherty Tower. . .and the splendid views across the sea to the Scottish coast. . .and Donegal, which she had seen with Sean on the mountain road to Limavady. The Irish way of doing things provided solace. Ireland was home—would always be home.

Renewed purpose flowed through her being. She would work hard here, or at whatever other position she could find, and save every cent. And as soon as she acquired sufficient funds, she would book her return passage for home.

Chapter 3

Rising at dawn's first light, Kiera quickly recited her morning prayers and completed her toilette, then hurried downstairs to the kitchen.

"Well, aren't you the early bird?" Cora Phillips teased, elbowing her husband in the ribs. Already dressed for the day, the couple sat at breakfast.

"I wondered if I'd be expected to take a tray up to the mistress," Kiera admitted. "I shouldn't want to keep her waitin'."

"You can relax on that score, lass," Kingsley assured her, idly fingering a tip of his short handlebar mustache. "Madam never opens her eyes before nine, and we see to her meals. But you come and have a bite with us."

"How about a nice coddled egg?" Cora stood and crossed to the stove.

"Sure and I don't expect ye to be waitin' on me, now. I can do for meself."

"No doubt," the cook answered. "But as it happens, our Louella hasn't made an appearance yet, so this one will soon go to waste."

"Then I shall have it, and I thank ye for it."

The stocky woman removed the cooked egg from the

warming oven and brought it in a small bowl to the table, where two more places had been laid out in readiness. She filled the coffee cups and smoothed her apron before re-claiming her seat.

Kiera smiled her appreciation and took a chair, but an awkward moment passed before she touched the food.

"Don't mind us, child," Cora said gently. "If you'd like to say your grace, you just go ahead. We've already prayed."

With a sigh of relief, Kiera murmured the prayer her family had always used:

Bless us, O Lord,
Bless our food and drink,
You who have so dearly redeemed us
And have saved us from evil,
As You have given us this share of food,
May You give us our share of the everlasting glory.

She thought she imagined a curious look pass between the older pair opposite her, but they made no comment as she helped herself to a warm scone from a plate in the middle of the table and dipped the sweet bread into the moist egg.

"Did you sleep well, lass?" Kingsley asked.

"Oh my, 'twas the most restful I've been in ages. On such a grand bed, how could a body do otherwise?" She bit into the buttered biscuit and chewed slowly. "And did ye both have a good night, too?"

Cora nodded. "But we're expecting a busy day today. Master Landon and his bride are returning from their honeymoon and will be here for supper. He's the younger son," she added. "I'm sure Master Devon will be eager to hear about the wedding trip. And Miss Alexandria, what with her upcoming marriage to him, will make it a lively foursome."

"Well," snowy-haired Kingsley cut in, "if you ladies will excuse me, I'd best see to the garden. We'll need flowers for the centerpiece." He lightly tweaked his wife's kitchen cap, then smiled at Kiera. "You take your time, lass." With a last gulp of his remaining coffee, he got up, shoving the chair back with his legs. The sudden force sent it toppling.

Kiera almost choked. A chair falling when a person rose signified an unlucky omen. But the Phillips couple did not appear the least concerned as Kingsley righted the thing and took his leave. She blotted her lips on her napkin and vowed to be extra careful all day. To be on the safe side, she whispered her after-meal prayer when Cora went outside to shake the braided throw rug:

> Praise to the King of Plenty,
> Praise every time to God,
> A hundred praises and thanks to Jesus Christ,
> For what we have eaten and shall eat.

With no reason to hurry, Kiera lingered over a second cup of coffee, basking in Cora's quiet chatter before heading back upstairs to await Mrs. Hamilton's bidding. But when she reached her room, a virtual mountain of gray-striped boxes in assorted sizes all but blocked her doorway. Each had a burgundy lid, with the name Hamilton embossed across the top in gold script.

Seeing a red-faced Kingsley and a grinning Devon Hamilton approaching, their arms laden with still more, Kiera gasped. "Whatever is all this?"

"We expected to finish before you came up," the old servant blurted.

But nothing caught the man of the house off his guard. "You'll find that the boxes contain just a few things we hope you can use," he said with nonchalance.

"A few things, is it now? And how can I be takin' so much from ye, I ask?"

"It's not that much," he replied. "And surely nothing to trouble yourself over. After all, we do own the store."

Kiera, however, had a different opinion. *Take gifts with a sigh; most men give to be paid.* She could only wonder what particular payment she would be forced to render.

"Why, it's perfectly fine, lass," Kingsley offered in calm assurance. "The madam likes all the staff to look sharp and fashionable."

"Then I'm not to be let go, after all?"

"Far from it," Mr. Hamilton said. "I'm the one who hired you. You stay unless I personally give you the boot, and I'm not about to do so anytime soon." He turned to the older man. "Well, let's tote these boxes into her room, while we're at it. She'll want to put everything away herself, I'm sure."

Kiera stepped aside to allow the two free access. Never had she seen such a quantity of stylish boxes at one time, much less been the recipient. Watching the men as they neatly stacked the packages near the bed, her heartbeat quickened at the mere thought of peeking inside each one. New clothes. American clothes. . .for her. She hadn't expected any immediate personal benefits to her chore of tending a cross-tempered matriarch.

"Well, that's the last of them, Miss MacPherson," her employer announced while Kingsley brushed off the sleeves of his suit and returned to his duties. "If the buyer forgot anything, do let me know, and we'll rectify the situation."

For one terrifying moment, Kiera felt tears gathering behind her eyes. She swallowed the huge lump forming in her throat. "Y–yes, Mr. Hamilton. And. . .thank ye, sir. I've never. . ." Overcome, she lifted a hand in a mute gesture.

He gave an understanding nod. "We want you to feel at home here, Kiera. I trust you will approve the clerk's choices. She's quite knowledgeable about what women are wearing these days."

"But still. . ."

"Remember, as it says in the Bible, our heavenly Father knows when His children have needs."

Against her better judgment, Kiera could not help but speak her mind. "And where might it say that? Seems to me quite a few of those same children have been in need for some time, and still are, in truth."

His dark eyes softened with his smile. "Well, now, I'm not altogether sure of the passage offhand, but I'll look it up so you can read it for yourself, if you'd like."

"Aye. Thank ye. And I truly am most grateful for your kindness."

He grinned and tipped his head, then left, closing the door after himself.

Kiera surveyed her bounty. Where to start. Nibbling her bottom lip as she gazed at the largest parcels, she snatched a smaller one from the top of a pile, to work her way down.

Several pairs of soft kid leather shoes, camisoles, chemises, nightgowns, and bonnets to match a glorious array of summer gowns later, Kiera felt like a princess in a fairy tale. Nothing had been omitted, from lacy shawls to combs for her hair to modest jewelry with matching earbobs. She breathed a wordless prayer of gratitude over her good fortune and began putting her lovely new wardrobe away. All, that is, except for a lavender organdy day gown with embroidered daisies on the bodice. She would wear her favorite color when she greeted her mistress. Slipping off her own worn but serviceable attire, she returned them to the armoire, then donned the new dress, running her hands down the delicate fabric in awe. Even as she brushed her long curls and caught the sides back with ivory combs, she could hardly stop staring at her reflection. She only hoped the mistress would approve.

Soon enough, the bell rang.

Kiera started and jumped to her feet. Then, taking a calming breath, she went at once to the matriarch's bedroom, where she rapped softly and entered. "Top o' the mornin' to ye, mum. Will ye be takin' breakfast now?"

"Yes." The hazel eyes widened, then narrowed again as quickly. "I daresay, you're looking much more presentable today. Not so dowdy as before."

"Thank ye, mistress." Kiera supposed she would get used to the criticisms eventually. She pushed the heavy draperies aside to let light flood the room. "Just look," she exclaimed, admiring the gardens below. " 'Tis a grand mornin'. I'll go see about your tray."

But even as she spoke, Louella Banks appeared at the door with the woman's breakfast. A bit flushed, the servant seemed eager to be relieved of her burden.

Kiera nodded her thanks and had the invalid all set up in short order, somewhat gratified when her charge displayed a bit of appetite. From now on, Kiera determined, a vase with a fresh flower would brighten each meal tray—and perhaps an arrangement of fragrant blooms for the room. No sense in their wilting outside, unseen by the person who had likely planned that wondrous garden. She planned to discuss the matter with Kingsley.

"Is there anything in particular you'd like me to be doin' for ye when you've finished, mum?"

A weary sigh emerged. "Yes. My hair must look a sight. I should like it brushed."

"Certainly. And I can help you freshen up, if you'd direct me to your clean bed jackets. You'll be wantin' to look special for your son and his wife, I'd expect."

Mrs. Hamilton eyed her in contemplation, then gave a nod. "Yes, that is today. I'd forgotten." She paused. "Are you always so. . .cheerful?"

Kiera had to smile. "Morning is my favorite part of the day, mistress. 'Tis so bright with hope and promise, with so many good things likely to happen. To be sure, there's little sense in imagining clouds when the sunshine's so glorious."

"Indeed."

Amazingly, the remainder of the morning passed quite pleasantly, and Mrs. Hamilton, all washed and sporting a pale green bed gown, actually smiled while Kiera brushed and rebraided her hair. "You have quite a gentle touch, I must say. The others always seem to be in a hurry and invariably yank too hard."

"Well, I've no reason to rush. I'm here to make sure you're rested and comfortable, mum." Returning the costly silver brush to the dressing table, she turned. "Would ye like me to read now?"

But the crowning moment came at lunchtime, with the arrival of the lunch tray.

"A rose!" the older woman cried in surprise. "I'd almost forgotten the lovely garden fragrances, being cooped up in here for weeks and weeks."

Kiera merely smiled. "Perhaps 'tis time we take you out for some sunshine and a stroll around the grounds."

Mrs. Hamilton grimaced. "It's been too much bother for the staff to fuss over an old woman who needs to be carted around."

"Well, 'tis no bother to me. I'll speak to Kingsley."

A noticeable change in atmosphere settled over the sickroom from that point. And not long after eating, the invalid nodded off, providing Kiera with a little time to herself. She dashed downstairs to chat with Cora.

"Oh, just the one I wanted to see," the cook said when Kiera breezed into the kitchen. "Our Louella is a mite under the weather. Could you possibly help serve supper this evening? We do have company coming, if you recall."

"Aye, I remember. I'm as able to be helpin' out as I am to sit in me room with a book, I'd say."

"Thank you, child. I'll get you a clean uniform. You're about the same size as she, though perhaps a bit trimmer about the waist. With a tuck here and there, her things should fit well enough." Going to a small room off the kitchen, she removed a complete outfit and brought it to Kiera.

"When should I be ready?"

"We'll be serving at eight. That's after the mistress has finished her own meal, of course. No doubt she'll excuse you so her sons can visit her awhile."

"Fine. I'll be only too glad to be lendin' a hand. In the meanwhile, is there somethin' I can do to help with the cookin'?"

She shook her head. "No, dearie, not a thing. I've seen to all of that, and there's naught to do but wait for it all to finish."

"And what about the table?"

"King helped with that awhile ago. I won't impose upon you until about seven or so."

"Oh, 'tis no imposition in the least." Kiera regarded the older woman, debating whether to bring up the subject of her morning, yet she saw no reason to avoid the matter. "I. . .suppose you've heard how I happened to come into an incredible variety of new clothing earlier today."

A knowing smile added two more creases in the plump face, and Cora reached across the worktable to give her an empathetic pat on the forearm. "Ah, Master Devon is as generous to us all often enough. Always eager to do for others less fortunate. That's just his way."

Just his way. Kiera pondered that concept as she left the kitchen and carried the uniform to her room. Would the brother Landon be similarly disposed? And what would her employer's fiancée, Alexandria, be like? 'Twould be interesting to see his taste in women. Not that it was any concern of hers. She'd just always been curious by nature.

Chapter 4

A t the immense walnut desk in the library, Devon raked splayed fingers through his hair and closed the tiresome accounts folder, pushing it aside. He reached for his Bible instead, opening to the New Testament. He had recently read the passage he quoted to Kiera, and he knew it was in the Gospels.

Sure enough, he came across the passage he sought in the sixth chapter of Matthew. *Consider the lilies. . . .* "Perfect."

Stretching a kink out of his neck, he leaned back in the leather chair and idly scanned the bookshelves lining two walls of the room. His gaze fell upon his grandmother's tattered Bible, the most precious memento of his childhood. Hard to believe a dozen years had passed since Grandma Hamilton had gone to be with the Lord. She had been such a presence in his world. Devon could still envision her spindly frame in her favorite rocking chair on the sunporch, aged head in a ribboned house cap as she pored over the Scriptures. So lovingly she had penned notes in the margins, writing down the insights gained during her times of quiet study and prayer. In the treasure house of his mind, the echo of that quavering voice still proclaimed God's goodness, still encouraged him to be a faithful follower of the Lord. How fervently she had prayed that one of her grandsons would go into the ministry.

Well, at least I came close to fulfilling her desire, Devon reminded himself as he exhaled. He had chosen to enroll in theological college at Princeton, rather than attending Columbia, as his parents preferred. But who would have expected Father to die so suddenly of a heart attack two years ago, leaving the entire Hamilton merchandising enterprise in dire need of a new head? As eldest son and having worked under his father's tutelage for quite a few summers, Devon could do no less than assume the responsibility permanently. Strange, the way life worked out, often so contrary to one's dearest dreams.

But this opportunity to search the Scriptures once more—even though not in the same depth he once did at college—brought back forgotten memories—and forgotten pleasure. Certainly the ministry had to be one of the most satisfying and valuable careers, guiding people in their life decisions, aiding in time of distress, doing something that counted for eternity. High time he made personal Bible study a habit again. Even a layperson could obey God's instruction to be a workman who needeth not to be ashamed, one ready to give an answer for the hope within.

"Someone in this very house needs some of those answers, Lord," he prayed in the quietness as his thoughts drifted to his mother's new companion. "Use me to help her find them."

He smiled to himself, recalling how Kiera Mac-Pherson had been almost overwhelmed at the paltry items the buyer at Hamilton's selected. A peaches and cream complexion like hers couldn't belong to someone more than twenty, yet those ocean-blue eyes contained experience and wisdom beyond her years. And, after listening to Dr. Browning relate the young woman's encounters with hardship in America, Devon felt compelled to make up to her for some of them. . .sort of assist those circumstances in working together for good, as the apostle Paul wrote in Romans.

"And perhaps that old Bible will have new purpose, too," he declared. "Grandma would like that." Rising, he strode to the bookshelf and took it down.

Kiera had never served at a formal supper before, but Cora's advice to stick close and follow her lead went a long way in lessening the possible nervousness. A dutiful step behind the cook as they brought the food into the dining room, Kiera tried not to stare in openmouthed delight. Everything looked exquisite in the light cast by the crystal chandelier—including the elegantly coifed women guests, whose gowns and jewels sparkled with every movement and whose soft laughs could be heard as they sipped lemonade from long-stemmed goblets. The heady perfume of the summer flowers Kingsley had placed in a cut-glass vase on the lace tablecloth almost overpowered that of the Cornish hens in orange sauce on Kiera's tray.

"Mmm. Cora, you have outdone yourself, as always," Devon Hamilton told her upon her approach. "If anyone ever tries to lure you away from us, just tell me, and I'll double their offer."

"Oh, pshaw," she said, obviously accustomed to such good-natured teasing. "As if I'd be happy anywhere but here with you and the madam." Placing one of the golden birds on his plate, she moved on to serve the willowy honey blond to his right.

Noting the perfect oval face, delicate features, and full, rosy lips, Kiera surmised this was his fiancée, Alexandria. The young man occupying the foot of the table had eyes only for the shy, fragile-looking brunette next to him, whose hand rested lightly atop his, their fingers loosely intertwined.

As Kiera drew closer, the blond raised her lashes, revealing the bluest eyes Kiera had ever seen. Though somewhat lacking in warmth, they contained more than a little interest. "And whom have we here, darling?" she asked, favoring Devon with a dazzling smile. "Has little Louella been replaced?"

Seemingly taken aback at the sight of Kiera, Mr. Hamilton tipped his head toward his fiancée. "Actually, this is Mother's new companion, Kiera MacPherson." But confusion colored his tone, and he glanced toward the cook.

"Louella fell ill this evening," she supplied. "I imposed upon the lass to help out."

"Ah."

"Your mother requires a companion?" Alexandria asked him. "When did all this come about?"

He gave a noncommittal shrug. "It was my idea, dear heart. The staff's been so busy lately, she was feeling neglected."

"Oh, what a shame, when something as simple as moving our wedding date forward might have forestalled such a need." Her gaze assessed Kiera more closely. . .as did the others at the table.

"Miss MacPherson has been a real godsend to us," her fiancé quickly added.

The center of attention and discussed as if she wasn't even present, Kiera felt her face heating. She tried not to wilt under everyone's scrutiny while Cora served the remaining hens, then they both returned to the kitchen. Bringing in the vegetables mere moments later, Kiera was thankful the family's lively conversation had turned to a subject other than herself.

"Paris was ever so romantic," the newly married woman gushed. "What we saw of it, of course, having scarcely left our suite." She blushed daintily.

Her husband, slighter in build and with lighter hair than his older brother's, chuckled. "But then, it's all lovely during the summer, Madeline, my love. I doubt we missed much."

"Yes, I've visited the city several times," Alexandria said wearily. "I'm hoping Devon and I will honeymoon in the Greek Islands."

"Assuming your wedding transpires in our lifetime," the younger son quipped. "Seems my big brother is set on having the longest engagement in history."

Not everyone chuckled.

Kiera remained expressionless as she set the mashed potatoes and gravy in place. But any relief she felt over the fact that this was the last trip she'd be making into the dining room for a while vanished when she happened to catch Alexandria's cool stare on her way out. . .one tinged with ill-concealed distaste and something else. *Could she possibly feel threatened by a newcomer's presence in the house?* Kiera wondered incredulously. Why a woman of quality should look upon an insignificant household servant in such a way was a mystery.

The very thought of trying to compete with such perfection almost made Kiera laugh. After all, she was here only temporarily, at best, determined to flee America at the first opportunity. And besides, she knew her place. Far be it from her to form some foolhardy attachment to her employer, of all people. She was seeking neither close friendships nor love—especially considering the sorry fate that had befallen everyone she had cared about in her life. Obviously she was being punished for something—what other possible explanation could there be for her misfortune?

But thankfully, the evening would not last forever. All Kiera had to do was endure removing the plates and serving dessert. After that, with any luck at all, her path might never again cross that of Mr. Hamilton's betrothed.

❧

Weary and footsore by the time she could turn in, Kiera trudged up the stairs. On the floor just outside her door lay an old Bible. A folded note had been tucked between some of the pages. With a yawn, she stooped to pick up the Book and carried it into her room.

The hour was late, and the house incredibly quiet, for after visiting with the lady of the house, the foursome had gone for a drive in Landon Hamilton's new motor car. Kiera shed the now-wrinkled uniform and donned her nightgown before crawling into bed. But she felt compelled to open the tattered Book despite her tiredness. Pulling the bedside lamp a bit closer, she unfolded the handwritten note.

Kiera,

Please feel free to make use of this Bible during your stay here. It belonged to my grandmother, who was an avid student of the Scriptures. I have marked the passage mentioned earlier and trust that some of her insight may help to clear things up for you. There is a similar account in Luke, chapter twelve, for you to compare. If you have any other questions regarding this or related matters, do not hesitate to let me know.

Cordially,
Devon H.

The fact that her employer had been thoughtful enough to provide a copy of the Bible for her own personal use pleased Kiera. Now, she could search for the answers to the perplexing issues she had raised earlier. And, she could also study the Psalms, which her mistress seemed so fond of, so she wouldn't stumble over the unfamiliar, archaic words.

Stifling another yawn, she noticed that he had marked the ending portion of the sixth chapter of Matthew's gospel, beginning with verse twenty-five. She read the passage through three times, paying particular attention to the phrases and sentences that seemed to stand out. Just as Mr. Hamilton had told her, the Bible did say that God looked after His own. But what did the phrase, "seeking after righteousness," mean?

Hoping the rest of the passage might enlighten her along that line, she turned back to the first verse and read the entire sixth chapter. But the extra verses only added more questions to her original one. Who exactly did God consider a hypocrite? And what did He consider vain repetitions? Could this pertain to the short prayers she had recited all her life?

Trying to decipher these new ideas, Kiera's head began to ache. Perhaps in the morning all this would make more sense. Using the note as a bookmark, she closed the Bible and turned off the lamp. Then, with only a slight hesitation, she whispered her customary nighttime prayer as she lay her head on the pillow.

❧

"And you actually believe this girl is an asset to the household?" Alexandria asked.

As the car motored along, Devon watched the play of light and shadow from the street lamps now dancing across his fiancée's fine cheekbones. The night was too pleasant to spoil with an argument. . .something which the two of them seemed to do a lot lately. "Yes, Alex, I do. You heard yourself how Mother sang her praises when we stopped in to chat—and Kiera only arrived two days ago. I've never seen such a drastic change in her disposition."

"All the same, I feel it's *my* place to cheer up your mother. And I will, once we marry. Can't we please set a wedding date?"

Following her line of vision as she turned forward, Devon observed the obvious devotion displayed by the newlyweds in the front seat. He knew Alex only wanted to experience the same heady newness of marriage. And why shouldn't she? After all, they had been engaged for almost three years now. The daughter of his mother's very best friend, Alexandria epitomized Mother's expectations for the bride of her eldest son. She wanted them to marry and produce some grandchildren for her to spoil while she still could. He cupped Alex's cheek with his palm and gently pulled her head nearer to rest on his shoulder. "Soon, sweetheart."

Her soft lips curved into a smile as she raised them to his.

Chapter 5

After breakfast the next day, Kiera ventured outside, the borrowed Bible tucked under her arm. A gathering of clouds appeared to be moving in from the east. But the temperature remained pleasant as she strolled the perimeter of the grounds, admiring the placement of grand shade trees and flower beds, the hem of her periwinkle skirt whispering softly over the grass with each step. The magnificent greens and colorful blossoms made her long for Ulster, with its freshening ocean breezes and mossy places. She hoped that she might soon set sail for her homeland. She hadn't given any thought as to what she would do after she returned to Ireland. . .she only knew she had to go.

As she neared the house, the muted shush of cascading water drew her to the fountain, where glistening arcs spouted from the mouths of the marble dolphins into the fluted pool below. The relaxing sound all but begged to be enjoyed. Sinking onto one of the curved benches, Kiera opened the Bible to the book of Matthew and buried her nose in the passage that still worried her mind. She planned to examine the corresponding account in Luke also, as suggested by her employer.

Perhaps that would shed more light on the subject of God's provision for His children.

"Lovely morning, isn't it?"

Kiera sprang to her feet. She had been so absorbed in the Scripture, she hadn't heard Mr. Hamilton's footsteps. "I–I'm sorry. I shouldn't be here, I know."

"Nonsense." He gestured for her to be seated again. "You're not a prisoner here, Kiera. You may do anything you like in your free time."

"Thank ye, sir." The breath returned to her lungs as she regained her composure. "And aye, 'tis as ye said. Lovely."

He gave a polite nod and lowered himself to the opposite end of the bench, gazing off into the distance while he sipped from the coffee mug he held. "Do you come out here often?"

"Until today I've only looked at it from me window."

"My father designed all of this for Mother before the house was even built," Mr. Hamilton said casually. "He was extremely busy. Always at the store. And he wanted her to have grounds she could enjoy in her solitary moments. She occasionally liked to dabble in the garden herself, trying new varieties of roses to see how they'd fare in this climate."

Even as her gaze idly traced his strong, appealing profile, noting how the smart navy suit complemented his coloring, Kiera had no trouble deciding what Alexandria Fitzroy saw in him. She cleared her throat. "If you'll pardon me for speakin' me mind, 'twould do her good to get out again. I was going to ask Kingsley about a wheelchair."

His wide-set eyes turned right to her. "That's an excellent idea. We do have one out in the carriage house. Of course, as you might imagine, after her stroke, Mother adamantly refused to be confined to a contraption designated for the old and infirm. But she might have changed her mind by now. I'll have King dust it off and bring it to the house."

"I thank ye. I'll see that she takes some sunshine every day."

"As you say, it'll do her good." An affable grin spread across his lips.

Kiera lowered her lashes, lest he think her bold.

"I see you brought the Bible with you," he began. "Has it helped you at all?"

"In some ways, aye. In some, nay."

"Mind explaining what you mean?"

Kiera considered her words, hoping to express her feelings correctly. "I understand that the Almighty looks after the creatures He created. He feeds us and clothes us when we are in need. . . ."

"Because He also loves us," her employer cut in. "He knows each of us by name before we're born and numbers the very hairs on our heads. He watches His creation so closely He sees even the sparrow fall."

"It says that, too, in the Bible?"

"It does. I'll look up the references for you."

Kiera gratefully tipped her head, then averted her gaze.

"Then why are you frowning?" he probed. "What else is troubling you?"

She shrugged and drew a deep breath. "I don't

know how to put the harder things into words. Such as, if God truly cares for us so very much. . .why does He permit horrid things to happen? Why are there wars? Why do babies die or loved ones get taken from us? Does He care more for birds than He does for His people? And where was He when. . .when my Sean was killed?" Embarrassed that she had touched on her deepest pain, Kiera blinked quickly to stay rising tears.

When Mr. Hamilton failed to respond right away, Kiera feared she had overstepped her bounds. She bit down hard on the inside corner of her lip, wishing she had curbed her tongue. "Forgive me. You're angry that I spoke with such doubt, such disrespect."

Finally he emitted a long breath. "Hardly. You're not the first person who ever wondered about those mysteries, you know. I confess, most of us, at one time or another, wish we could explain them adequately. As to where He was when your friend was killed, I'd say exactly where He was when His own Son was murdered. . .and no doubt with a heart that ached all over again, right along with yours."

Kiera had to look at him as he paused before going on.

"Regarding the other matters, I've asked myself similar questions and come up empty. But tell you what. I'll get out some of my old books and study up. See what I can find out. . .for both of us."

Searching those mahogany eyes, his compassionate expression, Kiera knew he meant what he said, and that, in itself, provided great comfort. She smiled and stood. "Well, in no time a'tall, the mistress will be ringin' the bell. I must hustle up to me room. I thank ye for the—help." Lowering her gaze to the Bible clutched to her breast, she started for the back door.

"Perhaps we'll talk again, another morning," he called after her.

Without turning, Kiera nodded and, with a wave of her hand, went inside.

The deeper he got into his study, the freer Devon felt in his spirit. How he wished this could have been his vocation. At the store he seemed surrounded by one frustration after another. Trying to keep the staid, older men on the board of directors satisfied with the accounts receivable. The future innovations he and Landon envisioned for Hamilton's. Entire shipments of goods delayed en route, some never arriving at all—or if they did, arriving damaged beyond repair. New stock items, in which they'd invested heavily, scorned by the customers and relegated to discount sales, practically given away. Trusted high-level employees leaving, unexpectedly, for greener pastures. Female employees deciding to stay home with their children or provide new additions to their families. Endless hours confined in that huge, stuffy office.

But here, at home in the quiet, his very soul soaking up the Word of God, he felt a fulfillment that the rest of his life lacked. However noble his intentions, had he made the wrong choice after all? Surely his younger brother expressed more enthusiasm than he, himself, had ever experienced for the family business. But Landon was four years younger than Devon. That fact alone prevented him from finding any opportunity to prove himself worthy of the store's challenge. Perhaps the time had come for him to become more than a mere junior partner.

With a shake of his head, Devon blew out a whoosh of air. Where was he before those conflicting thoughts tangled up his mind? Ah, yes. Romans. Still trying to unearth adequate explanations for Kiera's questions. Would she think it trite if he explained that three wills—God's, Satan's, and man's—were at war on this earth, or that heartaches often came as a result of one's own bad choices? Or that God's thoughts are higher than man's, as the prophet Isaiah had written?

In any event, he doubted he could help her to understand something so complicated by merely passing on a few Scripture references. This kind of thing was better dealt with in face-to-face discussion. And it called for being well prepared. Furthermore, the thought of doing just that exhilarated him beyond measure.

And so did Kiera MacPherson's thirst for spiritual knowledge. That purely lovely face of hers could be scrunched up in puzzlement one moment, and then as understanding set in, every line of concern would dissolve, leaving her expression relaxed in sweet—almost tangible—innocence again. . .the likes of which Devon had never encountered before.

Something about that young woman touched him deeply, stirring chords in his soul that until now had never had a voice.

❧

Over the next several weeks, Kiera settled gradually into

her new environment, growing accustomed to Mrs. Hamilton's mood swings and the routine of the household. She enjoyed quiet chats with Cora and Kingsley. She admired the unassuming Louella's efficiency as she smoothly ran the household affairs. And she knew enough to stay in her room when the brothers entertained their ladies at family dinners one night a week. With the mistress still confined to the house, Kiera preferred to stay with her on Sundays rather than go with the rest of the household to church. But that hardly seemed a deprivation—considering all that she was learning from one day to the next.

Mr. Hamilton was off managing the store a good deal of the time. Often during the evening he wouldn't come home until the hour was late. No doubt keeping company with his betrothed, Kiera imagined.

But mornings were another story. True to his word, he began meeting her at the fountain after breakfast each day, weather permitting. He listened patiently to her every question then provided explanations which somehow turned the most complex doctrine into simplicity itself. And she heard his counsel, going over various passages with him, then studied them later on her own. Little by little, things were starting to make sense, about God's sovereignty and His holiness, about His infinite wisdom and purpose for mankind. But she couldn't quite grasp the matter of man's need for salvation, how it couldn't be earned, but was a gift freely given by God.

"Ye sound almost like a preacher," she remarked almost in jest after he had finished responding to yet another question she'd asked on the subject.

His gaze clouded over. "Perhaps that's because I almost became one. Lately, I'm beginning to regret not seeing the vocation through." He drew a troubled breath.

In that moment, Kiera caught a glimpse into Devon Hamilton's soul. She recognized that he had shared a confidence with her—one which he hadn't discussed with anyone for a very long time, if ever. Before she realized the words were tumbling from her lips, she was telling him all about Sean. And about the beautiful promises that had fallen by the wayside with his death.

She realized something else, too. No longer did she feel the inferior servant daring to converse with the master. They had come very close to crossing the invisible line into actual friendship. . .a line she knew she had no right to cross.

Kiera deliberately reverted to propriety. "So you're sayin', Mr. Hamilton, that Jesus Christ provided a way for mortal man to reconcile himself to God. And that way is by the Cross, not by our own efforts to find acceptance." The concept, still new to her, bore further pondering within the sanctity of her room.

"Precisely. The third chapter of John explains this truth far more clearly than I ever could. And for pity's sake, Kiera, why don't you call me Devon? Hanging on to that cumbersome formality is more of a hindrance than a necessity, especially when we're trying to sort out the Scriptures."

"Nevertheless," she said, suppressing a blush, " 'tis best I remember me place. And that you do, as well."

Now more than ever, she almost blurted out.

"Your place." He tucked his chin. "You happen to be part of this household."

"But not part of the family. And as such, I'll be takin' no liberties."

He regarded her steadily for a timeless moment, then acquiesced. "As you wish. Well then, getting back to today's passage. . ."

But Kiera rose even as he spoke. " 'Tis time for me to be seein' to your mother. She'll be wantin' to get dressed for our stroll in the garden."

Mr. Hamilton gave a compliant nod. "I see. Tomorrow, then, we'll take up where we left off." He sobered suddenly. "Oh, wait. I plan to go away for a couple days. We must postpone our next get-together until I return."

"Fine. Top 'o the mornin' to ye, sir. And. . . Godspeed." With a small smile, Kiera traipsed off to her duties. But the day suddenly seemed only half as bright and the thought of the coming morning brought no enthusiasm.

You're gettin' yourself in too deep with this man, she lectured herself. *Ye can't be gettin' so attached to him that a day without his presence is like a day without the sun itself.*

All the way upstairs, she silently reiterated her intention to return to Ireland. The wages she had put aside would, already, more than cover the cost of passage. The time had come for her to revert to her original plan. The longer she put off her departure, the more difficult her task of bidding farewell to Mr. Hamilton.

For, if the truth were told, she had been calling him Devon in her heart for some time now.

Chapter 6

Seems a lifetime since I smelled moist earth beneath my fingers," Mrs. Hamilton remarked as Kiera guided the wheelchair over the smoothest route she had found through the grounds, still within sight of the flower beds. "Time was, I'd be out here almost every day, clipping unwanted sucker branches from my rose bushes, choosing just the right gladiolus or dahlias for the evening supper table, tea parties out on the lawn. . ."

Stopping in the shade of a huge maple, Kiera smiled and plopped onto the grass, her ecru muslin skirts ballooning about her. "No doubt the place has been missin' your touch, mum. 'A garden grows best for the person who loves it most,' me dad always said."

"Strange, to think someone of your tender age is all alone in the world," the older woman said kindly.

"I scarcely think of meself as alone. I've always had people to care for. And I've nothing but good memories of me parents, rest their souls." A soft breeze played around them, tossing a light brown curl in front of Kiera's eyes. She brushed it away and glanced up to the canopy of leaves above, where songbirds flitted through the branches, trilling their choruses.

From the direction of the house, masculine foot-steps approached.

"Well, well," Dr. Browning remarked, striding up to them, a twinkle behind his spectacles as he tipped his head toward his patient. "Aren't we looking sprightly these days? Much better than last week when I came by."

"Yes, I'm feeling much improved, thank you. Not quite ready to trust these old legs just yet, but in this thing I make an appearance at the supper table now and then." A droll almost-smile appeared when she tapped an armrest.

"Good. Good. I rather expected you'd flourish under the care of this wee lass." He beamed at Kiera, making her blush.

Her mistress emitted a low laugh. . .the first Kiera had ever heard from her. "I must admit, this slip of a girl wasn't content to let me wallow in pity, despite the injustices of life. She began whipping me into shape the first minute she set foot in my room."

"Sure and ye jest, mum," Kiera gasped, looking up in denial at her mistress. "I was only tryin' to help ye get well again, so ye could be tendin' the roses. As the old saying goes, 'You'll never plow a field by turning it over in your mind.'"

"Indeed." The aged hand reached down and patted her shoulder. "And well I know, it's thanks to you that I've been regaining my strength. But I am feeling a bit tired just now, if you'd take me inside."

The rail-thin physician stepped forward. "No trouble at all, Daisy. We'll see you back to your bed. It's about time for your nap anyhow." He grinned at Kiera, and she rose from the ground and fell into step beside him.

❧

Devon left home without the foggiest notion of where he was going. He needed to get away—from everyone and everything—long enough to do some serious thinking and praying. Thankfully, Landon's shiny Oldsmobile made that possible. With a tank of gasoline and a suitcase in the back, the miles chugged past in a blur of green hills and valleys liberally dotted with farms and small towns. Occasionally, he passed a picturesque lake shimmering beneath the azure sky, reflecting cloudless glory back to the heavens.

For a brief moment, he wondered how well his brother would handle the business affairs in his absence. But as quickly as the thought had come, the realization overtook him—Hamilton's Department Store had survived the loss of their father, and it would survive Devon's truancy for a day or a week. Even a month, if necessary. *What about a year? Or forever? Would marriage settle his younger brother down enough so that he might take over the store for good?*

Scarcely able to breathe around that possibility, Devon unbuttoned the stiff collar pinching his neck and averted his attention to distant mountains. Row upon row of them in a misty panorama of bluish green. . .the exact shade of a certain pair of Irish eyes he couldn't quite banish from his mind.

And just for a moment he didn't make the attempt.

❧

Having been encouraged by her employer, at their last

morning study, to study the third chapter of John's gospel, Kiera spent so much time reading the passage that she could almost recite it from memory. And the story of Nicodemus would not leave her alone. As she lay on her bed in the balmy darkness, she pictured the wealthy ruler, stealing through the night to see Jesus, perhaps on a night like this one, questioning Him about matters beyond the man's understanding. Kiera, too, wondered what it meant to be born again, of water and spirit. Yet, the way Mr. Hamilton had explained man's need for reconciliation to his Maker, and the purpose for the Cross, did make sense.

The thought of God's incredible love for mankind moved her in a way nothing ever had. She tried to fathom the Almighty Father sacrificing His only Son—the Crown Prince of heaven—sending Him to suffer and die an excruciating death for people who neither believed nor cared. These sinful humans deserved nothing less than the eternal wrath of God. Yet, even so, many rejected His gift of love.

But in her heart, she knew it was true. All of it.

And I, too, must make a choice, she admitted. *Whether to remain among the throng who spit upon Him and cried for Him to die. . .or be like the thief on the other cross, who realized in his final moments that he was in the very presence of the Son of God.*

She knew one thing for certain. The short, recited prayers she had uttered dutifully throughout her life had never instilled her with any sense of peace or the presence of God. But since she'd been here, discovering new truths in His Holy Word, witnessing in Devon

Hamilton a living, personal relationship between a man and God, the Lord seemed near enough for her to reach out and touch. . .if she would but do so. And suddenly she wanted to do that more than anything in the world. "I choose Jesus Christ," she whispered. And slipping to her knees beside the bed, she confessed her need for the Savior.

❧

After three days of prayer and fasting, Devon purposely returned to the city in time to join the next family supper. He swung by Hamilton's to inform Landon he was back. Then, he drove to see Alexandria and tell her that she would be picked up as usual. Strangely, her ardent embrace failed to stir him the way it once had. But he supposed that was to be expected. He was different now. His priorities had changed. So had his goals. And tonight he must tell the family. He just didn't know how.

He failed to encounter Kiera as he made his way to his bedroom to freshen up and change into his supper clothes. But that was fine. He wasn't quite up to facing her just yet, either. He still had a lot of very personal praying to do.

The afternoon flew by, and all too soon, the supper hour arrived. Family members gathered around the table. . .Mother, Alexandria, Landon, Madeline, and himself.

Even through Devon's befuddled mind, the heady essence of the roses mixed with the tantalizing aroma of Cora's pork roast assailed his senses as he took his seat at the dinner table. Louella served with her usual flair. But in his present state, he could only pick at the food before him, wondering all the while when he should make his announcement. He did notice that his mother's gown matched the asparagus spears, smothered as they were in Hollandaise sauce. In hopes of preserving her good mood, he used this as a springboard to conversation. "You're looking quite well, Mother. I must say, it's been wonderful having you with us at supper of late."

Her cheeks plumped with her smile. "Yes, it's grand to be among the living again. . .even if it is but once or twice a week."

"Soon enough, we'll have you every day," Alexandria gushed, with a subtle flutter of her long lashes in Devon's direction. "Won't we, darling?"

"And when will the happy event take place, big brother?" Landon asked tongue in cheek, while he cut a generous slice from the meat on his plate and forked it to his lips.

Only Madeline remained silent, still retaining her shyness around her new family. Between bites, she sipped delicately from her goblet, seemingly content to let the others converse.

"Well," Devon hedged, "that's what I wanted to discuss with you tonight, while we're all here." Intending to sample another stalk of asparagus, he glanced down at his plate, only to discover it was empty, save for a puddle of sauce. Oddly, he could not remember taking even one bite.

Alexandria swung a puzzled gaze at him. "Don't you think it would be better for the two of us to talk in private, sweetheart?"

He covered her beringed hand with his, hoping she

would absorb a measure of the calmness he hoped he portrayed. In truth, however, his insides felt like a dike after a deluge, ready to give way at any second. He drew a long, slow breath.

"I did a lot of thinking while I was gone," he began.

"And where was it you went on this impromptu getaway, dear?" his mother asked. "I'm sure we'd all enjoy hearing exactly where you ended up, wouldn't we?" She circulated a questioning glance and received a trio of nods.

"I headed south," Devon replied. "But that's not important. What is important is that, while I was away, I made some decisions you all should know about."

Alexandria's countenance brightened considerably, and she swallowed a chunk of the roll that she had been nibbling.

Devon knew she undoubtedly surmised he was about to announce their wedding date, and he squelched a twinge of guilt. But he could do little about that now. Nor was there any point in putting off the inevitable. He might as well quit his hedging. "I've decided— I–I—no longer want to run Hamilton's." There. He'd said it. Part of it, anyway. . .

His mother's demeanor froze somewhere between confusion and horror. "I beg your pardon?"

"I'm sure you heard me," he said quietly.

"But–but that's preposterous," she countered. "What would you do, if not head the business your father left you, the business he poured his very life into, in order to provide you and your brother with a prosperous future?"

"I want to go into the ministry."

Two forks clinked onto two china plates. Mother and Alexandria both stared at him aghast, as if he had just informed them he had contracted the bubonic plague.

Landon smirked, one eyebrow hiked, then returned his attentions to his dinner plate.

Madeline's huge gray eyes didn't even blink as she looked from one person to the next.

"I've always admired pastors and their work of eternal value," Devon went on evenly. "The greatest joy comes over me when I study the Bible. I can almost sense God smiling down on me. I did go to Princeton, if you recall. . .and my intention was to prepare for a career in the Lord's service. That's what I've always wanted—more than anything else."

"I have never heard a more ridiculous statement in all my life," Mother finally said, portraying a certain conviction that her eldest son would either come to his senses or she would have his head.

"I agree." Rosy circles came to the fore on Alexandria's high cheekbones. "Why, the last thing I wish to be is the wife of a minister. . . . Just imagine, an entire congregation watching my every step, measuring my every word. Meanwhile, my husband is apt to be called out of our warm bed in the middle of the night to go counsel some drunk or scoundrel who suddenly wants to get religion before drawing his last boozy breath. Pastors put others' needs ahead of those of their own loved ones. No family event is more important than any stranger's request. No, thank you. I don't see myself sharing my husband, my very life, in such a fashion."

"Don't you fret," his mother told her placatingly. "Obviously my son was out in the sun far too long—those automobiles shouldn't be all open like that, you know. All that sun is bad for the mind."

Relief settled over Alexandria's flushed features.

"Wait a minute," Landon piped in. "I happen to find this all quite interesting. I think we should hear what Dev has to say." He switched his attention to Devon again. "Come on. Out with the whole story, man."

Just then, Cora and Louella breezed in from the kitchen. "Is everyone ready for coffee and strawberry shortcake?" They stepped to the table to remove dinner plates, but sensing the somber mood of the family, their movements halted in midair.

"Not just yet, Cora," Mother said, her expression signaling the unlikelihood that anyone would partake of dessert tonight. As the two made as unobtrusive an exit as possible, Mother turned an imperious scowl on Devon.

He felt his neck warming. "I'm sorry, Mother," he told her. "Perhaps the supper table wasn't the wisest place for this discussion; I don't know. Nevertheless, I've spoken openly and honestly. And, in all seriousness, I assure you, I meant what I said."

"Then, I shall be equally serious," she grated, her tone so cold the ensuing words dropped from her mouth like shards of ice. "I will not tolerate such dishonor to your father, who worked so hard to give you every advantage. If you persist in this nonsensical delusion, you will do so with neither the blessing nor the financial support of this family." And with that, she unlocked the wheels of her chair and backed away from the table.

For a full minute after the family's matriarch rolled herself out of the dining room, no one spoke.

Alexandria, her spine rigid as a broomstick, came to her feet. "You made this decision without even discussing it with me. Without a single consideration for my feelings."

"I most certainly did consider your feelings," he told her quietly. "But I can't turn my back on my calling. . .even for you."

"Well, *I* can't live such a thankless life, even for you!" She tore the engagement ring from her finger and dropped it into the watery remnants of lemonade in Devon's goblet, then flounced from the room.

"Well, Dev," Landon said, in a predictable brotherly gibe, "looks like you just managed to throw yourself out into the cold."

Chapter 7

Amidnight thunderstorm drenched the grounds and Kiera awakened to rainy skies. Filled with the joy of her newfound faith in the Lord, she refused to allow something so insignificant as inclement weather to dampen her enthusiasm. She donned her brightest morning gown, a cheery daffodil yellow, and tied her hair at the nape of her neck with a ribbon of the same hue.

"Top o' the mornin'," she said airily upon entering the kitchen a few moments later.

Cora, at the table with her husband and the house-keeper, peered up at her with a lackluster smile. No one appeared to be eating.

"Why, you've circles under your eyes," Kiera exclaimed in surprise. "All three of ye. Did ye not sleep through the storm?"

"That squall was nothing, compared to the one that blew through the dining room last eve," Kingsley supplied miserably.

"It's Master Devon," Louella said, her fair complexion so white her myriad freckles stood out in prominence. "He's done something that has the mistress all upset."

"Thought you might as well be warned," King added. "This is one storm that will take awhile to blow over."

Helping herself to a fresh muffin and some coffee, Kiera mulled over their words, wondering what on earth could have transpired in a single evening that would have such a profound effect on the household. Thankfully, whatever it was had nothing to do with her. And with all this wonderful new joy bubbling up inside her, surely she had more than enough to share with the lady of the house.

Shortly thereafter, brave hopes notwithstanding, Kiera paused for several moments outside the green bedroom before moistening her lips and rapping lightly.

"Who is it?" Mrs. Hamilton snapped.

"Kiera, mum." Opening the door, she entered without a sound. "I've come to help ye freshen and dress for the day."

"I prefer to stay abed."

"Would ye care for a wash, then? Perhaps a bathin' might make ye feel better."

"Humph. Nothing can make this day any better." She muttered unintelligible phrases, short huffs of breath punctuated with audible exclamation points.

Scarcely able to decipher but a few words here and there, Kiera could only nibble her lip. It had been weeks since she had seen the madam in such a state of mind. Risking her very position here, she ventured on. "Pardon me for askin', mum, but is there something I might do to help?"

"No," she rasped, lying motionless under the light blanket. "No one can help." She went back to mumbling.

". . .stubborn. . .deluded. Ministry, my foot. . .ridiculous notion."

Tidying the room, Kiera held her tongue.

After a short lapse, the volume of Mrs. Hamilton's voice went up a notch in a scornful mimic, as if oblivious to Kiera's presence. "Always loved studying the Bible, did he? Had a dream to go into service for the Lord, did he? Humph. I'll be dead and buried before I see him become some threadbare minister. The ingrate. After his father worked to build that store into something that would ensure a comfortable future for both our sons."

Adding up the various tidbits of information, Kiera felt a chill course through her. Perhaps she had been wrong to assume this trouble in the family had nothing to do with her. In fact, it just might have *everything* to do with her. She'd been the one asking those hard theological questions. Gotten him digging for answers. Quite likely, she'd provided the catalyst for this whole affair. "W–would ye be wantin' your tray, mistress?" she asked, unable to manage more than a whisper.

"No. Nothing. And you may return to your room."

"Aye, mum."

After informing the others not to prepare a breakfast tray, Kiera headed for the library. Her jitters were getting the better of her. She doubted that she'd be able to focus on her daily Bible study. Perhaps amid those endless shelves fairly sagging beneath the wondrous collection of books, she'd find a volume of poetry or a novel, something to take her mind off the tension which seemed to permeate the entire house. And, moreover, assuage her own guilt in the matter. Entering the high-ceilinged room, she began perusing the multitude of titles.

❧

Devon, dozing lightly on the couch facing the library fireplace, stirred from his sleep with an awareness of another's presence. He cautiously inched up a little, just enough to peer over the divan's back. *Ah. A friendly face.* He smiled as he watched Kiera browse the rows of leather bindings, now and then plucking a volume from the rest and leafing through a few pages before returning it to the shelf.

"Looking for something in particular?" He rose to a sitting position.

She nearly jumped out of her shoes. "Forgive me, sir. I didn't know ye were in here." She whirled around in order to make a hasty exit.

"There's no reason for you to leave, Kiera. Make a choice, at least."

Obviously flustered, she inhaled sharply and snatched the nearest title.

Devon chuckled. "*The Care and Feeding of Thoroughbreds?* I had no idea you had an interest in horses."

Despite her flaming cheeks, she calmly replaced the book and slid him a sideways glance rife with chagrin. "Do ye have this entire library memorized?"

"No. But I have a general idea of what's in the various sections. You happen to be standing in front of the animal husbandry books."

Kiera glanced over her shoulder, then turned back, her expression admitting he was right. A small smile tweaked her lips as she visibly relaxed. "Ye had a safe trip, I see."

He nodded. "Right up until I got home, actually." He cocked his head back and forth. "No doubt the entire household is aware by now—the oldest son and heir to the Hamilton empire has gotten himself into hot water."

A tiny shrug indicated her only response. She looked away.

Watching her toying with a fold of her skirt, no doubt wishing she were anywhere but here, Devon couldn't help wondering if she, too, would consider his decision foolhardy. "I. . .told them all I wanted to quit the store," he confessed candidly. "That I wanted to pursue the ministry again."

All the color fled her face. "Ye didn't."

"Yep. Afraid I did."

" 'Tis no wonder your mother seeks that handsome head of yours served up on a platter, then."

"That bad, eh?"

She pursed her lips into a grim smile.

"And what about you? Do you think I've lost my sanity?"

"That's not for me to be sayin' one way or the other."

"Why not?" Hardly caring that she made no reply, he allowed his gaze to linger on her lithe, yet tantalizing frame, on curls that had to be as soft as the finest silk spun in China. . .on those eyes. Eyes that the most able-bodied man could drown in. Suddenly her opinion mattered to him—far more than the opinions of those at supper last night. He moved to one end of the couch and gestured for her to take the other. "Talk to me, Kiera."

"I. . .I don't know what to say," she whispered.

"Then just listen. No one else seems the least interested in anything I have to say."

After a slight hesitation, she took the seat he indicated, folding her hands in her lap.

"Did you learn anything interesting while I was gone?"

"In the Bible? Aye. So much that me poor mind is in a whirl."

He grinned. "Sometimes the truths prove more than one can absorb all at once. Still, nothing ever brings me such pleasure as I find in studying the Word, comparing one passage with another, digging for the clearest meaning. The searching makes me feel. . .alive."

"Aye, I know exactly what ye mean. But what's more important than that, ye have a gift for explainin' things to others," she offered. "I know that for sure."

Devon watched her as she raised her lashes. When she met his gaze, his heart all but stopped beating. Some quality within her eyes lingered unspoken, as if the two of them shared a secret apart from everyone else.

"It's what I was meant to do, Kiera. I see that now as never before. And I've renewed a promise I once made to the Lord. I intend to serve Him all the rest of my days."

᠊ᢙ᠊

A jumble of emotions assaulted Kiera as Devon Hamilton disclosed his innermost thoughts to her. "But. . .what of the cost?" she had to ask. He could find himself cast out from them all. For good and for always. It just wasn't right, when the whole thing was her fault, not his. Never his. She couldn't bear the thought of his banishment from his own family.

His expression flattened noticeably. "Mother has already informed me of the price she will exact for my brash intentions. Naturally, I wish she felt otherwise. I long for the support of the people I love most—at least emotional support, if not financial." He raised a hand, palm up. "What am I going to do, Kiera? No one understands. None of them." His voice broke on the words and he bolted to his feet. Crossing the room to the window, he slid his hands into his pockets and stood staring into the rain.

The sight of those manly shoulders sagging in defeat and dejection was more than Kiera could endure. She had no right to care for him. She hadn't planned to care for him. But, gradually, without her realizing it, deep respect and admiration had grown beyond their boundaries and blossomed into something that must never be. She rose and went to his side, knowing that the only comfort she dared offer would be insufficient, at best. Nevertheless, she had to try. Had to say something. "Perhaps. . .in time. . ."

With a low moan, he pivoted and drew her into his arms, burying his face in her hair. For an eternal moment he held her. Wordlessly. His strong, warm arms crushed her against himself so tightly she could hardly breathe. Then, with no warning, he took her face in his palms and covered her lips with his, in a kiss of passion, of desperation.

Kiera's heart skipped in bittersweet joy even as she closed her eyes against the brimming tears. Wishing and dreaming were useless in light of their two different worlds. No matter how special he made her feel when they shared those precious morning discussions, she must put an end to them. Better she accepted that now and seek God's strength in forgetting him. He was merely seeking comfort from the only friend he thought he had, and she would not deny him that. She would savor this one embrace, no matter the cost. . .but it would be all that fate allowed.

When he eased away and brushed a hand down his face, she felt utterly bereft.

He raked his fingers through his hair. "Forgive me," he said incredulously, his tortured eyes searching hers. "I–I'm sorry." And with that, he charged out of the room.

Watching him depart, her own insides a quivering mass of jelly, Kiera envied Alexandria Fitzroy with every fiber of her being.

It's as foolish to let a fool kiss you as it is to let a kiss fool you, the old saying taunted cruelly. Even as the words rang through her mind, Kiera marched straight to her room—to pack.

Chapter 8

W here would you like me to take you, miss?" Dr. Browning asked, his confusion evident as he snapped traces across his mare's back and pulled away from the Hamilton mansion. The rain had stopped within the last hour, but Madison Avenue remained slick and shiny in the late afternoon light. The gentle breeze carried the promise of autumn.

"Carry me anyplace where I can rent a room until a ship sails for Ireland."

When the old gentleman had happened by, Kiera inwardly declared his arrival providential. While he had called upon Mrs. Hamilton, Kiera stole downstairs with her bags, unseen by anyone. Knowing she could never manage to bid farewell to the dear friends she had made during her stay, she waited outside near the physician's buggy until he reappeared. Then, she prevailed upon his good nature to drive her away.

"I thought you were happy with the Hamiltons," he said, breaking into her thoughts.

"Aye. I was, takin' me in the way they did."

"So why is it you're running away, child?"

The blunt question put Kiera on the defensive. "I'm

not runnin' away. Not exactly. I planned from the first to save me money until I had enough to return home to Ireland. And that I have. In fact, I've more than enough. 'Tis time I go back where I belong. Leave them to. . .sort things out on their own."

He chuckled. "Yes. Daisy informed me about Devon's latest escapade. He's sent her into quite a state, to be sure."

Kiera turned to meet his gaze. "Not that 'tis any of me own business, mind ye. . .but do ye think things'll turn out right for them?"

"Wouldn't be a bit surprised, young lady. There's a lot of the adventurous Maxwell Hamilton in that son of his. Just as his dad took a small bit of capital and used it to carve out a name for himself as a merchant, Devon will realize his own dreams. He's a fine lad, one who's likely to succeed in whatever he strives to do. So he plans to step out 'in faith,' as did Abraham of old." The old man chuckled. "Leaving the old life of comfort behind to follow God's call."

The idea of his being cut off from the family he loved so dearly and banished from the home as well cut Kiera like a knife. "Ye think he truly is called to be a minister, then?"

The physician smiled gently. "Now, that's not for me to say, is it? It's between Devon and the Lord. But I'll tell you one thing. . .if God laid something on my heart, I wouldn't want to refuse to do His bidding. Would you?"

She shook her head, and the old straw bonnet she had worn upon her arrival in America felt strangely dowdy, after the more elegant ones she now left behind. Those and all the lovely gowns which had graced her life during the past few months remained in the wardrobe of the guest room. None of those stylish things really belonged to her. Besides, such finery would be out of place in the Old Country.

She switched her attention to the passing traffic, always constant, and counted off the landmarks that had become familiar during her New York summer. Oddly enough, she found herself committing them to memory.

The buggy turned off the street at the next corner, allowing Kiera one final backward glance at the Hamilton mansion in all its red brick splendor. With the dark-haired master of the grand house in mind, her heart breathed an old Irish blessing:

> May the road rise to meet you,
>   May the wind be always at your back,
> The sun shine warm upon your face,
>   The rain soft upon your fields,
> And until we meet again
>   May God hold you in the hollow of His hand.

Only, she couldn't quite picture her path ever crossing Devon Hamilton's again. Not in this life. . .and she hadn't even told him of her newfound faith in Christ. She swallowed her tears and turned forward.

❧

The hard mattress of the waterfront rooming house provided Kiera precious little sleep the next two nights—especially considering the noisy patrons a mere floor below who were intent on drinking and cavorting the long hours through. Still weary when she rose the next morning, she dressed and went down to settle her bill. Then, bags in hand, she made her way along the wharves, past an endless variety of ships until she reached the dock where the vessel *Sea Princess* lay at its moorings. She mounted the long gangplank leading up to the passenger deck of the worthy-looking ship scheduled to weigh anchor for Europe within the hour.

The sky lacked the usual cheerful blue she enjoyed, but perhaps was more typical with fall coming. She only hoped for calm seas and that the voyage would be favorable and swift. And she prayed the Irish winter would be mild, so the whin would stay in perpetual flower. She had missed the yellow blossoms which graced the fields and hillsides and longed for their sweet coconut-like smell again. A consolation prize for the heart she would be leaving behind.

Once on board, a young steward in white uniform took her luggage and ushered her to a cabin. "Here you go, miss. Trust you'll be comfortable during the voyage. There's a schedule for meals posted on the wall, along with a map of the decks. If you have any questions, just holler."

"Will I be havin' a cabin mate, do ye know?"

"Don't think so, miss. We seem to have far more passengers sailing *to* New York than *from* it."

"I thank ye." Nodding, she closed the door and sat on one of the two narrow berths lining the walls. The last thing she planned to do was watch the New York skyline and the Statue of Liberty fade into the misty distance as the ship left the harbor. To think of all the hopes she had brought with her to America. . .yet none of them had been fulfilled. All unkept promises. Every one.

As the quietness of her cabin settled around her, she wished she'd brought a book to read. That wonderful old Bible with all its handwritten comments would be one of the two things she would miss most.

The other, she would not allow her thoughts to visit.

❧

A loud commotion roused her from sleep. Kiera startled to the realization that she had dozed off and the too-short nap made her head throb. She sat up and blinked to clear her vision.

The cabin door crashed open. "There you are!"

Gaping at the wild-eyed apparition that resembled Devon Hamilton, but with rumpled clothes and hair askew, Kiera had the impression she hadn't awakened after all.

Except he didn't vanish from view, the way mirages were known to do.

And the arms that reached out and drew her to her feet felt amazingly real. As did the muscular frame that nearly swallowed her up in an enthusiastic embrace. And the heart thundering against her own.

"Wh—what are you doing here?" she finally managed, her voice in an unfamiliar, squeaky-high range.

"Looking for you, of course," he replied wryly. "Where are your bags?" He glanced around the small confines of the tiny room, and releasing her, he seized the one most prominently in sight. "Is this all?"

"Devon," she gasped, scarcely realizing she had used

his Christian name. "Put that back. I need it."

"No, you don't. Are there any others?"

"Yes. No. Oh, stop! This is crazy. I can't even think." Turning away from the man she was determined to forget, Kiera grasped her temples in her hands.

She heard him express a frustrated breath. But when he spoke, his voice was in a calmer tone. "Look, I didn't mean to startle you, Kiera, but there's no time for a leisurely chat. The ship's about to embark. After a good deal of pleading, I was able to prevail upon the captain to let me aboard so I could take you off."

"But–but I–I'm sailing for Ireland. Going home."

"Home, my dear Kiera, is here. In America. Where I can see you, talk to you, and where we can be together."

"What did you say?"

He grinned then, an amazingly mischievous grin that set her heart to doing unbelievable things. "I'll explain things more clearly in a few minutes. Now, *Kiera, my dear,* must I ask you again to get your things?"

Unable to take her eyes off him and knowing somehow she should do as he wanted, she nibbled her lip that was so insistent upon smiling. "My other bag is there on the floor by the window."

With a sigh of relief, he grasped both travel cases in one arm, then looped his other around her. And together they ran down the plank to shore, just as the seamen loosened the heavy ropes and raised the wooden walkway.

Devon set her bags into the back of Landon's car. Then he led her around to the passenger door. But before he assisted her inside, he smiled and drew her into a warm embrace. "Thank you. Oh, thank you," he murmured against her ear, "for getting off with me. I don't know what I would have done if you hadn't. I'd have been on the next ship; I do know that much."

"Ye'd have been takin' a lot for granted, I must say," she teased, hardly able to move in her present position and realizing a girl could get used to not breathing. . . .

"No, I was acting strictly by faith," he said seriously, drawing her back to earth. "One of the things the Lord has convinced me of lately is that this life of mine—which has taken a far different turn from what I'd once planned—included a different woman than I'd thought was to be my mate. I have a very strong impression that my future bride is someone with whom I've grown quite close in the recent past. I'm hoping she might feel the same." Suddenly he held her at arm's length. "That is. . .if she'd settle for a poor minister as her husband. Would you?"

He was actually proposing? To her? Was this truly happening? Yet, despite that incredible realization, some of the light seemed to evaporate from the sky with the admission of her worst fears. "So your mother actually did cut you off, then?"

He nodded. "For the time being, at least. Still, you know Mother. She may yet come around. But if she doesn't, I'll take good care of you, somehow. I promise."

I promise. So far, Kiera hadn't had much luck with promises. Yet, gazing into those eyes mere inches above her own, she decided to give this one a chance. Borrow some of Devon's faith. Trust the Lord to work things out. Somehow, this felt more right than anything she'd ever done before.

The driver of a horse-drawn wagon blew a horn as he came up behind their automobile, and Devon waved. "Listen, we have to talk some more. Are you hungry?" But without waiting for her answer, he dashed to the front of the vehicle and gave the crank a few mighty turns before hopping into the driver's seat to start the motor.

A few minutes later, they sat across from each other in a charming tea house overlooking the Hudson River. All the while, Kiera drank in the sight of him, awed at the way this day—her very life—appeared to be turning out. "You never did tell me how you found me," she remarked while they lunched on chicken sandwiches and hot tea.

"Well, it wasn't until quite late in the day that I discovered you were missing," he confessed. "I'd taken a book up to your room, thinking you might find it enlightening. . .only you weren't there. No one had an inkling where you might have gone. And when you didn't show up for hours, I really began to panic. I simply couldn't bear the thought that I might lose you forever. I realized that cabs don't normally frequent our neighborhood but recalled that Doc Browning had paid Mother a visit. So I went to see him.

"Of course," he went on, "as luck would have it, the man was off on a call. I had to hang around his office for heaven knows how long before he finally returned. From there, my search took me to that pathetic excuse of a rooming house. . .and you know the rest."

"Almost like a knight of the realm," she said, half in jest. But remembering the sacrifice he was making, her smile faded. "But what will ye do, Devon? How will ye live?"

"I'm hoping you mean we."

A flush mounted her cheeks.

"Actually, I have some money of my own that should last awhile," he continued. "A trust fund set up by my grandmother. And Landon, of course, says he'll do what he can—as long as Mother doesn't catch wind of our schemes. But I'm not worried. I'm healthy; I can work, if need be. I'm aware it may take awhile before I'm actually established in a church. You'd be taking a lot on faith if. . ."

His gaze warmed as he studied her. "You have yet to answer my question."

"I know."

"Are you ever going to?"

At his incredibly vulnerable expression, her heart contracted. She nodded. "The answer is aye. Be it in the ministry or out of it, with a fortune or in the poorhouse. I love ye, Devon Hamilton. The way ye reached out to a poor Irish girl and showed me how to become a child of God, never makin' me feel beneath ye, always lettin' me speak me mind. . .the way ye look at me sometimes, like now. . . . I'd be proud to be takin' your name."

As the man of her dreams stood and held out his hand, she placed her fingers into it, to be drawn into yet another embrace. The few other patrons in the homey establishment looked on in amusement, but Kiera cared little.

Placing a dollar on the table, Devon led her outside again. But before he helped her into the automobile, he raised her chin with the tip of his index finger and looked deep into her eyes. "There's one more thing I have to tell you, Kiera MacPherson—besides the fact that I love you so much I can hardly see straight. I know you were disillusioned more than once when you first came to America, but I intend to spend my whole life proving something to you. I always keep my promises." Then lowering his lips to hers, he kissed her breathless.

Aye, her heart fairly sang. . .*I believe ye will.*

Chapter 9

Theirs wasn't the grand society wedding she'd envisioned that Devon would be part of a few short months ago. But to Kiera it seemed somehow. . .better. It was hers. . .and so was he. She would never cease praising God for His goodness.

Dr. Browning, in a gesture so sweet it brought tears to Kiera's eyes, had arranged for the use of a parlor belonging to another of his wealthy patients. The owner had filled the room with flowers and candles to celebrate this wondrous evening.

The one thing that might have made everything perfect would have been Mother Hamilton's presence. But that was not to be. Landon, however, agreed to be best man, though not even Madeline knew of his taking part in the nuptials. But three other dear people knew about the ceremony and came to show their loyalty. Kingsley, Cora, and Louella. . .the threesome provided the cake and punch to be enjoyed after the ceremony.

Wearing her mother's fragile wedding gown, which she had brought with her from Ireland, and a lace veil adorned with white roses with a bouquet of pink and white rosebuds, Kiera felt as elegant as any bride. When the first strains of music drifted up from the parlor, she placed her hand on the physician's arm and all but floated down the stairs to join her husband-to-be.

Her breath caught at the sight of Devon, resplendent in a crisp black suit, wavy hair neatly combed in place, and the light of love radiating from those sable eyes she adored. As she stepped to his side and placed her hand on his, she felt him tremble. But he smiled then, that special smile that made her heart crimp in exquisite pain. . .and she forgot everyone else.

Somewhere in her consciousness she was aware of the candles' glow and the fragrance of the flowers. And the faraway drone of the minister's voice, the repeating of her vows. Then the pronouncement that they were husband and wife, and the permission for them to kiss.

"I love you, Kiera Hamilton," he whispered when they drew apart. . .and she reveled in the sound of her new name.

"We wish you every happiness," Kingsley said, swamping the two of them in a huge hug. Beside him, Cora could only offer a teary smile, but Louella kissed them both on the cheek.

"Just like a fairy tale. Cinderella and her prince," the servant whispered for Kiera's ears only.

But Devon overheard. "More like the princess and her pauper," he said with an optimistic grin. "But at least I know she loves me for myself."

After the refreshments, Devon put Kiera's wrap on her shoulders, and they headed out to his brother's automobile. . .the motor already running in readiness to speed them on their way.

"I'm so glad they all came," she murmured as they waved and took their leave. "I'll always remember this day."

Devon reached over and draped an arm about her with a slightly wicked smile. "And so will I, my love. Today shall be only one of many treasured memories. . . and that I promise."

SALLY LAITY

Sally spent the first twenty years of her life in Dallas, Pennsylvania, and calls herself a small-town girl at heart. She and her husband Don have lived in New York, Pennsylvania, Illinois, Alberta (Canada), and now reside in Bakersfield, California. They are active in a large Baptist church where Don teaches Sunday school and Sally sings in the choir. They have four children and twelve grandchildren.

Sally always loved to write, and after her children were grown she took college writing courses and attended Christian writing conferences. She has written both historical and contemporary romances, and considers it a joy to know that the Lord can touch other hearts through her stories.

Having successfully written several novels, including a coauthored series for Tyndale, five Barbour novellas, and six **Heartsongs**, this author's favorite thing these days is counseling new authors via the Internet.

Freedom's Ring

by Judith McCoy Miller

Dedicated To

June Coombs
Ann Dunn
Jesse Grant
Ramona Kelly
Barbara Langham
Connie Long
Betty Marshall
Letty Meek

The friends who have prayed me through good times, bad times, and looming deadlines. The Thursday Evening Women's Care Group, Maranatha Baptist Fellowship, Topeka, Kansas.

Chapter 1

November 1, 1840

Hannah Falcrest stood at the railing of the *Republic* and stared into the blackness of the water below. Flickering light danced from a mast lantern and the resulting play of eerie shadows on the ship's deck sent chills rushing down Hannah's spine.

Hannah had fervently prayed. She prayed as she prepared for her family's departure from their hamlet on the outskirts of Yorkshire. . .and during the journey to Liverpool. . .and while waiting three days in a boardinghouse for their ship to sail. As much as she loved her English homeland, she had been willing to forsake kith and kin if, by immigrating to America, there were a possibility of Edward finding contentment. Then, perhaps, his happiness would overflow and spill out to include their marriage. *Oh, Lord, make it so*, she had constantly, silently pleaded.

Now, her journey to America neared an end. No longer must she cook her meals and brew her tea at the communal fire supplied to steerage passengers. No longer need she worry about her provisions running low, the distant, raging storms, or the dreaded seasickness. And, no longer need she pray for a change in her marriage.

After forty-eight days at sea, and within four days of their scheduled arrival, the vessel dropped anchor in a New Orleans' port. Everything seemed to be going according to plan. Everything—except for the fact that Hannah was no longer the wife of Edward Falcrest and mother of two children. Instead, she was a widow. Her husband and young son lost at sea. All that remained as evidence of her marriage was her eight-month-old daughter, Elizabeth, and the small gold wedding band on her finger. With a surprising determination, she twisted the thin circle of metal from her hand and watched as the ring dropped silently into the water below.

"Not thinking of jumping overboard, I hope."

Hannah hastily turned and moved away from the railing.

"I'm sorry, Mrs. Falcrest. I didn't mean to frighten you."

"Mr. Winslow?"

"Yes," he replied, moving forward so that the lamplight illuminated his broad-shouldered frame. "I grew concerned when I didn't see you below with the other women. Mrs. Iverson said you'd ask her to look after your daughter."

Hannah moved a step closer to him. The glowing lantern mingled with the red-orange hue of an autumn moon to highlight William Winslow's well-chiseled features and send luminescent streaks of vermilion and gold through his ebony hair.

"Since my husband's death, I don't enjoy keeping company with the other women."

"They aren't helpful?" he inquired, a look of concern crossing his face.

"They are very nice. But—" She hesitated momentarily, gathering her thoughts. "But, the women expect me to grieve the loss of my husband.

"I don't wish to speak ill of the dead, Mr. Winslow. However, I have no tears for Edward. The only tears I shed are for my son, Frederick. Does that shock you?" she quickly added, lifting her head and allowing her gaze to meet his velvet-gray eyes. His gentle countenance astonished her.

"Few things surprise me, Mrs. Falcrest. Indeed, I realize there are many unhappy marriages—I'm just not sure what causes them," he tenderly replied.

"From my experience, it would be beneficial if the betrothed parties loved each other, or at least liked one another, prior to the marriage."

"I would have to agree, ma'am. Am I to conclude, then, that your marriage to Mr. Falcrest was a loveless one?"

"Our marriage was nothing more than a business transaction—arranged to settle my father's gambling debts with Edward. But God blessed the union with two lovely children. For me, that proved sufficient compensation for the cruelties imposed by my late husband." Hannah's shoulders sagged with the weight of regret as she spoke. "Now, Edward is no longer alive. But neither is my precious Frederick." Her voice wavered at the mention of the boy, and she turned her gaze back toward the murky water that was gently slapping the sides of the ship.

"Tell me," Mr. Winslow asked, his voice once again filled with the quiet tenderness she had earlier detected, "what are your plans?"

"I've come on deck to get a much-needed breath of fresh air and to seek counsel in the matter," she replied, giving him a reticent smile.

"Ahh. And whose counsel might you be seeking?"

She watched as he glanced about, as if expecting to find someone lurking in the nearby darkness. "God's," she responded simply.

"And has He supplied your answers?"

"Not all. But at least the most urgent ones."

"I wish I could say that God answers *my* questions so directly."

"Perhaps you're just not listening," she suggested. "Or, perhaps, you don't like the answer and choose to pretend the answer is not from God."

His eyes seemed to twinkle in response to her comment. "You may be correct, Mrs. Falcrest. May I inquire as to when you and your baby will be returning to England?"

"I shall remain in America," she firmly replied, straightening to her full height with an air of stubborn determination.

"Would it be fair to assume that this is one of those answers from God that *you* would rather ignore?"

A small smile tugged at the corners of her full, pink

lips as she glanced toward the beckoning lights of New Orleans in the distance. "I suppose that would be a fair assumption."

He threw his head back and gave a deep, resonant laugh that filled the night air. "You are truthful to a fault, my dear lady."

"I would certainly like to think so," Hannah responded.

"Forgive my laughter, but I find your forthright answers refreshing."

"That's an interesting comment, Mr. Winslow. I like to think that truthful, forthright conversation is a common practice. You speak as though the opposite were true."

"Perhaps I've spent too much time associating with the wrong people. I'll need to see if I can change that," he replied.

"A week or so after we set sail from England, I believe my husband mentioned he had visited with you."

As Mr. Winslow's face broke into a smile, Hannah attempted to recollect what Edward had told her about him. She raised her eyebrows in question and asked, "Didn't he tell me that you've previously visited the United States?"

"That would be correct," he replied cordially.

She had hoped that Mr. Winslow would elaborate without being quizzed. Hannah lacked the skill of engaging in small talk, especially with gentlemen, but she felt a desperate need for knowledge about this new country that would soon become her home. "Are you planning to settle in America?" she ventured.

"My dear lady, I've already made my home in the United States. I was back in England only briefly in order to meet with some business associates."

"So you've found them agreeable?" she inquired.

"Found what agreeable?"

"The United States."

"Yes, of course. Quite agreeable."

"And where do you reside, if I may be so bold as to inquire?"

"We've settled in New Orleans," he answered.

"We?"

"My mother lives with me."

Although she waited for what seemed an inordinate period of time, he said nothing further. Hannah could restrain herself no longer. "Mr. Winslow, only minutes ago, you told me that you appreciate forthright and truthful conversation. Is that not correct?"

"Yes, I did."

"Then why do you persist in giving me only the most meager of answers to my questions? Is it not obvious that I desire information about the United States and what I may expect in this new land?"

"I apologize, Mrs. Falcrest. But something tells me that once I provide you with the answers you desire, you'll scurry back below deck and I'll not see you again. I found myself mostly alone throughout the course of our journey and I much prefer your company, even if I must gain this pleasure by devious means.

"However, I must confess. You have succeeded in making me feel remorseful. Please, ask me your questions, and I shall answer them as fully as possible. But, with one provision," he quickly added. "You must agree to accept my assistance once we land."

Hannah chose to ignore his final remark. She needed information—information that Mr. Winslow could provide.

Before they embarked on their journey, Hannah's husband had not been lax in gathering facts about America. Quite the contrary. In truth, many folks had scoffed at Edward's determination to investigate all aspects of this venture before leaving England. But, although her husband had shared some of his newly acquired knowledge with Hannah, she knew that they would encounter unexpected circumstances at every turn. Edward's death had not been among the unforeseen situations she had considered. That event seemed to magnify every uncertainty the two of them had weighed only days before their sojourn.

"Prior to our departure, my husband was in correspondence with several people living in the United States. He decided that our best opportunity to start a new home was in a place called Illinois," Hannah explained. "We sailed to New Orleans, rather than one of the Eastern ports, in order to avoid crossing the Allegheny Mountains, for Edward felt that such a trip would cause undue hardship with the children and our belongings. Someone suggested that we sail to New Orleans and then take a steamer up the Mississippi River, where we could board a boat at St. Louis to traverse the Illinois River."

Mr. Winslow nodded his head in agreement. "Sounds like a good plan. What was to be your final destination?"

"Edward learned of good land to be homesteaded not far from Pike's Ferry, near the Big Blue Creek. Are you familiar with that area?" she asked, her deep blue eyes alight with anticipation as she waited for his answer.

"No, I can't say that I am. I've traveled the Mississippi to St. Louis and farther north, but I've not sailed the Illinois River or been to Pike's Ferry. So your husband was a farmer, planning to homestead?"

"We planned to homestead, although my husband had little farming experience. We were told that a person who was not afraid of hard work could succeed. My husband wanted to own a piece of land and make his way in the world. That opportunity was not possible in England."

"Please don't think me unfeeling, but surely you don't intend to follow your husband's previous plan."

"What else can I do? We have already invested considerable money in the land, and I can ill afford to throw it away. Besides, I have no family left in England. At least I own land in America."

"Your husband purchased land sight unseen?" Mr. Winslow inquired with a note of disbelief in his voice.

"Edward had been writing to Mr. Henry Martin, who lives on the adjoining property. The land came highly recommended by him—eighty acres of improved land with sugar maples and some of the acreage broken up for sowing wheat, and another portion ready to be sown with Indian corn and oats. Of course, I'll want a vegetable garden near the house and perhaps a small flower garden."

"I don't mean to discourage you, ma'am, but I still don't see how you're going to farm the land, what with only you and the baby left. Why don't you see if you can find a buyer and plan to settle in the city? You won't be able to plant and harvest the crops by yourself. It's hard enough to eke out a living with both husband and wife working the land."

"Who do you think is going to buy the land, Mr. Winslow? As you already stated, land is rarely purchased sight unseen. The only person expecting our arrival is Mr. Martin, and the only place I have to call my home is this land in Illinois. Unless my situation changes, I see no other recourse but to continue my journey. I find little pleasure to think of leaving this ship and the few people who have befriended me throughout this voyage. They represent my last link to England."

"Since you earlier agreed to accept my assistance, let me make a. . ."

"You misinterpreted my silence for agreement, Mr. Winslow. I agreed to nothing," Hannah interrupted.

"William," he replied.

"Excuse me?"

"My name is William. Why don't you call me William? If we are to be friends, I think it would be acceptable to address each other by our given names. What is your first name?"

Hannah stared back at him, her earlier argument forgotten with this latest suggestion. "My name is Hannah, but. . ."

"Well, Hannah, as I was saying, why don't you let me do a bit of checking to see if I can find someone to purchase the land? You could then remain in New Orleans—or return to England, as the Lord so directs," he added.

She shook her head. "I firmly believe that I'm to go to the farmstead, Mr. Winslow."

"William," he corrected.

"William or Mr. Winslow—makes no difference—I believe I am to make my home in Illinois, not New Orleans, and not England."

"You certainly are privy to explicit directions, aren't you?"

"Not always."

"But this time, you're absolutely certain that God has said, 'Hannah Falcrest, I want you to go to Pike's Ferry and live on that eighty acres of land.' " A tone of amusement edged his voice.

"God didn't actually say the words, Mr. Win—William. I just *feel* it, in here," she said, pointing to her heart.

"I see. Well, do you feel in there," he asked, while pointing toward her heart, "exactly *how* you're supposed to care for yourself and Elizabeth on that land? Or do you expect to receive that information on another day or in some other way?"

"Are you intending to shock me by your blasphemous questions, sir?"

"They're not meant to be blasphemous. I am a God-fearing man, Hannah. But I need you to clarify this matter. I believe God intends us to use the brains He has given us, as well as clear logic, to figure out what to do in situations such as this. And, to be honest, your decision defies logic."

"So you think me to be an irrational woman incapable of making a sound decision?"

"I beg to differ with you! I never said that," William retorted. "You've twisted my words. I merely stated that, given the circumstances at hand. . ."

"That I have made an irrational decision," she said, completing his sentence for him.

"Think this through, Hannah. How do you think you'll be able to survive in the wilderness? How will you plow the land, plant and harvest crops, care for a home, and take care of an infant? Even if you had spent your lifetime on a farm, it would be impossible. You don't even have experience growing flowers. Tell me how you plan to succeed," he persisted.

"God will provide a way," she answered calmly. "I know this is what I'm supposed to do."

There was an assurance in her voice and a set to her jaw that seemed to signal the end of the argument. Hannah knew that she would make the journey to Pike's Ferry. And she wouldn't tell William Winslow how frightened she was, no matter how many times he forced her to confirm that decision.

"If that's your final word on the matter, I beg you to make one small concession," he requested.

"If I am able."

"Permit me to accompany you. Once you've seen the land, you can make your final determination, but I feel it would be unwise for you to travel into uncharted territory by yourself."

"But it isn't uncharted territory, William. Mr. Martin

lives but ten miles away, and I'm sure that there are other neighbors."

"Did Mr. Martin mention other settlers?"

"Not that I can recall, but I'm sure that there are others nearby."

"I don't want to appear argumentative, Hannah, but I must once again disagree. There are probably very few settlers in that area, which will make it even more difficult for you to survive. Will you permit this one compromise?"

Hannah remained silent for several minutes, allowing the impact of William's words to take hold. The company of another person would give her great comfort—even a person she had known for such a short time. And, no doubt, Mr. Winslow could be of great assistance. On the other hand, how could she possibly travel in the company of a man who was not her husband? How could he remain with her once they reached Illinois? There would be no impropriety on her part, but such behavior would certainly set tongues to wagging. And, she reasoned, that was no way to begin a new life.

"What do you say about my proposal, Hannah?" he asked when she delayed her response.

"I realize that I have no control over your comings and goings, William. However, I believe such an arrangement would be improper. And what of your business? Surely it would be impossible for you to trek off on a sojourn into the wilderness and leave your employment."

"Being away from my business is the least of my concerns, dear lady. I am in a joint venture with several other gentlemen from Liverpool who now live in New

Orleans. Believe me, my presence is not required until such time as an occasional document needs my signature. Otherwise, I wouldn't be sailing with you right now," he explained. "As to the impropriety of the situation, I'm merely offering my assistance. There's nothing improper about that."

"I see. But I still don't think it would be prudent," she quietly replied. "Now, I must go below and check on Elizabeth. I'm sure that she is sleeping soundly, but I don't want to take advantage of Mrs. Iverson's kindness."

❧

William remained on deck long after Hannah had gone below. What about this particular woman made him feel that he must throw a cloak of protection around her? He had certainly courted women of higher title and more beauty. But there was something about her that begged his attention—perhaps the fact that she seemed unwilling to accept his assistance. No matter the reason, an undeniable urge to come to her aid now welled deep within his being.

Perhaps God is speaking to me, he pondered for a fleeting moment. Then, just as quickly, he brushed the thought from his mind.

"Are you all right, Mr. Winslow?" the captain inquired as he walked toward William.

"Yes, just enjoying the night breeze. I am glad to be back in port," William replied.

"Aye, as am I. In all likelihood, we will disembark at first light. But I could get one of my men to row you ashore now if you're anxious to get back on land," the captain offered.

"Thank you. That's very kind, but I'll wait until morning like the rest of the passengers."

"As you wish. Did I see you speaking with the Widow Falcrest earlier?" the captain inquired.

"Yes, you did."

"Poor woman—such a tragedy. I had not lost a passenger on my last five voyages, and then to lose both Mr. Falcrest and the little boy. Terrible!"

"You had no control over the situation, Captain. Mrs. Falcrest holds no one to blame."

"I know, I know." The captain shook his head slowly back and forth. "Still, what a waste of human life—the boy so young and all. . . ," he stated, his voice trailing off with uncertainty.

"Right. Well, storms are uncertain things, and with the little boy already asleep on the bowsprit, little could have been done to save him, although his father mounted a valiant try."

"I'm not so sure Mr. Falcrest wouldn't have done better by his family had he not tried quite so hard. Don't misunderstand. I applaud his efforts. But his death makes things doubly hard on Mrs. Falcrest, what with losing her husband *and* son."

"That's true. However, I'm sure her husband was thinking of nothing but saving the boy from the unforgiving depths of the ocean."

"Now, those waters are the resting place for the both of them," the captain concluded.

William nodded in agreement. There was nothing left to say. The event had struck fear in every one of the passengers, most of the parents now guarding their children with renewed vigor, while husbands and wives gave thanks that it had not been their mates who had perished.

"Is she returning to England?" the captain inquired, disturbing William's thoughts.

"No. She says that she'll carry on with the plans she and Mr. Falcrest made before leaving home."

The captain appeared dumbfounded by William's reply. "What? Can she not afford passage for her return?"

"I doubt she has enough for passage, but that isn't the issue. She tells me that she's had a word with God about her situation and He intends for her to carry on as planned," William confided.

"Do you think she's gone bleary-headed, what with her husband and the boy dyin'? Such things happen— grief causing a person to go insane."

William gave the captain a hearty laugh. "She's not insane. In fact, she is probably more sane than most of the people I know, Captain. At best, I'd say she's a woman determined to follow God's leading; at worst, I'd say she's pigheaded."

The captain appeared unconvinced of William's assessment concerning Mrs. Falcrest's mental stability, but he questioned the matter no further. "New Orleans is a far cry from a country home in England. She probably won't take long to change her mind and return to the homeland," the captain surmised.

"Ah, but she's not planning on remaining in New Orleans. Mr. and Mrs. Falcrest had made arrangements to homestead eighty acres of land in Illinois, and she intends on following through with those plans—alone."

"You're pulling my leg!" the captain replied as he

slapped William on the back. "That's a good one, all right."

"I am not joking. She fully intends to establish a homestead near a place called Pike's Ferry."

"Off the Big Blue Creek?" the captain inquired.

"Yes. Do you know the area?"

"That I do. My sister and her husband homestead near Springfield. I travel that direction when I visit them. Pretty desolate country around Pike's Ferry. Not many settlers. For her own good, she ought to consider living nearer to Springfield."

"Unfortunately, that isn't an option." Concern etching his face, William shook his head slowly from side to side. "Ever heard of a Mr. Martin? Evidently, Mr. Falcrest had been in correspondence with a man named Martin and sent him money toward the purchase of land near Pike's Ferry."

"No. Don't believe I've heard the name. But I could make some inquiries the next time I'm heading that direction," the captain offered.

"No, that's not necessary," William replied.

"I've got a few things to finish up before I turn in for the night, so I'd best be moving along. Have a pleasant evening, Mr. Winslow."

"Thank you, Captain, and you do the same," William absently answered as he stared off toward the blinking lights of New Orleans, again wondering why he felt compelled to help this woman and her child.

Chapter 2

Hannah bit her lower lip, hoping to hold back the tears now threatening to spill over their banks. Bidding farewell to her beleaguered fellow travelers would prove difficult. Many of them had become friends. They had shared their hopes and anxieties about moving to a new land, laughed and cried together, cooked together and shared meals— and they had held a fitting memorial service for her husband and dear son after their drownings at sea. Most important, they had shared her grief at the boy's death. She prayed that leaving her fellow passengers wouldn't rekindle the deep aching within her.

Earlier, the passengers had listened as the captain announced that the customhouse officers would be delayed in their examination of the ship and its contents. Explaining that more ships than normal had arrived within the last week and that the officials had fallen behind schedule, he encouraged the passengers to be patient for just a little longer.

The bleak pronouncements were met with groans of dismay and more than a few angry words. The already-weary immigrants were anxious to leave their floating habitation, and several of the men quickly blamed the captain for the delay. But William was at Hannah's side before the ship's officer finished relaying the ill tidings.

"You have nothing upon which a duty can be levied, and the captain signed a document on your behalf for the inspectors. The captain knows me and knows that I am a man of honesty. We've had previous business dealings, and I merely requested his assistance. The matter is as simple as that. Now, please let me help you," William urged.

"I feel like a traitor leaving the other passengers on board. Besides, the captain said that the inspectors wouldn't be here for several days," Hannah argued.

"This document will be given to a custom's official who will meet us at the dock. And you mustn't think you are a traitor, Hannah. If any of the other passengers were given an opportunity to leave, they certainly would do so," William quietly explained.

Hannah turned and met William's gaze. His tone was soft, his eyes filled with tenderness. He seemed to sense her agony. "Please," he gently added, "let me carry the baby."

The kindness overwhelmed her, and now the tears rolled freely as she handed him the tiny child. Without a word, he pulled a linen handkerchief from his breast pocket and tenderly wiped her cheeks. She failed miserably in her endeavor to return his smile, but somehow she knew that he understood and that no words were necessary.

Once they had reached the dock, Hannah allowed William to take charge. "Wait here. I'll hail a carriage and arrange for storage of your belongings. If you have money that you wish to have exchanged for American dollars, I can do that for you," he offered.

Hannah hesitated only a moment and then reached into her reticule. She pulled out her money, all in English sovereigns, and handed the cash to William.

"You can wait over there while I speak to the inspectors," he said, pointing toward a bench not far from the dock. Hannah watched as he entered a small building and then, a few moments later, returned to the dock. After briefly talking to a lanky man wearing a bright bandanna around his neck, William beckoned for her to join him. In less than an hour, they were in a carriage moving slowly away from the waterfront.

"I thought today was Sunday. I must have gotten my days confused," Hannah remarked, peering at the vendors who hawked their wares along the muddy street. She shuddered at the sight of several black men, shackled together, as they were prodded along toward a large open area where many people were gathered.

"It *is* Sunday," William replied. "I'm afraid you'll find that the general population of New Orleans doesn't hold the Lord's Day in much reverence. Don't misunderstand—there are those who are attempting to correct the situation. My mother staunchly supports reform."

"What's going on over there?" she questioned, unable to look away from the unfolding scene.

"Slave auction," he replied, without further comment.

"And you, William, do you support reform?"

He hesitated for a moment. "I must admit, I am not as adamant as my mother. I'm not quite as offended with the 'business as usual' attitude."

There seemed to be a note of caution in his reply. "Does that mean you observe the Lord's Day but have little concern for the eternal salvation of others, Mr. Winslow?" Hannah asked.

"Ah, I see I've struck a chord."

"What makes you say that?" she inquired while shifting positions, her chin jutting forward just a fraction.

"You addressed me as Mr. Winslow rather than William," he replied, with a slight smile playing at the corner of his lips.

"I suppose I did," she thoughtfully answered.

"Your religious convictions haven't gone unnoticed, Hannah. I'd be a total fool not to realize that a woman who looks for divine intervention in her decision making would disapprove of the New Orleans lifestyle—and working conditions," he quickly added.

"There's no denying that I believe Sunday is a day that should be dedicated to worship and rest. But there are those, even in England, who don't share my belief. Apparently, however, many of the people of New Orleans have taken liberties far beyond what I would have imagined possible."

He nodded. "For many, it's not because they want to work on Sunday. Undoubtedly, a great number of these folks would prefer to be at a worship service. But they have been forced to make a choice—earn a living or attend church. With families to feed and immigrants arriving daily who would gladly take their jobs, the choice soon seems simple enough."

"Perhaps they've placed their faith in the wrong

things," Hannah quietly replied.

"Easily enough said," William replied as the carriage came to a halt in front of a two-story home on the outskirts of the city. He stepped out of the carriage, took the baby into one arm, and lifted the other to assist Hannah down.

Hannah quickly observed the house and surrounding area. From outward appearances, William and his mother must be comfortable, but not overly wealthy. The house boasted a large front porch that wrapped around the house and a small sitting porch on the second floor that overlooked a flower garden. Hannah decided the sitting porch attached to the master bedroom.

A tall, thin black man graciously greeted them at the front door as if it were a commonplace event for William to arrive home with a strange woman and her baby in tow.

"My mother?" William inquired, stepping into the foyer.

"At church," the man simply replied. "Have you eaten? I'll have breakfast prepared," he offered.

"Please," William replied. "Let me show you upstairs where you can freshen up and see to the baby," he said, turning to Hannah.

They ascended the wooden staircase and turned down a hallway. A narrow strip of worn floral carpet was centered down the hall; bare wooden floorboards peeked out from either side.

"I hope you'll find the accommodations bearable. This house leaves much to be desired," William said, pushing the door open to permit her entry.

Hannah stared about the room. A small sitting area led into a larger bedroom, which overlooked the flower garden she had admired earlier. Beyond the garden and grassy lawn, there were several run-down outbuildings and what appeared to be a vegetable patch.

"What are those?" Hannah asked, pointing out the window.

"At one time, they were slave quarters."

"Were?"

"The previous owner of this house was engaged in slave trading. He housed slaves in those buildings until they were sold," William replied.

"And what of your slaves, sir? Don't they also reside in those buildings?"

"We own no slaves, Hannah," William simply replied.

"Really? What of the man who answered the door? And who is cooking our breakfast?"

"I employ servants, Hannah. They are not slaves. I don't own them, and they are paid for their labor," he replied, immediately turning to leave. "Come down and have something to eat when you are ready. I'll see to a cradle for Elizabeth."

"William—I'm sorry. My comments were rude and inconsiderate. I have no right to question the manner in which you run your household. Please forgive me," she begged, though her tone sounded more like an urgent plea than she intended.

"There's nothing to forgive," he said while giving her a quick smile. "I'll be downstairs. Take your time."

She had just begun to chastise herself for her boorish

behavior when Elizabeth's cries demanded her attentions. With experienced hands, she quickly replaced the baby's wet nappy with a dry one, tightly wrapped her in a blanket, and gently lifted the child to her breast. Elizabeth's eyes fluttered between wakefulness and sleep until her tiny belly was filled, then Hannah carefully placed her sleeping child on the bed.

Discovering a towel and washcloth on the commode, Hannah poured water into the basin and dipped the cloth into its depths. She held the cloth to her face and inhaled the cool dampness. The air seemed hard to breathe, a stifling humidity lingering in the air. She had heard stories of the difficult climate and yellow fever that seemed to plague New Orleans and the surrounding countryside, but she hadn't been prepared for the permeating heavy air. Her dress seemed oppressive as she slowly descended the stairs and entered the dining room a short time later.

William was seated at a highly polished mahogany table; behind him, a gleaming silver coffee service graced a buffet along the wall. A kind-faced woman rapidly waved a fan back and forth in front of herself, and she appeared to cling to William's every word.

"And here she is now," William said, rising from his chair. A smile spread across the woman's round face as Hannah entered the room.

"Mother, this is Hannah Falcrest. Hannah, my mother, Mrs. Julia Winslow."

Hannah offered her hand in greeting. "So nice to meet you, Mrs. Winslow."

"Address me as Julia, please, and the pleasure is mine.

William has been filling me in on the details of your journey. My deepest sympathies, dear child."

"Thank you," Hannah replied softly. "And has your son mentioned his many acts of kindness to me? I don't know how I would have managed had he not come to my aid."

"William doesn't tell me much about himself—he speaks only of others," she remarked as she gave her son a knowing look. "William tells me that you hold a deep faith in God. I admire that."

"Sometimes my faith isn't as strong as it should be, I'm afraid. But I attempt to seek God's will for my life, and I pray for opportunities to share my beliefs."

"The Lord apparently has heard your prayers," Mrs. Winslow commented.

"What do you mean?"

"He sent you to New Orleans. If ever there was a city that needed God's hand at work, it is New Orleans. Personally, I can't wait to shake the dust of this wicked city from my shoes, but it seems that there is always something holding me back," the older woman replied.

"Oh, I'm not remaining in New Orleans. This isn't where God intends me to be at all. I am going to Illinois. But with the humidity in this region, I doubt that you'd ever encounter any dust to shake off your shoes," Hannah said with a gentle chuckle.

Mrs. Winslow gave her a halfhearted smile, although William laughed aloud at Hannah's wit.

"William tells me you plan to homestead. Quite an undertaking for a single woman with an infant. Have you considered that you might want to give that decision a little more thought? Perhaps talk to some people who have homesteaded—hear about the hardships and adversities they were forced to endure while living in the wilderness?"

"Such conversations might prove helpful," Hannah answered, "but they wouldn't change my decision."

William smiled at his mother. "Hannah has prayed about this venture, and God has told her that she is to settle in Illinois."

"You needn't make me sound like a raving lunatic, William. I did not set sail from England without any knowledge or planning for my future. My husband and I had. . ."

"Yes, William told me that your husband had purchased land in Illinois." Several minutes passed as the older woman unfolded and then carefully refolded a lace handkerchief that lay in her lap. "Don't misunderstand, Hannah, for I share your belief that God has a plan for our lives. But sometimes in our haste to hear from Him, we—how shall I put this—misinterpret what we think are divine answers."

Hannah thoughtfully nodded her head and pushed away the half-eaten plate of food. Carefully wiping the corners of her mouth with an embroidered linen napkin, she met Mrs. Winslow's gaze. "I understand and respect your opinion, Julia. However, you cannot dissuade me from what I know I must do."

"I didn't expect that I could, but I felt the need to test your reaction. Apparently, you and William are in for quite an adventure," she responded.

"Well, I don't think William. . .that is to say, traveling

together. . .homesteading. . .wouldn't be proper for the two of us. . .unmarried. . .and all," she stammered.

"Quite so," Mrs. Winslow mused. "However, when the Almighty has a plan, nothing is impossible," she quickly added, with a glimmer in her eyes.

"If you'll excuse me, I must check on Elizabeth," Hannah said, rising from the table. "I won't be long."

"Bring her down if she's awake. It has been too long since I've held a baby. No matter how often I nag at this son of mine, he ignores my pleas for a grandchild," she said, now directing her eyes toward William.

Hannah didn't know how to answer the comment, so she quickly exited the room, glad to remove herself from a discussion between Mrs. Winslow and William—at least any discussion that had to do with his producing grandchildren for the older woman.

❧

"Really, Mother! That remark was uncalled for," William chided. "You're certainly lacking in manners today."

"I spoke only the truth. If it makes you uncomfortable, so be it. I like that young woman. She has backbone—and the courage of her convictions. She's pretty, too," Julia added, almost as an afterthought.

"I've pursued prettier," William replied. "But I agree. There is something special about her. Perhaps it's her diminutive figure or the subtle appearance of golden streaks in her cinnamon-colored hair."

"Or her quick smile and upturned nose," his mother said with a laugh. "I'll tell you one thing, William—you may have courted woman who were a trifle more comely, but never one with half the gumption of Hannah

Falcrest. She makes all the others appear fainthearted. Besides, I'm certain you've never courted a woman with her deep belief in God."

"That goes without saying. In fact, I don't believe that I've ever known, much less courted, a woman her age with such beliefs."

"I'd say that a rare opportunity is knocking, Son. Don't rush her, of course. She's still in mourning for her husband. In due time. In due time."

"She mourns for her child, Mother, but not her husband. From what she told me, her marriage was an arranged one. Her father used her to pay off a gambling debt, so to speak."

"Surely not! Why, the poor dear, she can't be more than nineteen or twenty years old. How old was her son?"

"He was four," Hannah answered, walking into the room with Elizabeth in her arms. "And I am twenty-four."

"Only two years younger than William," Julia said, her cheeks flushing pink.

"No need to be embarrassed, Mother," William teased. "I'm sure that Hannah grew accustomed to people meddling in her affairs on board the ship. Didn't you, Hannah?" William asked, hoping to put his mother in her place.

"She's not meddling, William, and her curiosity isn't ill-placed. Your mother is most gracious. I would want the same information if the situation was reversed and strangers were residing in my home. Feel free to ask me anything, Mrs. Winslow," Hannah offered.

"Only if you promise to tell me when I'm being

intrusive," Julia replied, giving William a gleeful look.

"Does that offer go for me, as well?" William asked.

"Of course not, Mr. Winslow—I fear your inquiries might be most unacceptable," Hannah replied. "I don't think your mother will ask me any objectionable questions."

William leaned back in his chair and snorted boisterously. "Obviously, you don't know my mother, Hannah."

"That will do, young man," his mother cautioned from across the table. "Now keep your voice down. You will frighten the baby. Hand her here," Julia ordered as she stretched forth her arms to receive the child. "Oh, just look at her. What a sweet little darling. We're going to become great friends," she cooed at the infant. "William, why don't you take Hannah out to see the garden? I'll look after Elizabeth."

Hannah glanced first at Julia and then at William, trying to interpret the silent communication taking place between mother and son. "I'm sure Hannah would rather stay indoors," William answered, choosing to ignore the look his mother threw him. He knew what she wanted. Julia had used those looks as her silent form of communication throughout his life.

"Of course she wouldn't. She'd like to see the garden. Wouldn't you, Hannah?"

"If William would like to show me the garden, that would be lovely," she replied, obviously unsure what answer she should give.

"Certainly. This way," he said, rising from his chair and motioning toward a door at the side of the house.

Once outside, William led her through the garden to a small, shaded pavilion graced by two small fountains.

"You didn't want to show me the garden, did you?" Hannah finally asked.

"Oh, it's not that. I'm twenty-six years old, so I tend to resent my mother's attempts to direct my life. I am pleased to spend time with you, Hannah. But I had planned to attend to several other matters this afternoon. My mother doesn't approve of my Sunday activities," he answered.

"And what are your Sunday activities, if I may be so bold as to inquire?"

"Sometimes I handle business that can't wait. Today I was planning to check on the schedule of steamships heading up the Mississippi."

"Certainly that can wait until tomorrow," she calmly answered.

"But will you feel that way if I miss the opportunity to book passage on a steamer because I waited an extra day?"

"Of course. I would never want to be the cause of someone conducting business on the Lord's Day, William. However, if you desire to go into town, don't let my presence stop you."

"So if I were able to make the arrangements today, that would be acceptable?"

"You're putting words in my mouth. If the only reason that you are going into town is to conduct business concerning my passage up the Mississippi, I would prefer that it wait until tomorrow. Does that clarify the matter?"

"It's as clear as the sky above me," he replied. "Now, since we have the balance of the day, would you care to see the vegetable garden?"

Hannah chuckled. Obviously William found it difficult to spend time at home.

Chapter 3

W hat do you mean, book passage for four?"
William asked. "Hannah isn't even con-
vinced that she wants me to accompany her."
For the love of heaven, what had gotten into his mother?
In her mid-fifties, she thought she was ready to embark
on some grand adventure.

"Exactly my point," Julia responded. "Don't you see
the impropriety of the situation? We've discussed it."

"You've discussed it?"

"Yes, Hannah and I. She believes that, even though
you are well intentioned, it would be improper to travel
together. And then there would be settling the land.
You couldn't live together. Such brashness would ruin
her reputation. Surely you can see that, William?"

She was acting as though he were a complete ninny.
"Do you think I haven't given considerable thought to
the situation?" he asked. It took everything he had to
hold his temper in check.

"Honestly? No, I didn't think you'd give the issue
much thought whatsoever. Men don't think about such
things."

"Mother, please don't generalize. Perhaps there are

men who don't think about such things, but there are a few of us who give some thought to these matters. I know Hannah is a righteous young woman, and I wouldn't want to jeopardize her reputation. I would never want to do anything to cause her harm. Is that so difficult for you to believe?"

"No, of course not. But if you've given this matter your attention, then what, pray tell, is your solution?"

As usual, his mother had managed to put him on the defensive. He had given the situation some thought, although, truth be known, he hadn't dwelled upon the matter for long. Obviously, social impropriety fell further to the bottom of his list than that of his mother. Now she was giving him one of those motherly looks that said *I've caught you in a lie, young man.* Why didn't he just admit that his mother was right? It would be much easier, and it certainly would put a smile on her face.

"Well?" she questioned, breaking into his thoughts.

He shifted to his left foot, clasped his hands behind his back, and met his mother's unrelenting gaze. "We're going to be married," he blurted out.

"What? Married? Why, you never said. . .Hannah never mentioned. . ."

"We've known each other such a short time that she thought you would disapprove. I wanted to honor Hannah's wishes," he continued.

"When is the wedding to take place? You said you were planning to book passage right away. But you've not left the house long enough to make any arrangements for a marriage," Julia countered.

He could see his mother's mind at work. If he didn't

get out of her presence soon, he was going to be caught in his own web of deceit. "You're absolutely right, Mother. I was going to stop at the church and talk with the preacher on my way to book passage. Remember, Mother, we're talking about a simple exchange of vows, not an elaborate wedding."

"Wedding? Who's getting married?" Hannah inquired as she walked into the room while cradling Elizabeth in her arms.

"Family friends," William quickly replied.

"Sit down, dear," Julia offered, leading Hannah toward the brocade settee. "You know, Hannah, I think you are a lovely young woman. And, Elizabeth—well, it goes without saying that she is a delight."

"Mother!" William warned from between clenched teeth.

His mother gave him a syrupy sweet smile as she lifted Elizabeth into her arms. "Don't you need to go and make your arrangements, William?"

"I think they can wait a few minutes," he replied, dropping down beside Hannah on the settee.

"What do you think of your mother's suggestion?" Hannah inquired. "You have told him, haven't you?" Hannah asked, shifting her gaze toward Julia.

"Of course, I've told him," Julia responded. "I don't think he's particularly fond of my idea. Are you, William?"

"It's not that I don't want you to come along, Mother. It's just that it will be a difficult journey, and there's really no need for you to. . ."

"She was thinking of my reputation. How selfish of

me—I didn't give any thought to your health and well-being, Julia," Hannah apologized.

"Humph! My health is just fine, and I daresay that I could probably work longer and harder than either of you. I was looking forward to the adventure! As I told you earlier, Hannah, I would love to get away from New Orleans. But William tells me. . ."

"I hope you'll forgive me, Hannah, but I told Mother that we are to be married," William interrupted as he grabbed Hannah around the waist and pulled her into a deliberate embrace.

"You told your mother what?"

Hannah's voice pulsated between a croak and a shriek. William pulled her closer, hoping to silence her. His fingers tightened firmly around her rib cage. With his free hand, he took hold of her chin and turned her head toward him. Forcing his lips into a frozen smile, he furrowed his brow, met Hannah's questioning gaze, and threw her what he hoped was a look of warning.

"The announcement was necessary, my dear," William continued while still holding her chin, his steely-gray eyes demanding that she not turn away. "You see, Mother told me the two of you had been discussing the impropriety of our traveling arrangements. I realize that you didn't want Mother to know of our marriage plans, but in light of the circumstances, well, I felt it necessary to tell her. After all, I wouldn't want Mother to make a trip into the wilderness thinking she needed to save your reputation when your reputation was already protected."

Hannah looked so pitifully bewildered that he wanted to pull her into his arms, kiss away her concerns, and tell her that everything was going to be fine. He wanted to assure her that he would take care of her forever—that he loved her and would protect her.

Forcing himself to clear his head, William leaned down and whispered into her ear, "Play along with me, Hannah. I'll explain later." He hoped his mother would view the gesture as a show of affection.

Hannah's head moved ever so slightly, and her eyes seemed to register understanding. Inch by inch, William allowed his fingers to loosen around her waist until he had completely released his grip. Dropping his hand from her chin, he waited momentarily, not sure what she would do.

Hannah kept her gaze directed at him. He thought he detected a tiny glimmer in her eyes.

"I do understand, my dear. It was rude not to include everyone in the marriage plans. However, since your mother desires to go along, I can think of nothing more delightful than having her join us. Why, what a wonderful opportunity for us to get better acquainted. Don't you think so?" Hannah generously inquired.

She was giving him an ever-so-sweet smile, and her eyes seemed to dance with delight. "We'll discuss the matter further—in private," he added hastily.

"Why, thank you, Hannah. I knew I liked you from the moment we met. Didn't I say that, William?" his mother asked as she affectionately ran her fingers through Baby Elizabeth's curly blond hair.

Without comment, William rose from the settee and moved toward the windows that overlooked the garden. *Those two must certainly be collaborating.* They had to be!

How could this have happened otherwise? Only a short time earlier, he was a carefree bachelor. Now he found himself propelled into marriage, fatherhood, and a journey into the wilderness of Illinois. An excursion that would, of all things, include his mother. Unthinkable!

"Didn't I, William?" his mother insisted.

"What? Oh, yes, I suppose you did," he muttered, still trying to gather his thoughts.

"Is something wrong, William?" Hannah inquired.

Her voice seemed to vibrate with merriment. "Nothing that can't be attended to right now," he replied. "Mother, will you see to Elizabeth while Hannah and I take a stroll in the garden?"

"Of course, of course. You two lovebirds take some time for yourselves. In fact, why don't you both walk to the church and visit with Reverend Milrose about your wedding plans? No time like the present, I always say," Julia replied, a smile sweeping across her face.

"Right," William answered as he took Hannah's arm and led her toward the front door. "We won't be long."

"No, not long at all," Hannah added. "I'll need to feed Elizabeth soon."

"You just fed Elizabeth before you walked into the parlor and wreaked havoc," William replied, tightening his grip as they reached the street.

"I wreaked havoc? Surely you jest, Mr. Winslow. You are responsible for telling your mother those preposterous lies, sir."

She had turned to face him, her intense blue eyes appearing almost black. A tinge of crimson highlighted her cheeks, and her bottom lip seemed to quiver as she stood before him. Once again, he felt the undeniable urge to enfold her in his arms, cover her lips with his own, and promise her that everything would be fine. He lifted his finger and softly ran it down the side of her flushed cheek.

"You are so lovely," he murmured.

"And you, sir, are a. . ."

"Don't say anything you will regret," he admonished, his finger coming to rest on her lips.

"I never regret the truth," she sputtered around the index finger that he continued to press gently against her mouth.

"Why don't we stroll over to the park, and I'll explain this whole situation? I think our dilemma can be easily rectified."

"I don't appear to have much choice," Hannah answered.

"You certainly aren't the frail little thing I first thought," he said, surprised by her strength as she attempted to free her arm from his grasp. "Please don't be angry, Hannah, but when my mother told me the two of you were making plans for the journey, I had to think of something in a hurry. . ."

"And a big lie was the best you could do."

"Well, she caught me off guard. I hadn't planned to deceive her, but the thought of my mother traveling with us to Illinois—well, the idea was more than I wanted to even consider. Besides, our marrying isn't such a bad idea."

"Not such a bad idea? You truly think we should get married?"

He couldn't help himself. He laughed. A long, bois-terous guffaw that caused passersby to stop and stare.

"Would you please stop! People will think you crazy. Or worse yet," Hannah argued, "they'll think I'm crazy for being in the company of someone like you." Finally she stomped her foot. "Stop, William. Stop right now!"

Her tone warned that she would brook no non-sense. William immediately sobered and gazed deeply into her smoldering eyes. He knew that she was filled with anger, but her strong emotion made her only more beautiful. More desirable. More delightful. More the woman he had dreamed of all his life.

"Oh, yes, Hannah. I truly know that we should marry. And the sooner the better," he whispered, his voice husky with emotion.

"What has come over you, William? You make no sense whatsoever. Your mother has agreed to accompany us. Surely you find that more tolerable than entering into a marriage charade," she replied.

He continued to hold her gaze. He felt frozen in place, not a muscle twitched, not a sound penetrated his hearing except for the sweet sound of her voice.

"But don't you see? Our marriage wouldn't be a cha-rade, Hannah. I want to marry you, to be your husband, to be Elizabeth's father. Do you find that so hard to believe?"

Now Hannah burst into laughter, clapping her hands together as she exclaimed, "Oh, that was excel-lent, William. You should take up a career on the stage. Why, even your mother would have believed that little speech—I know I almost did," she continued, dabbing at her eyes with a linen handkerchief as she began to regain her composure.

"You think my words were all for show—a performance? That I was merely concocting a speech to impress you with my acting ability?"

"Or ability to deceive, if you prefer," she answered. "In any event, there's no need for this foolishness to go any further. Your mother wants to accompany us, and that takes care of any impropriety in our travel arrangements. That is, if you still intend to accompany me."

"Of course, I intend to accompany you. But my mother traveling with us doesn't take care of everything. I told her we plan to be married, and she expects a wedding to occur. I know you don't want to disappoint her. She has grown so fond of you and Elizabeth," he continued.

"Please don't exaggerate, William. She's only known us two days."

"Perhaps, but you must admit that she dotes on Elizabeth, and she's told me she thinks you're remarkable—and quite beautiful. We're in agreement over those facts," he added with a smile.

She hesitated momentarily and then met his gaze, her eyes serious. "William, even if I were to believe the things you've said, which I don't, you must realize that after one arranged marriage, I'd be a fool to jump into another. Do you remember that night on board ship when you approached me and asked if I was contemplating jumping overboard?"

He nodded. "I remember."

"Just before you spoke to me, I had removed my

wedding band and dropped it into the water alongside the ship. My fervent hope was that it would wash into the very depths of the ocean. I wanted nothing that symbolized my loveless marriage; I was arriving in a free land where I had the right to prayerfully make my own decisions. Freedom! You can't possibly understand what that word means to me, William. You've never been bound in cruelty to another."

"But, Hannah, this is completely different. It was your father who made the arrangements with that heinous Edward Falcrest. Surely you don't place me in the same category as your dead husband! I'm a good man, Hannah, although I must admit you're probably hard-pressed to believe that since I've seen fit to show you my worst characteristics in the past two days."

"So, telling. . ."

"Stretching the truth," he interrupted.

"I see. So, stretching the truth is your worst vice, William?"

"Well, I'm not in the habit of stretching the truth. That seems to have come upon me in full measure only since I've made your acquaintance. However, I'm not sure how the good Lord categorizes vices. I tend to believe that a vice is a vice, and He frowns upon all of them. But I'd like to think that most of my habits are pleasing to God."

"I believe you're a good man, William. Otherwise, you wouldn't have been so kind to Elizabeth and me. And I genuinely appreciate all you've done for us. But marriage. . ."

"Don't say anything just yet, Hannah. Would you at

least just think about my proposal? Better yet, would you pray about becoming my wife?"

"We'd better be getting back. I'm sure your mother has grown tired of being a nursemaid to Elizabeth."

"Hannah?"

"Yes, William, I promise I'll think about it—and I'll pray about it, too," she added.

They were silent as they returned to the house, each deep in thought, each unsure what the other was thinking, each afraid to break the silence.

"Here comes your mother," Julia cooed to Elizabeth as the couple walked into the parlor.

"Has she been crying?" Hannah inquired.

"Not a peep. She's been good as gold for her granny," Julia replied, kissing the baby's plump cheek. "She loves her granny, don't you 'Lizabeth?"

William and Hannah exchanged a quick look as Hannah reached for the infant.

"Well, what did Reverend Milrose have to say? When's the wedding?" Julia questioned.

"He wasn't. . . ," William faltered.

"We didn't talk with him, Julia. William and I had some matters that we needed to discuss privately. We didn't make it to the church. I hope you're not upset," Hannah interrupted.

"Of course not. There's ample time to take care of details. After all, it's not as though we're on a tight schedule. There are steamers up and down the Mississippi all the time. I'll see to dinner," she replied. "You two go ahead and continue your plans," she added as she walked toward the kitchen.

"You see, William? The truth wasn't so difficult, was it?" Hannah whispered as Julia proceeded down the hallway.

"No, not so difficult," he answered, his thoughts returning to the words he'd spoken earlier. Words of truth that expressed his deepest longing to make her his wife. Words of truth that she had chosen to believe were lies. He had to find a way to make Hannah his wife. She was made for him, and in his heart he knew it. All that remained was to convince her. Perhaps he was the one who needed to pray.

Chapter 4

Hannah gathered Elizabeth to her breast and stroked the baby's cheek as she nursed. This had been a long day, and Hannah was weary. Weary of trying to sort out the occurrences of the days since her arrival and weary of attempting to plan an uncertain future. Her thoughts wandered back to William and her earlier promise to pray about his marriage proposal. Did he really want to marry her? How could he? They barely knew each other. Yet when he had looked at her this afternoon, his eyes alight with what appeared to be desire, she had felt an urging deep within her, a longing to believe that what he said was true, to believe that he would protect her, to—dare she think it—love her. He could have any woman in New Orleans. His mother had as much as told her so. Why would he want to saddle himself with a widow and baby? Especially one that was determined to settle in the wilderness! Nothing seemed to make any sense.

Placing Elizabeth in the wooden cradle that William had thoughtfully brought to her room only yesterday, Hannah covered the baby and then knelt beside her bed. "Give me wisdom, oh, Lord. Show me what I am to do. I come seeking Your divine guidance, Father, and because You are always faithful, I know You will answer. You know my confusion, so I pray You will make Your answer crystal clear. I thank You for all Your blessings, Father," she whispered, her head now resting on the side of the bed. Forcing herself to rise, Hannah slipped under the covers and immediately fell into a sound sleep.

❧

"Who is it?" Hannah called out as she rubbed her eyes. Sun was shining through the curtains, and Elizabeth was awake, babbling softly and playing with her toes.

"It's Julia. Are you ill?"

"No, come in."

"I was getting worried when you didn't come down for breakfast. William left hours ago, and I didn't know whether to waken you or not."

"I'm fine, Julia. I'll join you as soon as I've fed Elizabeth and dressed."

"Good. We need to talk," she replied.

The older woman seemed distracted as Hannah entered the parlor a short time later with Elizabeth in her arms. "Here we are—finally," Hannah announced.

"Sit down, Hannah. I've something to tell you," Julia replied, patting the seat beside her. Reaching out, she took Hannah's hand in her own. "I don't know how to tell you this. I feel just terrible about it," she said while fiddling with a small brooch fastened to the collar of her dress.

"What is it, Julia? You look distraught. Surely nothing so terrible could have happened since last evening."

"Oh, but it has. We received word early this morning

that my sister is very ill back in England. She's asked that I return to see her before she. . ."

"Julia, I'm so sorry," Hannah said, embracing the older woman as she wept. "Of course, you need to go and be with her."

"But don't you see? I promised to go with you to Illinois, and now I can't go along." Once again she broke into unrelenting sobs. "I've let you down," she wailed.

"You haven't let me down. Everything is going to be fine."

"Of course it is," William agreed as he strode into the room, his hands filled with a sheaf of papers.

"What's all that?" Julia inquired.

"Shipping invoices, a purchase order for goods, steamer tickets, and an appointment to see Reverend Milrose," he said, waving one of the papers in the air. "We're to be married this afternoon at four o'clock— that way you'll be able to attend, Mother." Without missing a beat, he turned toward Hannah and added, "Mother's ship sails tomorrow morning, and our steamer departs midafternoon."

"We need to talk, William," Hannah said, nodding toward the other room.

"You're right; we do. Mother, would you look after Elizabeth for a few minutes?" Before his mother had an opportunity to answer, William grabbed Hannah's hand and led her to the garden.

"I believe God's answered our prayers," William began.

"Our prayers?"

"You did pray, didn't you? After all, you promised, Hannah."

"Well, yes, I. . ."

A smile crossed his face and he kissed her hand. "I know you did—don't look so serious. After all, we've already received an answer. The answer I prayed for, I might add."

"So you believe that your aunt's imminent death is an answer to our prayers?" an astonished Hannah questioned.

"Of course not. My aunt has sent for my mother three times in the last several years. She gets lonely and each time sends word that she's dying. Mother rushes back to England and they have a nice long visit, which seems to miraculously cure Aunt Birdie for six months or so."

"Hasn't your mother caught on to this ploy?"

"Yes, of course, but there's always the fear that this time it might be true. If she doesn't go and something should happen to Birdie, Mother would never forgive herself. It seems to me that we are meant to be married, Hannah. Don't you agree?"

She couldn't even sort out her thoughts, let alone make an intelligent decision. It was all happening so fast, yet she knew there wasn't time to delay. "I'm not sure. It would appear that all other doors have closed."

"Except the church door," William hastened to add. "I'm sorry. I couldn't resist," he grinned.

"We may as well remain lighthearted about the situation. Otherwise, I think I would dissolve into tears," she replied as she turned toward the parlor.

"Wait, Hannah. On a more serious note, there is one other thing I want to discuss with you."

She returned and faced him. What else could he possibly have up his sleeve?

"I purchased a wedding ring for you this morning." He reached into his weskit and pulled out a wide gold band. "You see, it has a heart engraved in the center," he said, tracing his finger around the delicately etched outline. "Quite unique, don't you think?"

"Yes, it's beautiful," she replied. "I didn't expect—I mean, you didn't need to. . ."

"You must have a ring, Hannah. It signifies to the world that you are a married woman. But this ring will also have a special significance to the two of us. When we are married, I will place the ring on your finger with the pointed end turned toward your heart. Until such time as you turn the ring and place the point outward, toward my heart, you will be my wife in name only. I shall not force myself upon you."

"William, I don't know what to say. That's most kind of you."

"I pray that it won't be long. But I give you my solemn oath that I will wait until you choose to be my wife."

"Thank you," she whispered, unable to immediately comprehend such loving generosity.

❧

Hannah settled herself beside William as the steamer chugged its way up the Mississippi. "What do you think of the country so far, Mrs. Winslow?" William inquired of his new bride as he took Elizabeth and placed her upon his lap.

"I believe this scenery could make anyone forget her

homeland. The landscape is too beautiful for words—except for that," she said, pointing toward a cluster of black workers cultivating land on one of the many plantations they had passed. "I thought this was a land of freedom," she murmured.

"For some but, unfortunately, not for all," William replied.

She nodded at his comment, but her gaze remained focused in the direction of the slaves until long after they had disappeared from sight.

Day after day they moved up the river, stopping frequently to obtain timber with which to fuel the steamer. After two days on board the boat, the three of them began going ashore at each stop, enjoying the brief respites to once again walk on firm ground and spend a few moments by themselves. The plantations soon gave way to more uncultivated land, and majestic forests replaced the date and plantain trees. Hannah marveled at the untamed beauty of it all until, twelve days and thirteen hundred miles later, the paddleboat hissed and shook its way into port at St. Louis.

"This isn't what I expected," Hannah told William as she attempted to gain a better view of the city. "I thought it would be much grander, with buildings of stone instead of wood. But still, it will be enjoyable to see what sights St. Louis has to offer and sleep in a decent bed for the night."

No sooner had Hannah uttered those words than a crewman called to William. "Best hurry, Mr. Winslow. "The packet headed for Pike's Ferry is leaving soon."

"We must leave immediately? And we're traveling

on that? I had hoped to visit St. Louis," Hannah complained as William led her toward a worn and unkempt boat.

"We've only a hundred more miles. Take heart, my dear. We'll soon be home."

Home? She returned his smile, but the less-than-adequate accommodations and chilly November air caused her to wonder what she had gotten them into. Wrapping another blanket around Elizabeth, Hannah once again gave thanks for the child's sweet disposition.

About nightfall the next day, the packet came to a halt, and a small boat was lowered into the water. "You folks need to collect your luggage and get into that boat," the captain explained.

"Excuse me? Why would we want to do that?" Hannah inquired.

"That's Pike's Ferry over there. My man will row you over and come back to get the rest of your belongings. Careful as you go, missus," he continued while pushing Hannah toward the boat.

"There's been a mistake," Hannah said, pulling away from the captain. "This can't be the place. There's nothing in sight but woods."

"No mistake, missus. That there is Pike's Ferry. Step lively, now. We need to keep moving."

"Come along, Hannah. Let me take Elizabeth," William offered. "Let the captain help you down."

"William! We can't go ashore here. It's nightfall, and there's not a dwelling in sight."

"This is where God told you to come, my dear.

Remember?" he whispered in her ear.

"Yes, William, I remember," she replied, pasting a smile on her face as she tripped and fell into the boat.

"Careful, missus. You don't want to get wet. You'll catch your death, what with this frosty night air," the captain warned.

"Thank you so much for your concern, Captain," Hannah replied.

"Was there a note of insincerity in that 'thank you'?" William inquired as the boat cut slowly through the water toward shore.

"Perhaps, just the tiniest bit," Hannah replied with a giggle.

By the time the small family and their belongings had finally been deposited at Pike's Ferry, Hannah's laughter had subsided. In fact, she was now attempting to hold back a floodgate of tears. She chewed upon her lower lip, but it didn't work. The tears rolled freely down her cheeks as dusk gave way to twinkling stars bursting through the darkening sky and the chill of a damp frost invaded the countryside.

"There's nothing in sight, William, not a sign of habitation. What are we going to do?"

"First of all, we're going to remain calm. The owner of the ferry must live nearby. We will probably find a homestead clearing just beyond these woods. I want you and Elizabeth to remain here. I'll go and see if I can find someone. Everything will be fine—you'll see," he said, placing a comforting arm around her shoulder and pulling her close.

The warmth of his body radiated through her like

the warmth of a glowing ember. She pressed tightly against him, drawing from his body heat and attempting to ward off the chill of fear that now attacked her very soul.

"Please, William. You can't leave us. What if something happens to you out there? What would we do? We'd never survive."

"Of course you would. Besides, nothing is going to happen. Remember who brought us here, Hannah. While I'm gone, perhaps you could ask for some divine guidance."

"Yes, William, of course. I'm being foolish. I'll be in prayer while you look for help. You're right. Everything is going to be wonderful."

"Now don't put words in my mouth, Hannah. I never said everything was going to be wonderful," he said as he gave her a smile. "I'd best be on my way before it gets any darker. You stay right here, no matter what. You understand?"

She nodded her head in agreement as he turned to go.

"William, wait!"

Without further thought, she rushed to him, pulled his head down to hers, and firmly kissed his lips. "Hurry back," she begged, the sound of her heart pounding so loudly that she could barely hear her own words as she spoke.

His eyes filled with a profound passion that ignited a spark of love deep inside her very being. Pulling her into his arms, he held her tightly, his mouth covering hers with kisses as he murmured her name, over and over again. Her knees felt as though they would capsize beneath her. She clung to him, hungry for his touch and craving his love with a raw emotion that she had never before felt.

Without warning, he pulled away from her, "I must leave now. Otherwise, I'm going to break my promise. I'll be back soon," he called over his shoulder.

Hannah dropped onto one of the trunks, her legs now unable to hold her upright. Her body was trembling, but not from the cool night air. What was happening? Was this the love God created for man and wife? Was it possible that she had fallen in love with her husband?

Dropping to her knees on the bare, cold ground, Hannah looked upward. "Oh, Father, I don't know why You want me in this place, but I'm trying my best to follow Your direction. I come now to thank You for sending William. I pray that You will protect him as he seeks help for us. I think I may be in love with him, and for that I'm eternally grateful. Show us Your will for our lives and what You would have us do in this place called Pike's Ferry, for it certainly escapes my humble knowledge, Lord. Thank You for Your provision thus far. Amen."

Pulling a quilt from one of her trunks, Hannah tightly tucked it around the soundly sleeping Elizabeth. The star-filled canopy of heaven hung overhead, while the deep, silent river ran in front of her and dark woods stood looming to the rear. There was no place to go, nothing to do—nothing but to trust in God. It seemed as though hours passed, but she had no way of knowing for sure. The sky grew darker. More stars hovered above. And the moon shone brighter and larger than when they had first arrived.

The sound of barking dogs in the distance caused Hannah to snatch up Elizabeth. As the sounds grew louder, she clutched the child all the more tightly, wondering where she could possibly hide should the wild dogs seek them out and attempt an attack. She certainly couldn't go into the river. And running into the woods wasn't practical. The dogs would hunt them down in no time.

Cradling the baby, she rocked back and forth, fear rippling through her body as the barking continued—growing louder and more incessant with each passing moment. Then she heard it, the breaking of nearby branches as the animals approached. She could hear them panting and see their eyes glistening in the moonlight as they coursed toward her with long, calculated strides. The first one arrived, closely followed by three others, forming a semicircle around her and Elizabeth as they howled to their master that they had found their prey.

"Back off, you dogs," a deep voice bellowed in the distance. "Get back afore you scare the poor woman to death," he hollered at the dogs as they chased back and forth between the approaching wagon and a tearful Hannah, guarding her daughter.

"Hannah! It's me, William. The dogs will do you no harm," he called out while racing toward her. "Are you all right?" he asked as he reached the small clearing where she stood cradling Elizabeth in one arm while holding a large stick in her opposing hand.

"Oh, William! I was so frightened. I thought they were wild dogs. I see you found someone," she panted, unable to gain control of her emotions as she stared toward the unkempt-looking man sitting atop a mule-drawn wagon.

"I did. This, my dear, is Mr. Henry Martin," William announced.

"It is? I mean, how do you do, Mr. Martin? It's a pleasure to meet you. My late husband was in correspondence with you. That is to say, we purchased land from you," she stammered.

"So your present husband says," the man dryly remarked as he spit a stream of tobacco juice from between his front teeth. "You planning to spend the night out here jawing, or you want to load up and get back to my place?"

"He's certainly rude," Hannah whispered to William.

"So I've noticed," William replied.

"We appreciate your invitation, Mr. Martin," she called out as the man jumped down and began tossing their belongings onto the wagon. "We'll do that, Mr. Martin. Some of my dishes are in those barrels."

"Ain't no need for fancy dinnerware in this part of the country. Couple of tin pans and some iron cooking pots will serve you better," he replied with a snort as he continued loading the wagon.

"I'll load those things, Mr. Martin. Why don't you see to your dogs, and then I'd appreciate your help with the heavier pieces," William diplomatically suggested.

"Yeah, guess I better get them dogs in tow, or they'll be off and chasing after raccoons all night." Jumping down from the back of the wagon, he began hollering and calling the dogs, with his temper reaching fever pitch by the time he'd gotten them under control.

Hannah was thankful that few items remained unloaded by the time Mr. Martin returned to the wagon with the animals. He helped William lift the last of the heavy furniture and ordered Hannah to take the baby and be seated in the rear. She did as she was told without a word. Obviously, Mr. Martin's manners matched his appearance and she was too tired to argue.

After a few unseemly words and the crack of his whip, the team of mules finally moved forward. The wagon creaked under its burden as they lumbered down an overgrown cattle track. When they finally came to a halt, Hannah stared in utter disbelief. She had seen the large plantation homes and even the slaves' quarters as they had traversed the Mississippi, but she had seen nothing quite like the dwelling that stood before her. The house, made of hewn logs, squared and notched to each other with gaping spaces between the timbers, defied any architectural structure she had ever seen.

The front door opened, and a small-framed woman came out to greet them. Her wispy gray hair appeared to shoot about in every direction, and a trail of smoke circled above her head as she puffed on a pipe held between tightly clenched teeth.

"Whatever have I gotten us into?" Hannah whispered as William helped her out of the wagon.

"I'm not sure, my dear, but I think we both should keep praying!"

Chapter 5

G et on in here," the sprightly little woman commanded. "It's too cold to hold this door open
much longer."

"Then close it! I can open it myself when I'm ready
to come in," Mr. Martin hollered back at her. "I never
asked you to open it in the first place!"

It seemed to Hannah that the woman found great
delight in slamming the door. Meanwhile, Mr. Martin
continued to unhitch the mules as though nothing were
amiss.

"Do you think this is their normal exchange of conversation?" Hannah whispered to William.

"As far as I've observed, it seems to be. They're a
strange couple," he advised in a quiet voice.

"You may as well go inside while I finish tending to
the animals. We'll leave your belongings on the wagon
unless there's something you need tonight."

"No, this one small trunk and the baby's cradle are all
we need," William replied. "Come along, Hannah. Let's
get you and Elizabeth by the fire. Don't expect much.
The inside of the house isn't any more attractive than the
outside," he quietly warned as he banged on the door.

"Let yourself in," Mrs. Martin called from inside.

William pushed open the door and stepped aside, permitting Hannah to enter. She knew that she was staring, but the interior of the cabin was so unsightly, so contrary to what she had anticipated, that she couldn't help herself. She could sense Mrs. Martin watching her, probably thinking her completely ill-mannered and rude.

"I know what you must be feeling," Mrs. Martin said, breaking the silence.

"You do?" Hannah questioned, knowing that she must now apologize.

" 'Course, I do. You're looking around here wondering just how long it's gonna take afore you and your mister have a place as fine as this. Well, I can tell you it's taken us nigh onto three years to get this place looking this good."

"Three years?" Hannah gasped.

"I know, I know. You just can't imagine having anything like this in a mere three years. Your place may take a mite longer, but if you work hard, you'll make it," she encouraged.

Hannah sat down on the rough wood bench and surveyed the room. A few boards had been nailed together in the form of a table and were attached by leather hinges to the timber walls of the cabin. Mrs. Martin proudly called it her "sideboard." In the center of the room stood another small table. This one, covered with a piece of coarse brown calico, appeared to be the dining table. The most respectable furniture was a set of four chairs with seats of plaited hickory bark. In addition to the chairs, there were two stools and the bench upon which Hannah was now seated. Along the entire end of the house, there was a grotesque stone chimney.

"Your chimney," Hannah said, but then faltered.

"It's a beauty, ain't it? All them stones was gathered off our land."

"I see," Hannah replied while trying to understand the woman's pride in such a crudely assembled object. "And what is it that you've used to hold the stones in place? It certainly doesn't appear that it's cement."

" 'Course not. It's a mixture of clay and mud. Same thing we use between the timbers of the house. We haven't finished that just yet."

"So I see," Hannah remarked while observing a clumsily fashioned candlestick made from an ear of Indian corn, two or three warped trenchers, and a few battered tin drinking vessels sitting on the hearth. In the far corner stood farm tools, made with the same poor workmanship as was evident in everything else in the house. Suspended from the roof were a variety of herbs alongside several smoked hams and sides of bacon, and a rifle hung over the fireplace.

"Oh, and wait 'til you see this. Put the baby down and come in here," she ordered. Hannah followed the woman into the adjoining room, where Mrs. Martin pulled four large earthenware pots of honey from beneath the bed. "This here's a real treasure. Ain't nothing like coffee with a spoonful of honey. And this is my hand loom, but I guess you knew that," she continued, pointing toward the weaving machine. "Come along and I'll show you the cellar," she proudly insisted while taking the candle from the hearth and leading the way downward. "We growed this tobacco ourselves," she announced as she pointed to a pungent mound of the product that appeared sufficient to serve an ordinary smoker for a lifetime. "We'll have an even bigger crop next year."

Hannah gave a weak smile. "Lard?" she inquired motioning toward two rough-hewn tubs filled with the solid whitish substance.

"Right you are, missus," the woman replied as she continued pointing to an assortment of dried vegetables and meat that were stored in the dark room.

Hannah attempted to appear dutifully impressed with the stockpile, but the pretense was growing more difficult by the moment. When Mrs. Martin was finally convinced there was nothing else that she could show Hannah, the two women returned to the main room, where Mr. Martin and William were deep in discussion. William appeared to look displeased, but why shouldn't he be? Hannah wasn't overly delighted, either. The Martins were certainly not the genteel people that her deceased husband had described to her back in England, nor was the homestead what he had depicted.

"Come sit down, Hannah," William said, looking toward her and indicating the chair beside him. "I know you are weary. I think we all are," he said, glancing about the table.

"That's a fact," Mr. Martin agreed. "We can finish our business come morning. You folks can make a pallet in front of the fire. Get some blankets, woman," he ordered his wife.

"Already done it," Mrs. Martin replied, indicating a worn quilt and a woolen blanket piled near the hearth. "Best I got to offer," she said. "No extra charge."

Hannah laughed. "Thank you. I'm sure we'll put them to good use. The night air coming through these walls. . ."

"If you don't like what we got to offer, you're free to go elsewhere," Mr. Martin interrupted.

"No, no. I only meant that we would use the blankets and appreciate your hospitality. I certainly didn't mean to offend you or your wife," Hannah quickly apologized.

The man nodded his head. "In that case, no offense taken. We'll be turning in for the night," he said, motioning his wife toward the bedroom.

Hannah and William waited until the Martins left the room, and then William unfolded the blankets on the floor, being careful to spread them far enough from the fireplace to avoid any embers that might escape.

"We need to talk," William whispered a short time later.

"Is something wrong?"

"Mr. Martin insists that Edward never sent any money for the land."

"That's a lie, William!"

"Keep your voice down. They'll hear us," William warned.

Hannah nodded, but, in truth, she wanted to rush into the other room and confront Mr. Martin at that very moment. How dare he say such a thing!

"Did you ask him how we knew about this place?"

"Of course. He doesn't deny that he corresponded

with Edward. He claims that the two of them had reached a final agreement, all except for the payment of the money. Now he says he'll sell us the land for the same price that he negotiated with Edward."

"Ohhh, the gall of that man!"

"I did gain one concession that I think will please you," William said with a mischievous smile.

"And what might that be?"

"Since tomorrow is Sunday, I inquired if we might ride along with the Martins to church."

"That does please me. I don't mean to sound judgmental, William, but Mr. Martin doesn't seem to be much of a Christian."

"Well, I don't know whether he professes to be a Christian or not, but he doesn't attend church."

"Then how are we supposed to go with them?" Hannah asked while trying to hide her exasperation.

"He gave me instructions on how to get to the church, and he said we could use his wagon and mules—for a price, that is."

Hannah shook her head. "That man has no conscience, William. Unfortunately, there is no way I can prove that Edward paid for the land. Why would God want me to come all the way to this place to be made a fool of by Henry Martin?"

"I doubt that was God's intention, Hannah. I'd say it's time we did some more praying about this situation. Perhaps you'll have another revelation," he responded and kissed her lightly on the cheek. "I think we'd do well to follow Elizabeth's example and get some sleep. Morning will come soon enough."

✎

"I can't go to church looking like this," Hannah mumbled as she attempted to straighten the wrinkles out of the rumpled dress she had worn for several days.

"Don't you have another in the trunk?" William inquired, motioning toward the small chest he'd brought in the night before.

"Yes, of course," Hannah replied, brightening.

"And you can use our bedroom to dress yourself and the baby. I'll fetch some water so you can wash yourself," Mrs. Martin graciously offered, much to Hannah's surprise.

"Why, thank you. That's very kind," Hannah replied. "I think I may have misjudged her," Hannah told William a few moments later when Mrs. Martin was out of earshot.

"Don't be too sure," William said with a smile. "While you finish dressing, I'll go and make sure that Mr. Martin hasn't forgotten our arrangement to use the wagon."

"Here we are," Mrs. Martin said as she entered the house, carrying a bucket of water. "I'll just heat some of this water while you're feeding the baby. That's a lovely dress you've got there."

Mrs. Martin seemed like a different person this morning. Perhaps it was because her husband was out of the house and she could act more natural, more like herself. *That must be it*, Hannah decided as she nursed the baby.

"Here you are, heated spring water," Mrs. Martin announced as she poured warm water into the pitcher for Hannah. "You better get yourself dressed. Would you like me to hold the baby?"

"Thank you. That's very kind," Hannah said once again as she handed over Elizabeth. *The change is truly amazing,* Hannah decided, giving the older woman a warm smile.

Mrs. Martin smiled back through her tobacco-stained teeth and nodded her head. "Church starts at ten o'clock, and the trip takes nigh unto an hour from here. You'll need to leave soon."

Working as rapidly as she could, Hannah washed, combed, and rearranged her chestnut-brown hair. Carefully, she stepped into the muslin petticoats and then pulled her dark green silk dress over her head. She placed a white embroidered collar around her neck and donned a matching bonnet with dark green ribbons. She had hoped to wear her black leather dress slippers, but the scuffed brown walking shoes would have to do. If she was careful, her dress would keep the shabby footwear hidden.

"My, ain't you just the sight," Mrs. Martin exclaimed as Hannah walked out of the bedroom. "That's just about the prettiest dress I ever seen."

"And just about the prettiest woman I've ever seen that's wearing it," William agreed as he entered the house with Mr. Martin.

Hannah could feel her cheeks flush at his remark. "I think we're just about ready. Mrs. Martin's been looking after Elizabeth. Her assistance certainly made it easier to get dressed."

"We do appreciate that," William said, giving the woman an appreciative smile.

"My pleasure. I just added it to your bill. By the time you folks leave here, I should have enough money to buy me a couple of them fancy dresses—matching bonnets, too," she added.

"Our bill?" Hannah stammered. "What are you talking about?"

"Surely you didn't think we was putting you folks up out of the goodness of our hearts, did you?" she asked with a greedy glint in her eyes.

"You mean—you're charging us to sleep here?" Hannah asked, horrified at the thought.

"Sleep, eat, tote your water, fetch wood for your fire, watch after your baby, tour my house and cellar. . ."

"Surely you're jesting. That's preposterous!"

"I don't know what that word means, but I can tell you this is no joke. You'll be paying and paying dearly for all we've done."

"That's enough, wife. They understand how things are," Mr. Martin said. "I'll be expecting you back here with my mules and wagon by midafternoon, no later," he said to William. "I don't want to turn you in as a thief."

William nodded as he helped Hannah onto the wagon seat and then handed Elizabeth up to her. "Don't worry. We'll be back," he replied as he hoisted himself onto the wagon seat and slapped the reins, setting the mules into motion.

"The nerve of those people. Can you believe them?" Hannah stormed.

"No need to get yourself all worked up. Your anger won't change anything, and it'll just ruin your time worshipping the Lord."

Hannah turned on the seat and scrutinized him.

"What?" William queried as she stared at him. "Well, am I wrong? Anger will ruin our worship, won't it?"

"I suppose it will," she agreed with a dainty smile.

"That's better," he replied. "Why don't you move a little closer? That way people will think you like me just a little. After all, we wouldn't want to make a bad impression the first time we meet these folks," he continued while giving her a wink.

Hannah felt her stomach flip-flop and her cheeks flush when he winked. This was, after all, the first time in her life that she had been courted, and she liked it! Inching closer, she turned, met William's gaze, and smiled as he held the reins with one hand while taking her left hand into his own.

"Your hands are cold. You should be wearing gloves," he said with a note of concern.

"I didn't realize the weather would be quite so cold. I probably should have worn my lined bonnet instead of this one."

"But you look absolutely beautiful in it. Besides, we'll be there soon. In the meantime, I'll be pleased to help keep you warm."

"You are such a gentleman, William. You would make your mother very proud," Hannah replied, a smile playing at the corners of her mouth.

"There you go again. Do I detect a hint of insincerity in your words?" he asked with laughter in his voice.

"You are a gentleman, William. Even though I was jesting only moments ago, I truly realize and admire what a gentleman you are. I don't think anyone else in this world would have been so good to me, done all that you have—and with such merciful kindness," she added, her voice now soft and serious.

"Thank you for those sweet words, my dear. If I've been merciful or kind, it's because of the mercy and kindness you've shown me. I admire your relationship with God, Hannah, and just being around you has caused me to realize that I need to depend on Him for everything. I'm seeking His guidance before I make decisions, which means I spend a lot more time in prayer. I've even found it much easier to overlook others' shortcomings than I did only a few weeks ago. Perhaps that's because God has been making me aware of my own imperfections as each day passes."

Hannah smiled. "Evidently, your faith has grown stronger while mine has grown weaker," she replied in a sad voice.

"I think we both need this worship service," William said as they neared the church.

"Perhaps you're right. I haven't attended church since leaving England. Those Sundays when I could worship God and fellowship with other believers helped make my life with Edward bearable, and I'm certain it will improve my disposition toward the Martins."

"Good morning and welcome," a middle-aged man greeted as they entered the church. "I'm John Keating, the pastor. You folks must be new to the area. Where are you homesteading?"

"We thought we had purchased the eighty acres adjoining Henry Martin's place. But, apparently, the payment for our land never reached him, so we're not sure what the future holds," William answered as he shook Reverend Keating's hand.

"Ah, I see," the pastor said, nodding his head. "Henry Martin's sold that same eighty acres to a couple of families—seems he never does get the money."

"You mean he's done this to others?" Hannah asked, anger beginning to bubble up inside.

The pastor nodded. "I think you'd be about the third family."

"What happened to the others?" William inquired.

"One family returned to St. Louis. I'm told the other one, a single man, was so disheartened by the situation that he took his own life."

"Oh, my!" Hannah exclaimed.

"Now, now, Hannah, things aren't so dire that we need think about anything like that. If we can't resolve the matter, we'll merely return to New Orleans."

"Before you plan to leave, let me introduce you to Millie Sutherford. She's from England, too," the pastor added. "The Sutherfords were one of the first families to homestead this area. They settled here about fifteen years ago. Millie has a lovely little farmstead not far from here and—well, I'll have her talk to you. I'm not sure if she's arrived yet, but I'll be sure to introduce you after church."

"Thank you," Hannah replied, uncertain exactly how meeting Millie Sutherford was going to help.

Chapter 6

"So you see why I believe you're an answer to my prayers?" Millie asked William and Hannah as the three of them sat around Millie's kitchen table drinking steaming mugs of tea. Their stomachs were full from a midday meal of ham, boiled turnips, and thick slices of warm bread slathered with freshly churned butter.

William was silent for a moment. "What if I can't keep the place running? I've never farmed before, ma'am, and I wouldn't want to let you down," William replied.

"You were planning on farming your own land, and if I'm any judge of character, you'll not let me down. Besides, you'll find that most folks will help out. I couldn't have made it these five months since my husband's death if it hadn't been for my church family. They've come and worked, helping me with everything from tending the animals to harvesting my crops. They'll do the same for you, if you need," Millie assured.

"You're sure this is what you want to do?" William asked again.

"Sure as I can be. I can't run this farm on my own, and I've been praying that God would send just the right family to take over the place. I want to return to England, spend time with my few remaining relatives, and visit the places where my husband and I first met. I'm not sure if I'll stay in England or return to America. But if I do return, I want to live in one of those big cities back East that I hear folks talk about, not out here in the country. Would you feel easier about making a decision if you took some time to pray about it?"

The woman's gentle sincerity spoke to Hannah's heart. "Could we go into the other room to talk and pray?" Hannah inquired.

"Of course. And while you do, would you permit me to look after this sweet child?" she offered. "I promise not to charge a penny," Millie quickly added with a soft chuckle.

The newlyweds had taken Mrs. Sutherford into their confidence, relating the events that had occurred since their arrival at the Martin homestead. The older woman had nodded knowingly, disclosing that she had been praying for the Martins ever since their arrival at Pike's Ferry. Millie longed to be God's instrument in helping to turn the lives of Mr. and Mrs. Martin toward Him. But, she lamented, thus far her prayers had gone unanswered. With chagrin she noted that, unfortunately, the Martins were as mean-spirited today as they were the day they first arrived in Illinois.

A short time later, William and Hannah returned to the living area where Millie sat playing with Elizabeth. "We've decided to accept your offer," William announced. "Provided you'll give me time to arrange for the funds."

"Of course. And I want you to move in here imme-diately. I can't bear the thought of your staying with the Martins another minute. Besides, just think how won-derful it will be to have someone to talk to—especially you," she said, hugging Elizabeth close and placing a kiss on the baby's cheek.

William looked at his pocket watch. "I need to get the wagon back to Mr. Martin, or he'll soon be turning me in for stealing and will be claiming our belongings as his own."

"Why don't you unload those things before you return the wagon? Hannah and the baby can stay here with me while you're gone. Just tie my mare to the wagon and ride her back."

"That would be grand," Hannah agreed enthusias-tically. "But we'd better hurry."

"You can take the bed and other furniture to the shed out back," Millie suggested.

The three of them worked at a fever pitch, and when they had finally accomplished the task, the two women bid William good-bye, with Millie promising a savory stew and dumplings upon his return.

Thankfully, the mules moved along at a steady pace as William turned at the road in front of the church and continued onward toward the Martins' place. Soon, the distinct odor of smoke began to permeate the air and the stubborn mules became skittish. When the mare began pulling at the rope that tethered her to the rear of the wagon, William, now growing increasingly troubled by the smoke, resolutely determined that he could prod the mules no further. Jumping down from the wagon, he tied the team to a nearby tree, still hoping that he could walk the remaining distance to the Martin homestead before midafternoon.

As he grew nearer, a thickening wall of smoke caused his eyes to water, and his breathing became more difficult. Pulling a handkerchief from his pocket, he covered his nose and mouth, knotting the folded triangle behind his head. Moving forward, he squinted his eyes while waving his arm in a futile attempt to clear away the thick haze.

"Who's that?" a raspy voice called out. "I see ya out there."

"Mr. Martin? It's me, William Winslow. What's happened?"

"Step forward and let me see your face," the older man commanded.

William moved carefully through the dense smoke, Henry Martin's voice guiding him as he attempted to discern the looming remains of what had been the Martin home only hours earlier.

"Are you injured? Where's your wife?" William asked as he endeavored to make some sense of the ruin that suddenly lay before him.

"Over there," Mr. Martin answered, pointing toward the weatherworn woman, who sat rocking back and forth on the ground, weeping. "She's beside herself—won't quit that bawling. It's her fault this happened and she knows it," he said a little more loudly, obviously wanting Mrs. Martin to hear his accusation.

If she heard, she gave no sign, so William looked back toward the man. "I've got your mules and wagon down the road a piece." He didn't know what else to say. Words couldn't bring back the loss of their farmstead, and he certainly didn't know how to lend comfort to the wailing Mrs. Martin. He now wished that Hannah had come along. At that moment, as he thought of Hannah, he knew what he should do. He bowed his head and prayed—he prayed more fervently than he'd ever prayed before, seeking wisdom, guidance, mercy, and God's blessing upon the Martins. When he finished, he lifted his head and met Mr. Martin's awestruck stare.

"You and your wife come with me. We'll take your wagon and return to Mrs. Sutherford's place," William said, taking command of the situation.

"I thought you went to church. What were you doing over at Sutherford's?"

"I'll explain on the way. You think you can get your wife settled enough to walk to the wagon?"

"Why are you helping us? You thinking you'll be able to write off what you owe me by showing us a bit of kindness? 'Cause if that's what you're up to, it won't work. I know exactly how much you owe."

"No, Mr. Martin, I'm merely trying to extend a helping hand. I don't know what Widow Sutherford will think about the fact that I've invited you to her home, but I believe she'll treat you much better than you may deserve. Now why don't you assist your wife, and let's be on our way. There's nothing to be done here."

William's tone left no doubt that the conversation had come to an end. Mr. Martin pulled his wife to her feet and half dragged, half carried her alongside him until they reached the wagon.

"Where's your belongings?" Mr. Martin queried, eyeing the empty buckboard. "And whose horse is that?"

"I said I'd explain on the way," William replied. "Help your wife into the back. You drive—I hope that these mules will move for you. At least we'll be heading away from the smoke."

When they were finally back on the crude path and Mrs. Martin's sobbing had subsided, William told Mr. Martin of his plans to take over the Sutherford homestead, adding that he had no intention of purchasing the land that Hannah's husband had secured.

"Even if Mrs. Sutherford hadn't made us this offer, after observing your conduct and the condition of the land, I wouldn't consider doing business with you, sir," William said as he concluded his explanation of the afternoon's occurrences.

Mr. Martin said nothing, but gave his wife a menacing glare when she began to speak.

"You can park the wagon over there," William instructed, pointing toward a spot near the shed.

"William! We were beginning to worry," Hannah called while opening the front door. As soon as the words were spoken, she came to a halt, with her mouth opened wide in obvious disbelief.

"I'm fine, Hannah. Would you ask Millie to step out here? I need to have a word with her," William asked.

A few moments later, Millie met William in front of the house. "I hope I haven't overstepped my bounds," he said, nodding toward the Martins.

"What happened? And what's that I smell? Smoke?"

"Their place caught fire while we were at church.

They are burned out. With the weather turning cold, I thought maybe. . .well, I didn't want to. . ." He stammered, hoping to find the words.

"They need a place to stay and you offered your home. Is that what you're trying to say, William?"

"I offered your home, Millie."

"It's not mine anymore. You agreed to purchase it, or have you forgotten so soon?"

"No, of course, I haven't forgotten, but I won't think of it as our home until I've paid for it," William answered.

"Well, if it were my home, I would have no objection. In fact, I'd say you have done what would be pleasing to the Lord."

William smiled and took her tiny hand in his own. "Thank you, Millie."

"No, thank you, William. You may have given me the opportunity I've prayed for all these years. I'll go talk to Mr. and Mrs. Martin; I think you'd better go visit with Hannah. She seems a bit perplexed."

"No doubt," he said as he ran toward the house.

"What are they doing here?" Hannah asked just as William bounded through the door.

"Sit down and let me explain," he replied, first swooping Elizabeth from her cradle and kissing her along the chubby folds of her neck until she giggled in delight.

Hannah wiped her hands on the flowered cambric apron tied around her waist, tucked a wisp of unruly hair behind her ear, and sat down at the dining table. "So explain," she said, giving him her full attention as he placed Elizabeth back in her cradle.

"Have I ever told you what beautiful eyes you have?" William asked, wishing that he could stare into her very soul through their ocean blue depths. He seated himself close to her on the straight-backed wooden bench. "And how I love the shape of your nose and your high cheekbones, the creamy texture of your skin, and the softness of your lips?" he continued. He lifted her fingers to his lips and then gently stroked the back of her hand. Suddenly, his eyes dropped to her fingers and then raised again sharply to meet her eyes.

A tender smile played at the corners of her mouth as his gaze returned to her hand. "When did you do that? How could I have gone without noticing?"

"You mean the ring?" she innocently inquired.

"You know I mean the ring. Are you going to become shy now that I've noticed? Because if that's the case, you need not," he said as he pulled her into his arms. His lips brushed hers with a wispy tenderness as he ran his finger along the side of her face. "How I've longed for this moment," he murmured. He felt her shiver beneath his embrace and pulled her more closely to him, meeting her lips in a lingering, passionate kiss.

"Oh, William," she whispered.

A muffled cough from the doorway caused them to scoot apart. "I hope we're not interrupting anything," Millie said with a broad grin on her face as she led the Martins into the house.

"As a matter of fact, you are," William replied. "But I imagine it's getting too cold to ask you to remain outdoors," he joked.

"Well, what do you think, Hannah? I told the Martins that this would have to be a matter we all agreed upon," Millie said, rubbing her hands as she moved toward the fire.

"We were, uh. . .discussing another matter, Millie. I haven't had a chance to explain the Martins' circumstances just yet," William interjected.

"Ah. I could see you were in the midst of a deep discussion about something when I walked in," she responded with a crisp laugh. "In that case, why don't we let Mr. Martin explain while I finish getting supper ready? I'm sure that everybody will be ready for a bite to eat. Mrs. Martin, would you care to clean up in the bedroom? You will find water and fresh towels on the bureau," Millie offered.

William observed Mrs. Martin look toward Hannah as she rose from her chair. Hannah smiled and nodded as if to add her agreement to the overture. He wondered if Mrs. Martin was thinking of her own miserly attitude earlier that very day.

"You want me to tell you about it, missus?" Mr. Martin asked as his wife moved off toward the bedroom.

"Yes, please," Hannah replied, giving him her full attention.

"Well, to start with, it's all her fault," he said, gesturing toward the bedroom. "You got something I can spit in?" he asked, tapping his tobacco-filled cheek with a dirty finger.

"We don't smoke or chew in this house, Mr. Martin. And you can rid yourself of that tobacco outside," Millie answered from the hearth.

He didn't argue but returned to the table a few moments later, the puffiness gone from his cheek. "See, here's how it happened. You might recall the missus was washing clothes when you left for church?" he said in a questioning tone.

"How could I forget?" Hannah replied, remembering how she had tried to encourage Mrs. Martin to observe the Lord's Day by waiting until Monday, when she would help.

"Well, she thought she could get the clothes to dry faster if she hung them inside. I told her it wasn't that cold outside—that they'd eventually dry. But, no. She refused to listen. So she commenced to stringing up a rope in front of the fireplace and draping the clothes across it."

Hannah nodded. She'd done the same thing back in England on damp winter days.

"Only it seems she's forgotten how to tie a knot. While she's out puttering around. . ."

"I was collecting eggs!" Mrs. Martin yelled from the bedroom.

"You keep out of this, woman; I'm telling this tale!" Mr. Martin hollered back.

"Then tell it right! Don't make it sound like I was out having me a good time, and I left the house to burn to the ground. I was working, just like you."

He ignored her remarks and continued in a lowered voice. "As I was saying, the missus is out and about somewheres, and the knot in her rope gives way. The clothes caught fire, the house caught fire, and the rest is history. We're wiped out."

"Well, you still have your land—and ours," Hannah added, glancing at William and giving him a faint smile.

"That's true enough, but with winter coming on, I won't be able to rebuild until spring. Winters around here are long and cold. When your husband made his kind offer, I have to admit I was surprised, but I thought it was provision sent from above."

"I see. So you believe in God?" Hannah inquired.

"Well, of course, I believe there's a God."

"That's not what she's asking, Mr. Martin," Millie interrupted. "She wants to know if you've accepted Jesus Christ as your Lord and Savior and invited Him into your heart. Do you know Him, or do you believe merely that He's up there just floating around in the clouds? I'm asking because it's your own eternal salvation that's at stake. You might want to give some serious thought and prayer to the matter—and your wife, too," she added, looking toward the bedroom door.

"She don't mince words, does she?" Mr. Martin whispered to William.

"Not about something this serious. Did you know that she's been praying for you and your wife since you moved to Pike's Ferry?" William asked.

"Why would she do such a thing? I never asked her to pray for me."

"Because she's a woman who wants others to have the same peace that she's found. Spend some time talking with her, Henry—both of you. I don't think you'll be sorry," he advised. "I think Hannah and I need to discuss things further, so if you'll excuse us for a few moments, I think we'll step outside," William added as he reached for Hannah's heavy woolen shawl.

"What do you think?" William tentatively inquired, once they were on the porch.

"I know it's the Christian thing to do, William. My heart says yes, but my mind says no. A part of me wants to treat them as badly as they treated us, but I won't do that. Millie has no objection, and apparently, you think we should help them."

"If it makes it any easier, Millie tells me that the old cabin she and her husband built when they first moved here sits back behind the tree line. With some cleaning and a little repair, she thinks it will be quite usable for the Martins until they rebuild. They wouldn't be living in the same house with us for long."

"Perhaps long enough that God will stir their hearts. How could I object?"

"You're sure? I don't want this to cause a problem between us, especially since. . ."

"Since I've turned the ring?"

"Especially since you've turned the ring," he agreed. "And you never did answer me. How long did it take me to notice?"

"Not long," she replied.

"Will you tell me—what made you decide?" he asked.

"Many things. Your kindness, your gentle ways with Elizabeth, your tenderness toward me, but primarily the fact that you permitted me the time I needed to fall in love with you.

"I must admit, I didn't believe you would be patient. Deep in my heart, I thought you would grow weary of my hesitation and force yourself upon me. Instead, with each day that passed, you grew more unselfish, more caring. How could I resist such compassion and love? I now know that you never intended me to feel obligated or bound to you out of necessity. This ring is a symbol of freedom, not bondage or servitude. You wanted me to come to you freely, to stand beside you as your helpmate, your lover, and your friend. I'm ready to do all of those things, William," she whispered as he pulled her into a fervent embrace.

JUDITH McCOY MILLER

Judy makes her home in Kansas with her family. Intrigued by the law, she is a certified legal assistant currently employed as a public service administrator in the legal section of the department of administration for the state of Kansas. After ignoring the "urge" to write for approximately two years, Judy quit thinking about what she had to say and began writing it and then was and has been extremely blessed! Her first two books earned her the honor of being selected **Heartsong Presents'** favorite new author in 1997. She has had two more **Heartsongs** and two Barbour novellas published since.

A Letter to Our Readers

Dear Readers:

In order that we might better contribute to your reading enjoyment, we would appreciate you taking a few minutes to respond to the following questions. When completed, please return to the following: Fiction Editor, Barbour Publishing, Inc., P.O. Box 719, Uhrichsville, OH 44683.

1. Did you enjoy reading *American Dream?*
   - ❏ Very much. I would like to see more books like this.
   - ❏ Moderately—I would have enjoyed it more if _____
   _____
   _____

2. What influenced your decision to purchase this book?
   (Check those that apply.)
   - ❏ Cover
   - ❏ Back cover copy
   - ❏ Title
   - ❏ Price
   - ❏ Friends
   - ❏ Publicity
   - ❏ Other

3. Which story was your favorite?
   - ❏ *I Take Thee a Stranger*
   - ❏ *Promises Kept*
   - ❏ *Blessed Land*
   - ❏ *Freedom's Ring*

4. Please check your age range:
   - ❏ Under 18
   - ❏ 18–24
   - ❏ 25–34
   - ❏ 35–45
   - ❏ 46–55
   - ❏ Over 55

5. How many hours per week do you read? _____

Name _____

Occupation _____

Address _____

City _____ State _____ Zip_____

If you enjoyed

American
DREAM

then read:

The Painting

A Timeless Treasure of Four
All-New Novellas

Where the Heart Is

New Beginnings

Turbulent Times

Going Home Again
